Intimate Deception

Intimate Deception

LAURA LANDON

The characters and events portrayed in this book are fictitious. Any similarity to real persons, living or dead, is coincidental and not intended by the author.

Published by Montlake Romance
P.O. Box 400818
Las Vegas, NV 89140

ISBN-13: 9781612184791
ISBN-10: 1612184790

To all my readers. I can't thank you enough.

Prologue

May 1853
London, England

Vincent Germaine, eleventh Marquess of Hayworth, ninth Duke of Raeborn, paced the hallway outside his wife's bedroom. Sweat beaded on his forehead, then ran down his face and into his eyes. He wanted to run, but there was nowhere for him to go. No place where her agonizing moans would not follow him.

He clenched his fists and walked to the end of the hall, his carriage every inch a duke's, even though inside he hardly felt like one. This was God's way of teaching mortal man the limits of his control. God's way of teaching man humility when he became too self-assured and self-reliant. And tonight, God had decided the Duke of Raeborn needed to be shown how powerless he truly was.

He wanted to rail to the heavens, rant against God for His unfairness. Instead, he offered up another prayer.

All through the night he'd bartered, offering God every earthly possession he owned. Even his own life. But his prayers had gone unanswered. For the second time in his life, Vincent Germaine was being brought to his knees.

He was one of the wealthiest, most influential men in all of England, yet tonight he was as helpless as a lowly street beggar.

From the moment he'd found out his wife was going to have a child, he'd prayed that this time the outcome would be different. Prayed that this time his wife would be delivered of the child safely and he would have an heir to carry on the great Raeborn name. He even promised God that if He brought his wife and the babe through this, he would never chance planting his seed in her again.

But his prayers had been for naught. It had been nearly two days and she still hadn't been delivered of the babe. Two days, and he knew Angeline would not live much longer if she did not soon give over the babe the doctor said was too large for her.

He shoved himself away from the wall, then froze when another gut-wrenching moan rent the air. Guilt and regret threatened to suffocate him. Fear more terrifying than he could withstand. She was weakening. Would that he could ease her pain. Would that the risk was not so great to get an heir. Would that he had never planted his seed in her womb.

Regrets born of desperation.

He swiped his hand over his sweating brow, then turned an anxious glance toward her room when the door opened. His heart thundered in his chest.

A maid rushed out, her arms laden with blood-soaked linen. Tears ran down her ashen face. Her gaze carried a helplessness he'd seen from his staff on a night similar to this five years earlier. The night his first wife had died trying to give birth to their babe.

Another muffled moan echoed from behind the door. Angeline's cries were weaker now, filled with even more pain and despair.

Vincent strode with determined steps toward the room where his wife lay struggling to give birth to his child. He would not allow her to die. He'd lost one wife trying to give him an heir. He couldn't live with himself if he was responsible for another woman's death.

He opened the door and entered.

His gaze moved to where she lay in the bed, and his heart dropped to the pit of his stomach. He slowly made his way toward her.

"You should not…have come, Your Grace," Angeline whispered, her weak voice filled with pain.

He sucked in a deep breath that broadened his already massive shoulders. "I'm your husband. This is exactly where I should be."

Angeline attempted a smile.

His heart twisted in his chest as a part of him died. He reached for her hand and held it. "I've come to tell you I have waited long enough. I demand you cease this procrastination and give birth to our babe."

She released a trembling shudder. "So like you to make demands of matters you cannot control."

"That is because I have always found doing so effective," he answered, brushing a stray wisp of hair from her cheek. Dear God, he didn't want to lose her. He couldn't say he loved her, wasn't sure he knew what love was, but oh, he cared for her. Could not imagine a life without her.

"I'm afraid your demands are quite useless in this… Your Grace."

He forced himself not to react. Forced himself not to tell her he feared the same.

Another wave of pain speared through her body. She attempted a scream, but the sound was reduced to a weak, pathetic gasp. He cradled her hand, and she held on to him even though she was so weak her clasp was negligible.

"Do you know how much I love you, Vincent?" she said when the spasm was over.

Tears burned his eyes. "Yes, Angeline. I have been the luckiest of men. Nowhere in all the world could I have found anyone more perfect than you. You have made me very happy."

"But I could not give you an heir. I know how much you wanted one."

"We both did," he whispered, his throat constricting.

"Yes, I did. More than anything."

Another spasm overwhelmed her. She gasped for air and held his hand. "Please, don't…leave me."

"No, Angeline. I won't leave you."

He sat in the chair beside her bed and held her limp, fragile hand in his. His chest ached with such pain it clenched his body with relentless agony.

"You don't have to worry about the babe, Your Grace," Angeline whispered. "I will take good care of him when we reach heaven."

Vincent swallowed hard. "I know you will." He leaned over and kissed her gently on the cheek.

She tried to smile at him one final time.

He brushed his fingers down her face and held her hand securely. What had he done? Was the desire for an heir worth even one life? Was having a child worth the risk a man forced a woman to take? Or the risk a woman felt obligated to take?

* * *

She was finally delivered of the babe—a son—a perfectly formed babe with plump arms and legs and thick black hair just like Vincent's. He was a beautiful babe that wore the look of peaceful bliss as he slept for eternity.

Vincent held his wife's hand long after it had grown cold. Long after life had ebbed from her body. Tears streamed down his cheeks. He let them flow with shameless abandon. She'd sacrificed everything to give him an heir.

With his dead wife's hand nestled in his, he vowed he would never allow another woman to take such a risk again.

Chapter 1

January 1858
London, England

Lady Grace Warren stood back from the crowd of well-wishers and watched her youngest sister, Anne, and her new husband greet their guests. After their wedding breakfast celebration, the groom would whisk his happy bride away from their father's London town house and they'd travel to their new home to begin a wonderful life together.

Grace breathed a heavy sigh. The relief nearly took her to her knees.

Anne was safe now.

Grace swallowed past the lump in her throat. The nightmare she'd lived with for more years than she wanted to remember was finally over. The last of her six sisters had husbands now to protect them. They were all safe. Finally out of his reach.

The euphoria she felt was indescribable. She'd been so scared that she'd fail and he'd somehow get one of them.

She watched Anne and her new husband, focused on the loving way they looked at each other, their timid touch, their longing gazes. Her heart ached with a painful yearning she thought she'd squelched long ago. She wouldn't allow herself to dredge up all the regrets and disappointments, all the wasted years she'd sacrificed to save them. Today was a happy occasion. Anne's marriage was the completion of the promise she'd given her mother on her deathbed—to make sure each of her girls found someone who loved them. Someone who would take care of them.

She'd fulfilled her promise, even though it had come at a price—a very high price.

She'd done everything she knew to do to keep *him* from getting them.

Even sold her own soul.

Grace pushed the gnawing terror aside and watched as, one by one, her sisters descended on Anne with congratulatory hugs. Only Caroline, Marchioness of Wedgewood, wasn't there.

That didn't surprise her. Caroline was in the family way again and had no doubt found a chair in which to rest.

Grace smiled. It wouldn't be long before her sisters and their families would have trouble fitting into one house. That should throw their father into a fine stupor.

She shifted her gaze to where her father stood talking to a group of friends and neighbors. Her heart dropped to the pit of her stomach when she saw the man standing next to him. Just the sight of him made her skin crawl.

"What is *he* doing here?" Caroline asked from beside her.

Grace gave a start. She hadn't heard Caroline approach. She put a smile on her face and turned. "Father invited him. He's a neighbor, after all."

"He's Satan masquerading as a messenger from God."

Grace suppressed a shiver and forced herself to concentrate on anything other than Baron Fentington. He was as repulsive and vile as the threat he posed. Grace pulled her gaze from Fentington and focused on Anne and her new husband. "They make a lovely couple, don't they?"

"Yes." Caroline placed her hand on Grace's shoulder and gave it a gentle squeeze. "Are you breathing a sigh of relief, Grace?"

Grace tried to look relaxed. "Yes, I'm glad it's over. There are always a number of last-minute details to see to."

"That's not what I'm talking about. As well you know."

A long silence stretched between them before Grace gave up her pretense of ignorance. "Yes, I'm glad."

She forced her gaze to shift back to the man standing beside her father. The baron. The man who'd wanted Anne for his own. As well as Mary, the sister older than Anne, and Sarah, the one older than Mary.

Although Fentington gave the outward appearance of being an upstanding member of society and a righteous nobleman, Grace and all her sisters knew differently. The man was inherently evil.

There were no lengths to which Grace hadn't gone to keep each of her sisters out of his reach.

Caroline leaned close. "You could almost hear a collective sigh from each one of us when Anne said *I do.* I had to grip the edge of the bench to keep from jumping to my feet and shouting for joy."

"I know. Me too."

"How did you do it, Grace? How did you keep our Annie out of his clutches?"

"It wasn't that hard," Grace lied. "I had a long talk with Father. Eventually he saw reason."

"Why don't I believe that?" Caroline said, her tone filled with skepticism.

Grace heard the obvious dislike in Caroline's words. It was the same when any of her other sisters talked of their father.

"What promises did you have to make to keep her out of the lecher's hands?" Caroline asked.

Grace looked around to make sure no one could overhear them. "Let's just say Father found it financially more advantageous for Annie to marry Wexley, even though he wasn't titled, than to marry Baron Fentington."

Caroline chortled a humorless laugh. "Wouldn't you know the weight of coins offered for Anne's hand determined to whom Father would give his daughter. Heaven forbid he put any of his children's well-being and happiness over his greed when making decisions that affected their futures."

"You're not being fair, Caroline."

"How can you say that, Grace? After all he's done to you."

"He hasn't done anything I haven't allowed him to do. It was my choice to take care of the six of you. And I don't regret a moment of it."

"Only because of the promise you made Mama."

"Stop talking as if I'm some sort of martyr who sacrificed her life."

"But you did."

"I did nothing of the kind. I was thankful to have someplace to go after I'd suffered through two miserable

Seasons without anyone offering for me. Taking care of my sisters was much more satisfying than the humiliation of being a permanent wallflower because no one would give me a second glance."

"It wasn't you, Grace. Father made sure you didn't get a match. I know he did. Although I don't know what any of us would have done if you had married and left us. You saved each of us from the disastrous marriage Father would have chosen for us."

"I just helped him realize it was in his best interest to let each of his daughters follow her heart."

"No you didn't. You convinced Thomas's father to give up that stretch of land to the east of Father's estate for my hand. And you bartered that prize racehorse Josie's father-in-law owned in exchange for her hand. And you haggled the Earl of Morningway out of the money that was to go to Francine on her wedding day and gave it to Father. And you—"

"Enough, Linny."

"Face it, Grace. Father would have sold every one of us into slavery if the price was right. But I thought this time we'd lost our Annie to the baron. I'm not sure I could have stood it if Father had forced her to marry him."

"You didn't have to worry," Grace said, still having to reassure herself that Annie was safely out of the baron's clutches. "I'd never have let him have her. Never."

"Oh, Grace. I don't know how Mama survived Father as long as she did. Seven babies in less than ten years. And all because he was desperate for an heir. Maybe that's why he resented us so. Do you think? Because not one of us was the son he wanted so desperately?"

"Could be, Linny. Every man with a title and land wants a son to pass it down to. Father is no different."

"Yes. But not every man will kill his wife in order to get it. I know even if Thomas didn't already have two sons, he wouldn't force me to bear another child if he thought it might kill me."

Grace focused on her sister's slightly pale face. "Do you still suffer from sickness each morning?"

"Not as much as I used to."

"I want you to know you nearly cost me that beautiful burgundy ribbon I bought to go with this gown," Grace said with a glint in her eyes.

"How so?"

"Anne and I wagered as to whether or not you'd make it through her wedding ceremony without having to leave because you were ill."

Caroline lifted her dainty brows. "Which side of the wager did you come down on?"

"That you'd have to leave during the ceremony, of course."

"What?"

Grace laughed. "That shouldn't surprise you, Linny. You handle the early months of pregnancy worse than any of your sisters."

"That's because my babes are half grown when they decide to make an appearance. At least Anne gave me a little more credit."

"No," Grace said with a smile. "Anne wagered that you wouldn't even make it to the wedding."

Caroline tried to look affronted. She failed, and Grace laughed again.

"Remind me to throw her words back in her face when she's suffering with her first babe."

"I remember Thomas's announcement after your last birth," Grace said. "He told us quite emphatically that little Robin was going to be your last."

"And if it were up to Thomas, Robin would be. But I'm giving him little choice in this matter. I want to try once more for my daughter."

Grace laughed. "And if this next one is a son too?"

"I will cross that bridge when I come to it. Besides, Josie already has three. And if the gazes she and her viscount exchange are any indicator, number four won't be long in coming." Caroline gave Grace a pat on the arm. "Face it, Grace. Not one of us seems to have any trouble providing our husbands with offspring. You are going to have to hurry and find a husband if you intend to catch up with us."

"I have no intention of keeping up with any of you. You are all too proficient at getting yourselves in the family way. I have no doubt in a year's time our Annie will prove she's equally capable."

There was a long silence before Caroline asked the question she knew her other sisters were too shy to ask. "What are you going to do now, Grace? Surely you don't intend to go back to the country and live out your life taking care of Father?"

"Perhaps. Living in the country wouldn't be so bad," Grace mumbled, pretending interest in the first of the guests bidding Anne and her husband farewell.

"Yes it would. You'd be nothing more than Father's slave." Caroline turned Grace to face her. "Stay in London with me for a while. I'll have need of you once I near my time. And who knows? Perhaps you will meet someone while you're here. Someone who will steal your heart and fall madly in love with you."

Grace shook her head. "That's a dream I've long given up. Falling madly in love isn't possible when you're an aging spinster."

"You're not that old, Grace. You're not yet thirty."

Grace smiled. "I will be next month."

Grace shifted her gaze to where her father stood. Baron Fentington was still there, watching them. Watching her. Her skin crawled and she wanted to hide from his probing gaze, from the way he had of undressing her with his eyes. She rubbed her hands against her arms, unconsciously trying to rub away the unclean feeling.

"Why is that repulsive man staring at us, Grace? I can hardly abide knowing he's in the same room with us, let alone ogling us."

"Ignore him, Linny."

"That's impossible. Have you heard? One of Josie's upstairs maids is related to one of the baron's servants." Linny paused. "She's with child. Fentington's child."

A cold chill shot the length of Grace's spine. The hairs at the back of her neck pinched painfully.

"Josie said the poor girl is only thirteen and that the baron nearly killed her when he forced himself on her. Then he beat her within an inch of her life when she threatened to go to Reverend Perry for help. Everyone's hiding the girl's condition as long as possible because they know as soon as he finds out she's carrying, he'll punish her."

Grace felt sick to her stomach. "We can't let her go through that alone, Linny. Someone has to—"

Caroline reached for Grace's hand. "I've already sent for her. I'll take her in as soon as she turns up on my doorstep."

"Oh, thank God. I should have known you wouldn't let someone that young suffer alone."

"What I'd like to do, though," Caroline said, glaring at the baron, "could get me hanged. Look how pious he wants people to think he is." Caroline's tone dripped with contempt. "He's dressed in all white, as if his outward appearance will hide the rot and maggot-ridden soul inside."

Grace gave her sister's fingers a gentle squeeze. Of all her sisters, Caroline was the most aware of Fentington's evil penchants.

"I wonder how righteous he'd try to appear if we informed the *ton* that he played a role in his first wife's death. Or that his second wife took her own life rather than submit to his cruelty and sexual depravity one day longer."

Grace breathed a trembling sigh. "He'd escape society's censure as he always has. People are always fooled by a person's outward appearance."

"Look at how he hangs at Father's side. I'd love to know what Father has that he wants."

Grace's blood ran cold. "I'm sure it's nothing." She turned her head and forced herself to breathe. "Look. Anne and her Mr. Wexley are about to leave. Let's hurry or we'll miss telling them good-bye."

Grace and Caroline made their way across the foyer to wish the bride and groom farewell. Caroline stepped into her waiting husband's arms, and Grace squeezed through the crowd just as Anne and her husband reached the door. Anne turned around one last time and, upon seeing Grace, raced back to give her a tight hug.

"I love you, Grace."

"I love you too, Annie. Always be happy."

"I will. Oh, I will."

Grace wiped a tear from her sister's cheek, then stepped away from the crush of people as her sister stepped back into her husband's arms and raced out the door and down the steps.

"How touching," Baron Fentington whispered from close behind her.

Grace fought the shudder that racked her body, the lurching of her stomach.

"Just think, Lady Grace. In only a few weeks you and I will be the focus of this same attention. Our friends and family will offer us the same congratulations, then wish us well as we race out the door to enter a lifetime of wedded bliss. I can hardly wait to have you all to myself."

Grace feared she would be ill. Baron Fentington looked at her as if he could see through her cool facade and gave her a sinister smile.

"Although I hesitate to admit you were not my first choice of a bride, I can now see you were right when you offered yourself in your sister's place. It is ever so much more rewarding to realize I am getting the better prize in you. You are, after all, a woman who's kept herself pure and untouched her entire lifetime. A woman above reproach and without a spot on her character. What more could a man who demands perfection want in a bride?"

Grace tried to step away from him, but he followed, closing the gap that separated them until he was so close she could feel his breath against her neck.

"I had my reservations, you know. But then realized I was indeed blessed. To have found someone of your years and maturity, still untouched by the sins of the flesh. To know I am the first."

Grace felt the pressure of Baron Fentington's fingers as he rubbed them against the bare flesh at the inside of her upper arm and fought the urge to jerk away from him. Instead, she turned to boldly face him. She lifted her chin and gave him her most haughty air. "If I recall correctly, you gave your word you would not press your suit until the wedding festivities were long over. They are far from over, my lord, and already you have broken your word."

The expression on Fentington's face turned serious, and the hardened look in his eyes caused her breath to catch in her throat. A wave of fear threatened to buckle her knees. Grace knew she had good reason to fear him. There was something truly evil about him. Something dangerous. He reached for her hand and held her fast. When she tried to pull out of his grasp, he squeezed harder.

"Oh, Lady Grace," he said, lifting the corners of his mouth in a sadistic grin. "I can see I made a good decision in offering for you. I will so enjoy curbing that tongue of yours and teaching you submission. But you are right. I did make a promise. So if you will excuse me," he said, lifting her hand until it touched his lips, "I will go home and await word that you are ready to be my wife."

Grace stood numbly as Fentington walked away from her. Her stomach roiled and she clamped her hand over her mouth, then raced to the nearest retiring room. She barely reached a chamber pot before she was violently ill.

Chapter 2

Grace stepped out of the carriage onto the rain-dampened cobblestones at the rear entrance of the large, imposing house halfway across town from her father's town house and willed herself to find the courage to do what she had to do.

"Wait here, Philus. I won't be long."

"Are you sure about this, my lady? A respectable lady like yourself shouldn't be anywhere near a place like this."

"It's all right," she reassured him, even though her heart thundered in her breast. "I'll be fine."

She pulled the hood of her cloak over her head and made her way to the back entrance. Before she could knock, the door opened and a regal-looking butler stepped back to allow her to enter.

"Good evening, my lady," the butler greeted, taking her cloak. He handed it to a waiting footman. "The mistress is expecting you."

Grace smiled a timid smile and entered her friend's home. The foyer was very similar to their own town house, yet even more elegant, with a rare shade of pink marble on the floor and a number of priceless paintings on the wall. In the center of the circular room a large Louis XV table supported a mammoth bouquet of fresh flowers. And overhead hung one of the most beautiful crystal chandeliers Grace had ever seen. The candles were all aglow, and they lighted the room as if it were day instead of the middle of the night.

Grace wasn't sure what she thought she'd find, but realized she hadn't expected anything this grand.

The butler led her across the foyer and down a long, well-lit corridor.

She'd never been here before. Hannah had always been protective of Grace's reputation and insisted they meet in private where no one would see them together. She also insisted Grace always leave first so no one would associate the one with the other. Tonight Grace was too desperate to care if the whole world saw her enter the famous Madam Genevieve's business.

At the end of the hallway, the butler stopped and rapped softly on a door. Grace heard Hannah's familiar voice bid them enter, and she stepped hesitantly through the opening.

"Grace?"

Grace looked across the room to where Hannah stood and stopped short. She knew it was her friend standing there, but this wasn't the Hannah that Grace was used to seeing. This wasn't the Hannah who always dressed in a plain yet fashionable day dress that drew no attention when they met. The Hannah who wore her hair in a modest yet stylish fashion that didn't cause heads to turn.

The woman who stood before her now didn't bear the slightest resemblance to that other woman—her childhood friend. The girl with whom she'd shared all her secrets, her fears, her dreams.

The woman standing before her tonight was more stunning than any female Grace had ever seen. No wonder the rumors surrounding the famous Madam Genevieve were legendary. They were true.

Madam Genevieve wore a low-cut gown of scarlet satin that revealed enough of her rounded breasts to be scandalous, yet not so much as to pass the line of obscenity.

Her hair was done up in an intricate style that allowed her golden tresses to cascade down over her shoulder. Shimmering wisps framed her heart-shaped face. Several scarlet satin ribbons twined through the loose curls. And there were scores of tiny rubies—whether real or not, Grace couldn't tell—throughout her hair. They sparkled like colored stars in the candlelight.

But it was Madam Genevieve's face that held Grace's attention. Hannah had always been beautiful. The creamy complexion of her face and midnight blue of her eyes set her apart from even the loveliest women society had to offer. No wonder her name was bandied about as the most notorious madam in London.

"This isn't how you're used to seeing me, is it, Grace?"

Grace shook her head. "I'm just not used to seeing you dressed so elegantly."

Hannah laughed. "You're used to seeing me as little Hannah from Sussex County. That's who I used to be. This is who I am now. Madam Genevieve from fashionable London. One of the city's most famous courtesans."

Grace lowered her gaze.

"Don't be embarrassed, Grace. I'm quite comfortable with who I am."

"I know. And it's all right. Really it is."

"But..." Hannah continued as she walked toward her, "there's enough of the prim, proper Lady Grace inside you that's more than a little shocked when you come face-to-face with an honest-to-goodness whore."

Grace was dismayed. "Don't call yourself that. That term is too demeaning for you."

Hannah laughed. "I see I've shocked your delicate sensibilities."

Grace smiled. "I was hoping I could keep them hidden."

"There's very little either one of us can hide from the other. We've been friends too long." Hannah reached for Grace's hands, then pulled her into a tight embrace. "So why don't you sit down and tell me why you're here," she said when she released her. "You shouldn't be, you know. It's not at all respectable. But those dark circles beneath your eyes tell me whatever brought you here must be serious."

Grace followed Hannah to a settee on the other side of the room. She lowered her gaze when she sat in order to hide the telltale signs of the last two sleepless nights. She wasn't sure she could go through with this, but she knew she had no choice. It was the only plan she could come up with to avoid the life of hell she would live if she married the baron.

"I'm desperate, Hannah. I need your help."

Hannah's concerned look focused on Grace as she sat next to her and reached for her hands. "Are you carrying a babe, Grace?"

Grace's eyes popped open. "I only wish it were that simple."

A frown deepened across Hannah's forehead. "Well, I'm relieved to hear you're not, but I'd hardly call being with child a 'simple' problem. If it's not a babe, then what is it?"

"I'm being forced to marry."

Hannah leaned back against the cushions. "I take it your father found someone to line his coffers adequately."

Grace nodded.

"But the man is not of your choosing?"

Grace looked away uncomfortably.

Hannah's brows lifted. "He must be terribly unsuitable if the idea of marrying him has brought you to me."

"He is."

"And none of your sisters can help?"

Grace shook her head. "No. They must never find out about this."

"The man your father promised you to must truly be reprehensible. I can only think of one person who would be so—"

Grace knew the moment her friend realized who her father intended her to marry. Hannah's body stiffened and her grip on Grace's fingers tightened. "Does this have anything to do with your sister Anne's recent marriage?"

Grace nodded.

Hannah rose from the settee and stood with her back to Grace. She absently stared at the logs still burning in the fireplace but kept her hands clenched at her sides. When she spoke, her words came out strained, as if it took an effort to speak. "He wanted her, didn't he? The bastard wanted Anne, and to save her you offered yourself in her place."

Grace didn't answer. There was no need. They both let the fragile silence buffer their anger, knowing no matter what happened, the hatred and bitterness they shared would not go away.

Grace clutched her hands in her lap. "He's coming to make the final arrangements next week. He will, of course, want my assurance that I am still a…a…"

Hannah slashed her hand through the air, the sharp movement stopping Grace's words. "Of course. That you are still a virgin. How like him," she whispered. "He will need to make sure his new wife is a vestal virgin before he sacrifices her to his demonic gods."

Grace shuddered. "I'm sorry, Hannah. I know this is painful for you, but…"

Hannah lifted her chin and faced Grace squarely. "Painful, yes. But I was only his daughter. I was able to escape. It is the poor women he marries who have no hope. Except to choose to take their own lives rather than live with someone so evil."

Grace lowered her head, trying not to think of the hell Fentington's two wives had endured. "I won't marry him, Hannah. I lied to him and my father and said I would to stall for time and save Anne. But there's no way I'll marry him."

"Nor would I let you," Hannah said with a vehemence Grace wasn't used to hearing from her friend.

Hannah stepped over to where Grace sat and knelt in front of her. "What do you want me to do?" she said, clutching her hands.

"I've thought for days, but I can't think of any way to escape marrying him except one."

Hannah's eyes opened wide when she realized what Grace meant to do. "Oh, Grace."

"Is there another way? Can you think of any other way, Hannah?"

There was a long silence before Hannah raised her head. When she looked into Grace's eyes, she wasn't Hannah any longer, but Madam Genevieve.

"No, Grace. That's the only way. The bastard will never want you if he knows you've already given your body to someone else."

Grace breathed a deep breath of resolve. "Will you help me?"

"You know I will." Hannah released Grace's hands and stood. "Do you know what this means, Grace? I mean…do you know what a man must do to take a woman's virginity?"

Grace tried to smile but couldn't. "Yes. I have six married sisters, none of whom have ever been shy when it comes to discussing even the private aspects of marriage. I also have eleven—soon to be twelve—nieces and nephews, more than half of whom I've helped deliver. Unfortunately, I'm only too well aware of what has to happen. Although I think this is one instance when ignorance might be blissful."

"Have you thought what you will do if you conceive?"

The air caught in Grace's throat. She wouldn't let herself even consider that possibility. "I won't."

Hannah shook her head. "I'm so sorry, Grace. I know this isn't how you wanted your life to go."

"None of us get everything we ask for. Some get far less. You know that as well as I."

Her friend gave her a quick hug, then stepped back, a serious look on her face. "Is there anyone special to whom you wish to give yourself?" she asked.

Grace felt her cheeks flame. "I don't want to know him, Hannah. Although, since I haven't been an active part of London's social life for more than ten years, I doubt that's a probability. And I don't want him to be younger than I am. It just wouldn't be right to give myself to someone who is as young as one of my sisters' husbands. And most of all," Grace said, staring down at the floor, "I don't want him to be married."

"Oh, Grace. I wish it didn't have to be like this."

"So do I." Grace hesitated, then said, "Have I asked for too much? Do you think there's anyone in London who fits my requirements?"

Hannah paced the floor, then stopped in front of the fire to stare at the flames. Grace fought her nervous anticipation while she waited for Hannah to answer. When Hannah turned, there was a serious look on her face.

"Yes, Grace. I think there just might be. I'll send my carriage for you on Thursday. There's no need for your driver to wait all night at the back entrance and risk someone recognizing your carriage."

"Thank you, Hannah." Grace swept away an errant tear that dared to tumble down her cheek.

Hannah narrowed her gaze, the harsh resolve evident on her face. "I should have killed him when I had the chance."

"No," Grace argued. "He's not worth it."

But a small part of her wished someone had done just that.

Chapter 3

Vincent Germaine, Duke of Raeborn, sat behind his mammoth oak desk and shuffled through the stack of papers in front of him. Bills. Each one of them another damning piece of evidence that outlined his cousin's extravagance and waste.

When would he ever learn!

Raeborn dragged his hand across his jaw in frustration. He'd been his cousin's guardian for the last six years, since the lad's father died when he was sixteen. Being an only child, the boy had been raised with too much freedom. But Raeborn had hoped as his cousin reached manhood he would grow out of his spendthrift ways. That in time Kevin Germaine would mature enough to realize the great responsibility that would one day be his. That in time he would be worthy enough to hold the Raeborn title.

Instead, his spending had increased more recklessly by the month. Kevin was two and twenty now, and if something weren't done soon, the young man would be so far in debt even the inheritance that would become his on his twenty-fifth birthday wouldn't be enough to keep him out of debtor's prison.

Raeborn shoved back his chair and bolted to his feet. He looked down at his desk, then pounded a fist against the mounting pile of debts in frustration. What had gone wrong? How had he failed? Kevin was the only living Germaine left to inherit the dukedom and to head the Raeborn dynasty, and he didn't want to think what would happen to the wealth his ancestors had amassed once it passed into his cousin's hands.

A sickening weight lay in the pit of his stomach when he thought of how easy it would be for Kevin to lose it all on his excessive living, gaming, and steady string of mistresses. How quickly the thriving estates would fall to ruin. How recklessly Kevin had already squandered the money Vincent gave him as an allowance. Vincent broke out in a cold sweat just thinking of it.

He thumbed through the papers strewn on his desk even though he knew each of them by heart. Bills for a matching pair of blacks, for an emerald necklace and earbobs, the cost of which could feed and house a hundred families for a year. Numerous bills totaling hundreds of pounds to a half dozen of the finest modistes in London, plus thousands of pounds for gaming debts, household debts, tailoring...

The list went on and on. Vincent raked his fingers through his hair in an uncommon display of temper, stopping a vile oath just as the door opened.

"Mr. Germaine to see you, Your Grace," his butler said from the open doorway.

"Thank you, Carver."

Germaine burst into the room as if being announced were a formality for which he didn't have time in his busy schedule. Vincent felt the familiar fondness that surged through him every time he saw the lad, for who couldn't help but be drawn to the exuberance and zest for living that was such a part of Germaine's personality? And yet…

Vincent looked to the mounting stack of bills on his desk, then gave his cousin a cursory glance. He was dressed in the latest fashion, his exquisitely tailored jacket and trousers a dark gray and his waistcoat a lighter shade of dove gray. Vincent could see at a glance what at least some of his money had been spent on. Although the lad made a striking figure if one took note of how he was dressed, it was not the expense of the clothes draping his body that caused a second look. Not his extreme good looks that endeared him to nearly every female in London, married or not. It was the easygoing expression on his handsome face, the devil-may-care twinkle in his eyes that acted like a magnet.

"Kevin," Vincent greeted, hoping to see some serious inclination.

"Your Grace."

He saw nothing that resembled it.

"Have a seat." Vincent lifted his hand, indicating one of the two leather chairs facing his desk.

There was a slight lift to his cousin's eyebrows as well as the audible sigh of—boredom?—before he sauntered to the chair and sat.

"What an…unexpected pleasure, Your Grace. Although I can't imagine the reason for the urgent summons."

"Can't you?"

Vincent picked up the stack of papers from his desk and placed them in Germaine's lap. "Perhaps these will enlighten you then."

Kevin Germaine gave the papers barely a glance before setting them back on Vincent's desk. "I'm twenty-two years of age, Raeborn. Surely you no longer expect me to account to you for every debt I incur?" He flicked his finger at an imaginary piece of lint on his jacket sleeve as if removing it were of utmost importance.

"No. Not every debt. Just the exorbitant debts that take you well over your quarterly allowance."

"Quarterly allowance? I've told you for years I cannot possibly live on the pittance on which you and my deceased father expect me to survive. I have a position to uphold. Certain standards to maintain."

Raeborn struggled to keep his temper in check. "That is not the point. You know the amount set aside for you each quarter is more than generous. Perhaps if you curtailed the amount you spent on your mistress, or limited what you lose at the gaming tables, you could see your way clear to pay your debts instead of expecting me to cover them."

A slow, innocent smile spread across his cousin's face, turning his handsome features into the face that had gotten him everything he'd ever wanted from the time he was a babe. "Isn't that what you promised Father you would do?" he asked, almost baiting Raeborn to deny it. "Didn't you promise him on his deathbed that you would always provide for me?"

Raeborn breathed a heavy sigh. He closed the gap between them, his determined steps making soft thuds on the thick Persian carpet. He did not let his gaze leave his cousin's, but honed in on him with the serious glare that was such a normal part of his demeanor. It was time to put his foot down. Time to put a stop to his cousin's extravagant spending.

"No. I haven't forgotten the promise I made your father. You, however, are the one who has misinterpreted what I promised."

Vincent saw a brief look of confusion on his cousin's face. That look was quickly replaced with the endearing smile that Vincent was so used to seeing.

"Spare me, Cousin," Kevin Germaine said, holding out his hands. "I remember vividly what you promised."

"Then you'll remember I gave your father my word I would see to your well-being."

Germaine shrugged. "I hardly see a problem. Just think of each bill as something essential to my well-being."

Vincent tightened his fists until they ached. His cousin instinctively knew just how to push him to the edge of his endurance. He would not let it happen this time.

The clock in the vestibule outside the door struck the quarter hour, then ticked on with unerring accuracy. The slow, steady clack of the pendulum pounded in unison with the painful drumming inside his head.

"Oh, come now, Your Grace. I am hardly intimidated by your hesitation. What is a meager thousand pounds or two to the overflowing Raeborn coffers? It's not as if you don't have enough to spare."

Vincent's shoulders stiffened. The blood thundered in his head. How had it come to this? Was his cousin truly such a wastrel that he thought there would never be a limit to the amount he could spend?

"What is it?" the young man said, rising and walking to the small table of liquor decanters. "Do you enjoy the dominance you have over me because you control my purse strings? Do you hope to see me beg?"

Vincent started. "I have never made you beg."

His young cousin threw the liquor to the back of his throat, then slammed the glass down on the table. "No. Never *quite*, Your Grace."

Vincent rubbed at the sudden tension in his neck. "Is that what you think I want?" His confusion as to how to handle his cousin overwhelmed him. "To see you beg?"

"What else could it be? You flaunt your air of supremacy, your condescending attitude, as if you have the right to make the rules to govern my life. You attempt to dictate my actions so I become the stuffy, staid, meticulously pompous member of society you are. God forbid I am condemned to such a boring life as yours. Well," he said, slashing his hand through the air, "enjoy it while you can. You only have three more years until I turn twenty-five. Then I will have full control over my inheritance."

Vincent turned on him. "At this rate, you won't have an inheritance to control!"

"Then I will have to continue to rely on the promise you gave Father, won't I?"

Raeborn couldn't believe his cousin's audacity. "Have you ever thought where the money you spend comes from? Ever considered the hours of labor that go into earning the fortune you waste every day? Ever considered the hard work it takes the tenants *you* are responsible for to earn even enough to pay for the clothes on your back?" Raeborn took a step closer to his cousin. "Evidently not," he said, his voice holding as much regret as anger. "Because you have always had everything handed to you as if it took no effort on anyone's part to provide for your pleasure. A mistake I intend to rectify."

The young wastrel had given him no choice. He needed to be taught a lesson. Needed to learn responsibility before it was too late.

"By making some changes now, perhaps by the time you reach your five and twenty years you will be responsible enough to manage your inheritance."

"And if I'm not? Are you implying that you will no longer come to my aid?" Kevin Germaine's lips curled upward in a daring grin. "I think not, Raeborn. You gave my father your word, and far be it from the Duke of Raeborn to ever go back on a promise. It's not in your character, Your Grace. You are far too noble. Far too…responsible."

Kevin poured another swallow of expensive brandy into his glass and downed it in one gulp.

Vincent waited until his cousin finished, then locked his gaze with his own. "Sit down."

"I prefer to stand, Your Grace. In fact," he said, returning to his former, lackadaisical self, "if you're close to being finished, I prefer to take my leave. I've an important engagement and I feel extraordinarily lucky."

Vincent lowered his voice, his command a serious whisper. "Sit down."

His cousin hesitated as if considering ignoring Raeborn's blatant warning signs. But his better judgment prevailed and he took a seat and waited.

Vincent picked up the thick stack of bills, then let them fall again to the top of the desk. "I will send a message to my solicitor yet today to pay each of these bills in full."

A knowing smile lifted the corners of the young upstart's mouth.

"Along with each payment will be a letter signed by me, informing every proprietor and tradesman that this will be the last expense accrued by his cousin, Kevin Germaine, that the Duke of Raeborn will cover."

Germaine bolted out of his chair. "What did you say?"

"You heard me, Kevin. You'll get no more money from me."

"You can't mean that! You promised my father—"

"I promised your father that I would see to your well-being," Vincent cut in. "I intend to do just that. You have a lot to learn and a huge responsibility that will eventually be placed on your shoulders."

Vincent walked to the sideboard and poured a generous amount of whiskey into a glass. He usually had one glass of brandy late in the afternoon before his evening engagements, but today he needed whiskey to calm his nerves. He took a long swallow, then turned to face his cousin.

"As of today, I will take care of the monthly rent on your town house here in London. I will also pay the yearly salaries for the…ten?…fifteen?…"

Germaine shrugged his shoulders defensively. "Twenty."

Raeborn arched his eyebrows. "Twenty servants you need to run your home. I will also deed you the Castle Downs estate. It is yours."

Germaine's disbelief was almost palpable. It came out in the form of a loud, demented laugh.

"The town house is yours to do with as you want," Raeborn continued. "You can sell it or keep it. It doesn't matter to me. Castle Downs, however, has belonged to a Raeborn for over four hundred years. It can never be sold. That will be in writing."

"And my quarterly allowance, Your Grace?" Germaine asked through clenched teeth.

"You will receive what your father set up for you in his will."

"You can't mean that! How do you expect me to live on that paltry amount?"

Raeborn ignored the hostile expression on his cousin's usually pleasant face. "Castle Downs has always provided the Raeborn family with an adequate income. If managed well, you should have more than enough on which to live."

Fire blazed from his cousin's eyes, his nostrils flaring wide. "I won't tolerate this. You can't expect me to exist like this. I have no intention of locking myself away in the country like some simpleminded fool."

"That decision is yours to make. I have given you the means to support yourself. What you do with the opportunity is up to you."

Vincent's young cousin fisted his hands at his sides and took a step closer. "Why are you doing this?"

"Because you are my heir! The only heir I will ever have!"

Tension crackled between them with as much force as a gunshot. Several long seconds passed and neither of them moved. When Raeborn spoke, his voice was calm and even, the tone more dangerous than if he had shouted.

"When I die, you will inherit one of the most respected titles in England. As well as enough wealth to maintain its greatness. I cannot take credit for anything I have been given. It was earned by those who came before me and passed down from one generation to the next. But this gift comes at a cost.

"The weight of responsibility is staggering. Hundreds of people rely on my judgment for their livelihood, for the very food that goes on their tables. For the clothes on their backs as well as the roofs over their heads. I have accepted this responsibility. But I'm afraid you see only what you can take from the gift. Not what is expected of you so that what you've been given prospers."

Raeborn paused, waiting for some sign his cousin concurred. He felt immense disappointment when no sign was forthcoming. Even though only ten years separated them, he knew the animosity Germaine harbored stemmed from a lifetime of jealousy and envy on the younger man's part. His cousin's next words emphasized it.

"You are only doing this because all the Raeborn wealth is already at your fingertips. Because of a freak accident of birth, your father inherited everything and mine nothing. Because of the mere eighteen minutes that separated their entrance into the world, your father inherited the riches while mine was left a pauper."

Vincent gripped the edge of the sideboard until his fingers ached. "Whether my father was born eighteen minutes before yours or eighteen years, it still made him the firstborn and heir. He was born heir to the Dukedom of Raeborn, as was I."

Vincent emptied the whiskey in his glass and filled it again. After he took another swallow, he spun around to face down his cousin. "I have given you all you are going to get."

"Damn you, Raeborn!"

"Enough! In time it will all be yours. Hopefully when it passes down to you, you will be responsible enough to appreciate the gift you have inherited."

"A town house and country estate are not enough. How dare you expect me to live like a country squire when I am your heir? Your heir!"

"Then be an heir I can be proud of!"

Vincent's retort was a rare display of his anger and frustration. He regretted his words as soon as they left his mouth.

It was at times like this that he'd give everything he'd inherited for things to be different. That he'd gladly hand over the Raeborn title and everything that went with it if the two women who'd sacrificed their lives to give him an heir were still alive.

Vincent gripped the glass until he feared the expensive crystal would shatter in his hand. "Any argument you pose is a moot point, cousin. The fact remains that, until my death, I am still the Duke of Raeborn."

"That fact is always in the forefront of my mind, *Your Grace*."

Vincent didn't react to the sarcasm in his cousin's voice. "A letter will be dispatched to my solicitor yet today to pay all your outstanding debts. The papers concerning your London town house and Castle Downs estate will be ready for your signature in a week's time."

The Duke of Raeborn slowly stood and, with his glass in hand, walked to the window. He turned his back on his cousin as a sign of dismissal.

There was a slight pause before Germaine stormed from the room, the heavy oak door slamming behind him.

Vincent slowly lifted the glass to his mouth and drank. He'd had far more than usual and was close to being drunk. Today, however, he didn't care. Too many of his cousin's words burned like acid in an open wound. Too many of his accusations were closer to the truth than he wanted to admit. He *was* stuffy and staid. He'd seen too much death not to be. Given up too much of his heart not to protect himself behind a cloak of detachment. Let the world think his heart was made of stone. It mattered not to him.

He picked up the half-empty decanter and walked back to the window. The sun was starting to set, afternoon shadows lengthening. He tipped the decanter to fill his empty glass and poured the liquid with hands that trembled almost uncontrollably. It had been a long time since past regrets waged an attack with such a vengeance.

The faces of both his young wives flashed before him. They'd both been tender and sweet in their own ways, as different as night from day, yet the same. They'd both been robbed of a lifetime of gaiety and laughter. A lifetime he'd stolen from them.

No. He would never marry again. Having a child was risk enough to any woman. Having *his* child was a death sentence. How could he condemn another woman to the same fate?

He took the bottle and his glass and sat down heavily in the large mahogany-colored wing chair. He propped his elbows on the padded leather arms and held the glass carefully in his hands, then rested his chin on his steepled fingers while his mind shifted to memories long buried. To the two beautiful, perfectly formed babes he'd cradled in his arms before laying them with their mothers for eternity.

* * *

Vincent sat in his chair and watched out the window as the sky turned darker. A footman set fire to the logs when the room took on a chill, and Carver replaced the empty whiskey decanter with a new one. He'd had more to drink than was usual for him. Far more than he was used to—something he never allowed himself to do. But he wasn't drunk. Just…numb.

With a sad smile, he admitted that tonight he did not care. That just this once, he would allow himself to wallow in a mire of self-pity.

He lifted the decanter he'd set on the floor and tipped more of the liquid into his glass. He took another sip of the whiskey and lowered his arm.

"Did Your Grace wish for his carriage tonight?" Carver asked from the open doorway.

Vincent expelled a weary sigh. "What function am I supposed to be attending, Carver?"

"It's Thursday, Your Grace."

He dropped his head back against the cushion of the chair and smiled.

Thursday.

"Yes, Carver. Have my carriage sent round."

Vincent set the glass on a nearby table and rose.

He was never in his life so glad for a Thursday.

Chapter 4

Raeborn stepped out of his carriage and maneuvered the walk and the five steps to the exclusive brothel he'd visited every Thursday night since his second wife's death. His legs felt strangely relaxed from the excessive liquor he'd already consumed. He couldn't remember ever losing such control except for the week after he'd buried his first wife. And another week after he'd buried his second. They were the only two weeks of self-pity he'd allowed himself before he stepped back into the ducal role he'd been born to live.

Tonight, his cousin and heir was responsible for his lapse of self-control. Bloody hell, but the boy had a lot to learn. If something happened to him tonight and Kevin became the next Duke of Raeborn, everything would be lost. The wastrel didn't have the slightest idea of the responsibility that would be placed on his shoulders. He didn't have the vaguest notion of the demands that would be thrust on his time. Vincent's blood ran cold just thinking about it.

He looked at the stylish London town house that was his usual Thursday night destination. Yes, he needed to be here. Needed this release more tonight than he had for a long, long time.

He needed to be able to bury himself deep inside a soft feminine body and slake his passion until he could forget all he'd lost—all he would never have. He needed to visit the place where he was least likely to leave a woman pregnant.

This was why he'd never taken a mistress. Not every woman who gave her body to a man in exchange for clothes and jewels and a fine house knew how to prevent a man's seed from taking root. So when he needed a release from this human side of his nature, there was only one place he felt comfortable going. One place he knew he could satisfy his physical needs without adding more emotional scars to his already riddled heart—Madam Genevieve's.

Madam Genevieve catered to only the most selective clientele, and her girls were, without exception, from a higher class than any of the other London bordellos. Some of them were actually less fortunate members of the *ton*, he was sure. No matter what their reasons for being here, and he assumed there were many, the girls who gave their bodies for a man's pleasure were here because they chose to be. They were eager and willing to satisfy a man's every desire, yet knowledgeable concerning every method available of preventing a pregnancy. And that was his primary concern, his cardinal rule.

After the death of his second wife, he'd vowed never to plant his seed inside a woman again. That he would never let another woman die birthing his babe. To guarantee this, Vincent added another safeguard. He always found his release outside a woman's body. It was a rule he'd made after Angeline's death. One he always kept.

Raeborn's body hardened in anticipation as his footsteps carried him toward the brothel. Before he reached the entrance, the thick oak door opened.

"Your Grace." A man clad in dark maroon livery bowed regally.

"Good evening, Jenkins. Is your mistress in?"

"Yes, sir. She's expecting you. In the Gardenia Room."

Vincent smiled. Oh, yes. He needed to be here.

"Thank you, Jenkins. I can find my way."

"As you wish," the butler said, then walked across the tiled foyer and out of sight.

Vincent walked past the curved stairway that led to the private rooms upstairs, then past a half dozen sitting rooms—the Daffodil Room, the Hyacinth Room, the Azalea Room, the Daisy Room, the Marigold Room. The Gardenia Room. He knocked softly, then turned the knob.

As usual, the smell of fresh flowers assaulted his nose. A dozen or more bouquets from recent admirers sat on tabletops and pedestal stands scattered throughout the room. He had to search for her amid the arrangements, but finally found her standing by the window.

She turned and smiled when he entered the room.

"Your Grace," she said, curtsying gracefully.

Raeborn let his appreciative gaze soak in her beauty. Genevieve was twenty-nine, perhaps thirty, with a small, voluptuous body he couldn't imagine ever showing the ravages of age. Her gown was exquisite, made of the softest shade of yellow and cut in the latest fashion.

She wore her hair swept up to the top of her head, then left to cascade downward in a riot of thick curls. She wore very little makeup. Only a spot of rouge on her cheeks and a hint of red to her lips. She was lovely in the most elegant manner. A beauty beyond compare. When she lifted her gaze to greet him, he couldn't help but smile. "Genevieve," he said, taking her hand and kissing it. "You look lovely tonight."

"Thank you. And you look…" She reached up and placed her palm against his cheek. "Ah. It has been a difficult day. Let me get you a glass of brandy."

Vincent smiled. "I think tonight I'd rather stay with whiskey. It might not be wise to switch at this late hour."

Genevieve raised her eyebrows and lifted the stopper on a crystal decanter of amber liquid. She poured each of them a drink. "You are late. I was afraid—" She cast a glance over her left shoulder and smiled. "The *girls* were afraid you would not come."

Vincent sat on the plush floral settee and rested one ankle atop the opposite knee. He always felt so at ease here. So comfortable.

She handed him a glass over his shoulder. When he took it, she rested her fingers on his shoulders and massaged his tense muscles.

"Do you remember the first time we met, Your Grace?"

"Of course."

Vincent took a swallow of Genevieve's excellent liquor and leaned back to let her work her magic.

"I was only nineteen and had just come to work for Madam Renée. You were a young man of what? Twenty-one? Twenty-two?"

"Twenty-two."

"You'd lost your first wife the year before and were still grieving."

"It was a difficult time for me," he said, remembering how devastated he'd been. How hard it had been to get over his loss. Genevieve had been a true friend then. Listening when he needed to talk. Loving him when words no longer helped. "You always knew what was going on in my head, Genny. How did you do it?"

"I understood you only too well, Your Grace. We're very much alike, you know. We both suffer from the same nightmares. Different in substance, yet the same—and equally terrifying."

"And what is your nightmare, Genny? You know mine. But you've never told me what horrors have you in their clutches."

Genevieve reached over his shoulder and took the empty glass from his hand. "My nightmares are best left where they are. Bringing them out in the open won't help either you or me."

She came around the settee and sat next to him. "We have been friends a long time, Raeborn. I want you to know how much I value your friendship. I would never intentionally do anything to risk losing it."

"Nor I yours." Her words confused him, but he wasn't sure why.

She gave him her most brilliant smile. "However, you did not come to visit with me. Did you?"

Raeborn smiled. "So who have you chosen for me tonight? Corrine?"

"No, Your Grace. Tonight you will have…Deborah."

A frown wrinkled his forehead. He realized he was far from sober, but that name was not familiar to him.

"Is she new?"

"Yes. But you will not have to worry. You will find her most eager to please. It is quite shameless the way my girls fight over you."

Raeborn shook his head. "I think what is shameless is the way you flatter me, Madam."

Genevieve laughed, the sound clear and melodious.

"Ah. You have discovered my secret." She rose and walked to the door. "I think it is time you met Deborah."

Vincent sat forward to rise and stopped. A sudden rush of warmth engulfed him. It wasn't the heat one associated with the warmth of the sun on a bright summer's day, but an unusual heat creeping to every extremity in his body. Down his arms and legs, then settling deep in the pit of his stomach. It was not an uncomfortable warmth, but a euphoric sensation that seemed to lift away the troubles and worries he'd brought with him.

"Deborah is waiting upstairs for you," Genevieve said, standing at his side. "In the Peach Room."

"Then I'd best go. I wouldn't want to keep the lady waiting."

Genevieve walked with him to the bottom of the stairs and gifted him with an open smile before leaving him. He felt strange, but pleasantly so, and with each step he climbed toward the private rooms above, his anticipation grew stronger. The desire to find release in a woman's warm, willing body grew more desperate with each footfall.

When he reached the Peach Room, he knocked quietly, then opened the door when a soft voice bade him enter.

The room was dimly lit, only the flames from the fireplace casting a light by which to see. He scanned the room.

His gaze stopped when he saw her sitting on a chair by the window. She rose when he entered.

He wasn't sure exactly what he expected, but he was somewhat surprised by the girl facing him. She didn't have the look most of Genevieve's girls had. She seemed softer, even delicate.

He stepped into the room and closed the door behind him. She took a tentative step toward him, then stopped, her air of innocence taking him quite by surprise.

She was exquisitely shaped, exactly the paramour most men of society demanded from a high-class establishment like Madam Genevieve's. But she did not seem as bold as most of Genevieve's girls. This one seemed almost shy.

Her long blonde hair hung loosely around her shoulders and flowed in beautiful waves that cascaded down her back nearly to her waist. A sheer white chemise, so thin he could see the outline of her shapely legs in the glow of the firelight, covered her body. She wore nothing beneath it.

For someone so slender, her breasts were round and full. Her waist was narrow and her hips fanned out with the fullness of age, but not unseemly so. She was not so very tall, but he knew when he stood next to her the top of her head would reach nearly to his chin. He was glad. He hated how he towered over most females. Hated the way he dwarfed them.

She was older, perhaps twenty-eight or -nine.

He smiled. It had been a long time since he'd met someone who didn't make him feel like he'd stolen her from a schoolroom.

He walked toward her, his fingers pulling his cravat loose. "Good evening, Deborah. Genevieve tells me you're new."

"Yes." She smiled a shy greeting, then took another hesitant step forward.

Her timidity was endearingly sweet, and he smiled in hopes of relaxing her. "Would you prefer to talk a while first?"

Her eyes widened. "No. I mean…not unless that is what you prefer."

He shook his head. "No. That is not what I prefer." He shrugged out of his coat.

She stepped up behind him and took his jacket from his shoulders, then placed it over the back of the chair. He removed his waistcoat next and handed it to her. Then his cravat and finally his shirt. She placed each item on the chair and watched him closely as he sat on the edge of the bed to remove his boots.

"Please, allow me to do that," she said, her voice soft and seductive.

He nodded and leaned back, bracing his hands behind him on the mattress. When she reached down to pull his boots from his feet, he noticed her hands shook slightly. That realization pleased him.

He stood when he was bare except for his trousers. "Should I light a candle?"

"Would you mind if we…didn't?"

"Not at all." He stepped closer to her and brushed the backs of his fingers down her cheek. "Making love in the moonlight is always more enjoyable."

She lowered her head and stepped toward him. She lifted her chin slowly, her gaze taking in his features. She didn't seem disappointed by what she saw, and Vincent felt an uncharacteristic warmth at the realization that he pleased her.

Their gazes locked and he couldn't move, couldn't turn away from her. For a moment they remained frozen until, in a slow, intimate gesture, she raised her hand and pressed her palm to his cheek.

Her movement was at first light and tentative. Her fingers trembled slightly as she traced the line of his jaw, then moved upward to lightly brush across his forehead. But in time she became more confident.

"You are a man who worries much," she whispered, rubbing a finger over his brow.

He smiled, something he didn't often do. But he'd had enough to drink that the smile came easily. Enough to drink that her touch affected him more than a woman's touch usually did. Enough to drink that he was completely enamored of the innocent warmth of the woman giving herself to him. "Only occasionally," he answered, forcing his hands to remain at his sides to keep from rushing ahead too quickly. His resolve didn't last long.

Vincent reached for the hand pressed against his cheek. Her hand seared his flesh where she touched him. He turned it over, then pressed his lips to her palm.

The intake of her breath affected him. A need so powerful he could barely control it consumed him. He wanted her. Wanted to bury himself deep inside her and take out his needs and frustration until he could forget all he'd lost.

He placed his palms on her shoulders, then slowly ran his hands up and down her arms. With a heavy sigh, he lowered his head and rested his forehead against hers.

"You're perfect."

"As are you."

She placed her hands on his chest and slowly moved them upward until her arms were wrapped tightly around his neck.

They shared a closeness he was loath to sever. He breathed in the clean smell of her, roses mixed with lilacs, then reached around her and pulled her into his embrace.

"I'm glad Genevieve gave you to me," he whispered, his voice sounding unnaturally husky.

He felt her tremble in his arms and held her tighter. Her arms moved, her fingers touching him, searing his naked flesh. The desire building inside him erupted into a blazing inferno. He lowered his head and covered her mouth with a hungry, desperate kiss.

Bloody hell, but he needed her. Wanted her.

* * *

Grace thought she'd been prepared. Thought she'd known what it would be like when he touched her, when he kissed her. But nothing had prepared her for this. For the heat that enveloped her. For the bolts of energy that spiraled through her. For the liquid fire that weakened her, consuming her at an alarming speed.

Strange and violent sensations moved deep inside her and dropped lower and lower and lower until they reached the very core of her body. A secret place she didn't even know was hidden deep inside her belly came alive. A shudder racked her body, and she leaned closer as if in search of something to which the man holding her held the secret.

She was on fire. Even though the only garment covering her body was a gown so thin and filmy she felt naked, it was too much. Too heavy. Too confining. Oh, heaven help her. She didn't know it would be like this.

He moved his lips over hers, touching her in a way she'd never been touched.

His lips were firm and warm. A fire she couldn't control ignited deep inside her. She prayed he'd never stop kissing her, never stop touching her. Never drop his arms from around her. And he didn't. He held her closer and deepened his kisses.

He opened his mouth atop hers, his tongue skimming her lips, then invading her mouth.

A thousand blinding lights exploded behind her eyes. His tongue touched hers and a loud moan echoed deep inside her. Her heart thundered harder than it had ever pounded before. Raced faster than it had ever gone before. And he kissed her again, drinking deeply from her. Demanding more.

A whimper was the only sound she was capable of making, and she wrapped her arms around his neck and clung to him.

"Ah, what magic you possess," he whispered, his fingers touching her face and his mouth following with tiny kisses. He worked his way down her neck to a tender spot at the base of her throat, then lower where a tiny satin ribbon held the front of her gown together. He pulled on the ribbon and pushed the silky material from her shoulders.

She barely noticed it falling to her feet.

He touched her breasts, molding them, lifting them, holding them in the palms of his hands. "You are beautiful," he whispered, rubbing the sensitive tips.

Her knees buckled beneath her and she clung to him with greater ferocity. What he was doing to her nearly undid her. She cried out, then arched her back, desperate to give him more of herself.

She knew she should feel shame, knew he probably thought her actions were bold and brash, then shoved such a thought from her mind. It was too late to turn back from the course she'd decided to take. Too late to stop now. She was in a brothel, playing the part of a prostitute. He would expect her to be experienced. Expect her to accept his touch without hesitation. Then he moved his mouth to her breasts and she couldn't have stopped him if she'd wanted.

"Touch me," he ordered, and she moved her hands over him, kneading the muscles at his shoulders. Her fingers, tentative at first, then turning braver, played with the thick mat of hair on his chest. Oh, what a strange feel. Not soft. Yet not coarse. She let her hands roam over his torso, touching every inch of him.

He let out a husky cry, then moved his mouth to suckle at her breasts. She gasped and dropped her head back on her shoulders, then arched up to meet him.

His hands moved over her. The feel of him on her flesh sent her soaring to a strange place. To a place where her mind no longer controlled her body. A place where his touch and caress were all that was important. A place where bending to his will, following where he led, was the only choice.

He took a step forward, forcing her to step back. She went gladly, willingly. He moved another step and another, until the bed stopped them from going farther.

"Lie down," he said, undoing the buttons and slipping out of his trousers while she got onto the bed. When he was as naked as she, he lay down beside her and looked at her. There was something tender in his gaze. Something that wiped away her fear, gave her courage to go through with this. It wasn't as if she had a choice. Wasn't as if there was an alternative.

"I'm glad you were the one tonight," he said, and he kissed her again while his hands moved over her breasts and her stomach. Then lower to the throbbing center of her. To the place that ached for his touch.

She cupped her palm to his cheek and brought his lips down to meet hers. He kissed her again then touched her with greater intimacy. She nearly bolted off the bed.

This was what Genny had explained to her. The place where he would enter her. The place she had to let him invade so she would no longer be a virgin. She rubbed her hands over his flesh, pulling him closer. Urging him to complete the act.

"Take me. Now."

"Not yet," he said with a ragged gasp. "You're not ready."

She wanted to argue, wanted to tell him she was. But she couldn't find the words. His mouth had settled on her breast again while his fingers touched her, rubbing that sensitive spot until she almost shattered. She writhed in wild abandon, whimpering until she was nearly in tears. She was desperate for something. And he alone knew what that something was.

"Please. Oh, please."

"Yes. I can't wait," he gasped, a film of perspiration covering his forehead. "I want you too badly."

Without hesitation, he positioned himself over her and entered her in one long thrust. The barrier broke and Grace clamped her lips together to muffle the cry of pain.

"What the—"

His body jerked upward and he bellowed a cry of denial. She could see the turmoil on his face as his mind struggled to understand what had just happened. Grace saw the recognition in his gaze, his eyes wide with confusion and disbelief.

"It's all right. Please. Don't stop."

He looked down on her, the fury evident in his gaze. But she couldn't let him stop. She couldn't let this be all there was. She wrapped her arms around his neck and held him, refusing to let him roll away from her the way she knew he wanted.

"Please, don't stop. Love me. Just this once."

He stared at her as if evaluating what his mind was telling him, then lowered his mouth and kissed her.

The mating of their lips was tentative, hesitant. Then he kissed her again, deeper, as if he realized how desperately she wanted him. Almost as if he wanted her just as much.

"You're sure?"

"Oh, yes."

He moved inside her, slowly, tenderly at first, then faster and faster until she could do nothing but hold him and let him take her on a journey to the stars.

She was desperate to have him. Desperate to give him as much of herself as she could. She matched him thrust for thrust and clung to him as he pushed her to the madness of mindless ecstasy. He drove into her again and again until she cried out her completion.

She was still gasping for air, her hands clutching his shoulders, her legs wrapped around him, when he stiffened above her. With a violent shudder, he let out a lusty cry and found his release.

He collapsed against her and she held him close, refusing to release him. Refusing to separate herself from him.

She heard his gasps for air as she ran her hands over the rippling muscles of his shoulders and down his arms, skimming lightly over the sheen of perspiration that evidenced the ferocity of their lovemaking.

Then she lifted her face and kissed his flesh while tears of elation and sorrow streamed down her cheeks.

* * *

Vincent awoke alone in bed.

He opened his eyes slowly, then looked around the room, trying to remember where he was and who he'd been with. He felt like hell. His head throbbed from a combination of the whiskey he'd had before he'd arrived and whatever it was Genevieve had put in his drink.

And it came back to him in a rush. The girl. Their incredible night of lovemaking. Her hands touching him, her lips kissing him, her legs wrapped around him, enveloping him. Her soft, willing body. The barrier he'd broken.

Bloody hell!

His mind raced to the hours he'd spent with her in his arms. He'd been powerless from the minute he'd kissed her.

Lost to her from the minute he'd touched her. Desperate to bury himself deep within her and never let her go. And that was where he'd found his release. Deep inside her.

He remembered taking her that first time and remembered taking her again later. Remembered her pulling him to her, remembered her urging him to move harder, faster. Remembered her crying out her release.

Remembered spilling his seed inside her.

The memory left him cold. A rush of panic washed over him, stealing the breath from his body.

His head bolted off the pillow and he looked around the room, thinking perhaps she might still be there. Knowing she wouldn't be. Only her robe still lay in a puddle on the floor where it had landed when he'd pushed it from her body.

He was desperate to find her.

He threw back the covers and swung his feet over the edge of the bed. His first attempt to stand ended in defeat and he sank back dizzily. He cradled his head in his hands until his vision cleared. When the world righted itself, he eased himself to his feet and reached for his clothes. He was just buttoning his waistcoat when there was a knock on the door. Genevieve stood in the open archway.

"You slept late, Your Grace."

Raeborn gave her his most intimidating glower, but she knew him too well to be cowed by it. The smile didn't leave her face.

"It's been a long time since you stayed the night. Years, in fact."

"Where is she?"

"Would you care to join me for breakfast before you leave?"

"Where is she?"

He heard her sigh. "She's gone."

His heart lurched in his breast. "What do you mean she's gone?"

Genevieve shrugged her shoulders. "She left early this morning."

"Where'd she go?"

"I don't know, Your Grace."

"You have to. You know everything about each and every one of your girls."

Genevieve didn't answer, and he looked at the stoic expression on her face. "She *is* one of your girls, isn't she?"

Genevieve turned away from him.

Raeborn felt a niggling desperation. He reached for a cup of hot coffee someone had left on the table earlier and drank some. "What did you put in my drink, Genny?"

She didn't answer.

"What?"

She walked to the open window and looked out. "Just something to help you relax. Nothing that could hurt you or make you do anything you ordinarily wouldn't."

He couldn't believe this. He needed to think but couldn't. His head thundered as if two teams of horses were racing through it. He rubbed his hands against his temples. "What's her name? Her *real* name!"

"I can't tell you that, Raeborn."

"Why not?"

"I gave my word."

"I don't give a damn about your word. She was a virgin."

"I know."

"Then you know I have to find her. I could have left her pregnant!"

A confused expression covered Genny's face. "That's not likely. You always pull away before you spill your seed. You never—"

Vincent raked his fingers through his hair. "Well, I didn't with her!"

A suffocating silence hung over them. "I see." She reached out her hand and braced it against the settee.

"Now tell me who she is. I have to know."

Genny shook her head.

"She may have conceived!"

"That is her problem, Raeborn. She knew the risks when she came here."

He stared at her, unable to believe she was saying something so cold, so heartless.

"Why?" he asked, pinning her with his glare. "Why'd she do it?"

"Do what? Give away her virginity?"

"Yes."

"Because she had no other choice."

"She's ruined!"

Genevieve dropped her hands to her sides. Her shoulders sagged in defeat. "Yes. She's ruined."

A long, agonizing silence stretched between them. In frustration, Raeborn slashed his hand through the air. "Why me?"

Genevieve smiled. "Who better, Your Grace? You were my choice. I knew you would be gentle with her and I thought—" She paused. "I thought there would be the least risk of a pregnancy with you." She smiled a halfhearted smile. "Perhaps that is still the case."

"I want to know her name. I need to find her. Talk to her."

Genny faced him squarely. "She doesn't want to be found."

"Then she bloody well shouldn't have slept with me! You more than anyone know that."

Genny held his gaze for a moment longer, then turned back to the window. "Perhaps you did not plant a babe inside her. It does not happen every time. Especially the first."

Raeborn fisted his hands. When he spoke, his words hissed through clenched teeth. "I want to know who she is. I need to make sure."

The famous madam waited a long time as if considering the meaning behind his words. "I will think about it."

"No! You'll damn well tell me."

Genevieve slashed her hand between them. "I will think about it. *If* you're still concerned, come back in two weeks."

"Two!"

"Yes."

"No! I'll give you one week. And only one."

She sucked in a harsh breath. "Very well. One. But I can't promise I will tell you where you can find her. I will have to think about it."

Genevieve looked at him, her chin thrust outward in fierce determination. "You are not the only one who risked much last night, Raeborn. You are not the only one who could come out the loser."

Genevieve walked past him, the clean smell of gardenias and roses lingering behind her. "One week, Your Grace. *If* you are still concerned."

Raeborn stared at the closed door and rubbed his temples.

And he'd thought yesterday had been a bad day!

Chapter 5

The walls trembled from the shouting coming from her father's study. Grace sat in her room with the door closed and the drapes pulled. To the outside world she knew it looked like she was hiding, that she was a coward. Perhaps that was true. She'd already done so many things that required bravery, surely she was allowed just one moment of cowardice.

The voices grew louder, then stopped. But the silence also held a certain terror.

She waited.

She was almost thankful when the angry voices continued. She knew that when the fury stopped they would send for her. Her father would demand she tell Baron Fentington there'd been some mistake. That she'd lied. That of course she was still a virgin.

She clutched her hands around her middle and rocked back and forth, unable to ignore the erratic jumping of her heart in that little indentation at the base of her throat.

She knew what she'd done and did not regret it. She'd thought the act itself would be the most terrifying, the most humiliating. But it had been far from terrifying even though the man Hannah had sent to her had been commanding in size. What he'd done to her had been anything but humiliating.

His dark features and large stature had frightened her at first, but then he'd touched her. His touch had been gentle, his voice soothing, his words comforting.

And he'd kissed her.

Grace touched her fingers to her lips and held them there. She'd never been kissed like that before. She laughed. She'd never really been kissed before. When she was sixteen one of Squire MacKenzie's sons had placed his mouth on hers, but he hadn't kissed her. Not like she'd been kissed by the stranger. Not a kiss where her legs seemed to melt beneath her and her heart thundered in her breast. Not a kiss where his mouth opened atop hers and his tongue searched out hers. Every fear and trepidation had faded when he kissed her, and she'd found herself filled with a desire so intense she couldn't control her actions. A desire she thought perhaps he'd felt as desperately as she.

She couldn't believe she'd done the things she had with him. Found it even harder to believe she'd let him do to her what he had.

Grace closed her eyes until her rapid breathing slowed. Oh, but it had been wonderful.

She refused to forget what it had felt like when he pushed her gown from her shoulders. What it felt like when he held her and touched her and kissed her. When he placed her on the bed and came over her. When he lowered his magnificently muscled body and entered her. She refused to forget even one small detail of that night. Even the pain. It was all part of her experience.

For one night, one brief and wonderful night, she'd been held in a man's arms and loved.

Oh, she knew he didn't love her—he didn't even know her name, just as she didn't know his. But he'd held her and kissed her and taken her as a man takes a woman. He hadn't been repulsed by her because she wasn't a great beauty, or been put off because she wasn't so very young any longer. She was, after all, nearing thirty. He'd only been confused when he realized she was a virgin. But he'd continued making love to her as if he couldn't have stopped even if he'd tried.

Yes, she had this one beautiful memory to cherish. She would never forget even one small detail of it. Never forget one moment of the time she'd spent in her stranger's arms. Never regret what she'd done. No matter what the consequences, it would be better than the certainty she would have faced had she not done something so drastic.

Grace leaned her head back against the cushioned chair and closed her eyes. She let herself remember his face, his dark scowl, his hooded expression, his high, broad cheekbones and wide, angular chin. He was every inch a strong, powerful male. Every inch rugged masculinity. She smiled, then sat up in alarm.

It was quiet below.

She clenched her hands in her lap and tried to keep her breathing even and slow. She said a quick, silent prayer that she'd done enough. That she was now unsuitable to become Baron Fentington's wife. That she would not have to come up with another, more desperate plan to escape a marriage that would be a living hell.

She ground her teeth together when she thought of Fentington. He thought no one knew. Thought his dark secrets were his own and no one was wise to his perverted acts. Thought he could keep his depravity hidden behind his outward show of religious piety. But Grace knew.

She and Hannah had grown up together. Had been best friends. She'd heard too many horror stories not to know what her life would be if she married him—the beatings, the endless hours on her knees in submission and prayer, his sexual depravity. From Hannah she'd even heard as fact that the baron's last wife had taken her own life to escape his cruelty. Had risked eternity in hell rather than a hell here on earth.

No. She would not marry him. But it was her father who concerned her more. He had successfully married off all six of his other daughters. Only Grace, the oldest, remained. The one not quite as pretty or quite as outgoing. The one more content to play her music and read her books than learn to flirt. The one who usually stood off to the side at any gathering and whose intelligence frightened most men away.

The one he'd made sure no one wanted so she would be left behind to be the mother her sisters no longer had.

She knew she'd always been a disappointment to him, but surely when his temper cooled he would realize she could not marry but would be more content single. Surely he would realize their home, Warren Abbey, needed a mistress to run it. That he needed her to be a comfort to him in his old age. He would let her stay here.

Surely he would.

Grace lifted her head at the soft knock at the door and inhaled a deep breath.

"Your father wants you to come to his study, my lady."

Grace looked at the serious expression on the maid's face and repressed a shudder. "Thank you, Esther."

"Baron Fentington is with him."

Grace steeled her resolve, then walked out the door with the same numbness as a prisoner going to the gallows. She braced her shoulders, taking each step with resolute determination. She would not give in on this. She would not let him force her into marriage. Not to Fentington. Not to anyone so reprehensible.

She made her way across the tiled foyer, suddenly feeling very sure of herself even though her stomach churned as if a hundred swirling whirlpools were rushing in opposite directions. She reached out her trembling hand and opened the door.

Her father, the Earl of Portsmont, stood behind his desk, waiting for her. His eyes were glazed with such fury that for the first time in her life she was afraid of him. Baron Fentington stood at the window with his back to her.

"Papa. Lord Fentington."

Neither spoke. Her father remained silent, as if his temper wouldn't allow him to utter any words. Fentington refused to acknowledge her presence, as if turning to greet her was so reprehensible he wouldn't soil his tongue by uttering such blasphemy.

"Come here," her father demanded, stepping out from behind his dark oak desk. He looked as angry as she could ever recall, as near to murder as she'd ever seen. He kept his hands fisted at his sides as if ready to strike out at something, someone. An angry muscle worked at the side of his face and he kept his jaw clamped so tightly he spoke through clenched teeth.

"Tell him. Tell Baron Fentington that you lied. Tell him you are still a virgin."

Grace held her father's intense scrutiny only a moment before lowering her gaze to the floor.

"Tell him!" he yelled, stepping around the corner of the desk. He grabbed her by the shoulders and roughly shook her.

"I cannot."

An angry vein stood out at the side of her father's neck, and for a fleeting moment, Grace felt sorry for him. It wasn't that she cared overly much for him. No more than he cared for her or for any of his daughters. They'd all been disappointments to him. Seven daughters and not one son. But since she was the only one left, all the disappointment and disdain was aimed at her.

Fentington spun around with a long, accusing finger pointed at her. "See! I told you, Portsmont. I told you your daughter was a Jezebel. A harlot. A whore!"

Before she could protect herself, her father reached out his hand and slapped her across the face.

Grace stumbled across the room and cried out in pain when her hip collided with the sharp corner of his desk. She clutched at the desktop, dazed and in pain, but was thankful she'd managed to stay on her feet.

It was the first time she could remember her father striking any one of them.

Whether it was the shock of his hitting her or the unleashed fury behind his attack, she knew she had created a chasm between them that would never be bridged.

"Come here!" he yelled, clamping his fingers around her upper arm and jerking her toward him. "Do you realize what you've done? You've ruined everything!"

Grace pressed her fingers against her stinging cheek and stared at her father. He released her with a shove and stepped over to where Baron Fentington stood. The baron's face piously looked toward heaven and his lips moved as if reciting a silent prayer.

Her father reached for some papers on his desk and took them to where Fentington stood. "It's not too late, Fentington. I won't ask as much for her now. She will come cheaper."

The air left Grace's chest. Blood thundered inside her head. Her father was taking money for her. He was selling her as if she were a head of livestock or a bushel of grain.

Fentington speared a look at her father that simmered with fire and brimstone. "She's used, Portsmont. Tainted. The devil only knows who all has had her."

Her father turned on her. "Who, girl? Who is it?"

Grace backed up until her legs hit one of the two matching leather chairs in front of the desk. Her father reached for her again, but this time she twisted to the side to avoid him. He kept coming after her.

"Father, stop! What are you doing?"

"Who is it, girl? Who have you been laying with?"

She knew he wouldn't give up without an answer. "You don't know him."

Her father looked at her as if he couldn't believe her, as if he thought she might be lying. "It doesn't matter who it is, Fentington. Who it is can't be of importance."

"Doesn't matter! The girl can't even assure us she isn't carrying."

Her father's head jerked back to her. "Are you? Are you carrying some man's bastard?"

Grace placed her hands on her stomach. Of course she wasn't carrying his child. They'd only been together one night. The odds were his seed hadn't taken hold. It had taken each of her sisters months of trying before they conceived. But she couldn't let Fentington know that.

She held her hands against her abdomen as if protecting something very special, then looked into her father's face. What she saw stole her breath. There was hatred there, a repulsion and disgust she'd never noticed before.

"Are you?"

She shook her head. "I don't know."

His arm swung out and he slapped her again. She tasted blood and touched her fingers to her mouth.

Her father drew back his fist again, then stopped as if he realized it was too late. The damage was done. He faced the baron squarely with his head high and his shoulders braced. "We can come to an agreement, Fentington. I know she's far past her prime and not nearly as pretty as the other six, but she'll still serve you well."

"Father, no!"

"She can be taught subservience. With you to guide and mold her, she can be an exemplary wife. She still has a few years of breeding left to give you the heir your other wives were unable to give you."

Fentington snorted a repulsive sound. "She's too old to be molded, Portsmont, and she's given herself as a whore. Any fool knows once a woman's gone down the path of sin and degradation she can no longer be trusted. You keep her. She is of no value to me."

"No. She still has value. Tell him, Grace. Tell him you'll be exactly the kind of wife he wants."

"Father!"

"Tell him!"

Grace felt the floor shift beneath her. "I'd rather rot in hell than let such a contemptible monster as Fentington anywhere near me. His sadistic penchants are so vile and revolting that even if half of the horrific stories about him aren't based on fact, the ones that are true are enough to send him to hell for eternity."

Fentington staggered back as if her words had been a physical attack. The loathing in his glare suggested an underlying evil that frightened her. Then he smiled. The sneer on his face was the most sadistic grin she had ever seen. "Perhaps it would be my Christian duty to wed your daughter to save her soul."

"Yes! Yes!" her father agreed.

Grace's blood turned to ice. "Like you saved your last wife's soul? Do you think there is even one person in all of Herefordshire who doesn't know she took her life to escape you? That death was preferable to living with you?"

Baron Fentington pursed his lips, grinding his teeth so loudly she could hear the grating noise in the deafening silence.

"It would serve you right if I married you and brought you down a peg. You need that viperous tongue stilled and that high-handed attitude subdued. You need your sinful ways beaten out of you and need to be taught humility and respect and contrition. God says—"

"God does not speak through you, Lord Fentington," Grace said, willing herself to find the courage to stand up to him. "And if you ever try to force marriage, I swear I'll go to Reverend Perry and tell him all your dirty little secrets. Perhaps I'll invite him to tea along with Hannah and His Grace, the Duke of Sherefield, our local magistrate. Your daughter can tell them how wonderful it was growing up under your roof."

"Quiet! Don't you mention that harlot's name in my presence. I have no daughter. She is dead!"

"No, she's not. She's alive and well and living the only life growing up in your house has left her."

Fentington's face turned a mottled red. His eyes glared black fury. She could see murder in them and felt a fear unlike any she'd known before.

"The devil has your soul, you spawn of Satan. I should—"

"Try to force my hand, Lord Fentington, and I'll spread the stories of your perverted penchants from here to London and back. And feel no regret while I'm doing it."

Fentington took a step toward her. Grace stepped back, fearing he would do her harm. Certain her father would not come to her aid if he did.

"You can keep your harlot daughter," he said, giving her a final malicious glare. "The devil owns her, body and soul." He turned his attention back to her. "If your father is wise, he'll rid himself and his home of you and throw you out on the street where you belong. You are nothing but a whore. And God will punish you as He does all evildoers for their wicked ways."

Grace lifted her chin and faced him squarely. She refused to be cowed by a man as repulsive as the baron.

"You have played me for a fool. I'll not forget it." His eyes turned blacker. "I've let it out that you agreed to be my wife and will now have to face the humiliation of being spurned. You'll pay for your betrayal. Pay!"

Giving her a last glare, he spun on his heel and stalked from the room. The door slammed behind him and Grace nearly collapsed from fear and relief. Her heart thundered in her breast and she had to reach out a hand and grasp the back of the leather chair to steady herself.

She'd done it. She was safe from him and could spend her days in quiet contentment here in the country, reliving her one magical night and dreaming about the man who'd given it to her. Grace let her throbbing head drop to her hands.

"Get out of my house," her father growled from behind her.

His words slammed against her with the force of a fist pummeling her stomach. The hatred in his voice stole the air from her and engulfed her in a fear from which she couldn't find an escape.

"You will not spend one more night under my roof," he continued, taking a menacing step toward her.

Grace grabbed a fistful of the leather on the back of the chair to keep from sinking to the floor.

"Father—"

"No!" he bellowed, slashing his hand through the air. "Do not call me that ever again. You are no longer my daughter."

She stiffened her shoulders as she faced him. "Were you that desperate for his money?"

He stepped around her, circling her as a hunter circles his prey. "You lied to me. You told me you would accept Fentington's offer once Anne was married."

"Only because you threatened to give her to Fentington if I refused to marry him. I could never have let our Annie marry such a monster."

"So you waited until she was married to drop this surprise on me."

"I waited until she was safe from him. And from you."

"How dare you," he hissed and reached out to slap her again. Grace twisted away quickly enough to spare herself the full brunt of his blow.

With a loud bellow, her father paced back and forth as a man demented. "Do you know what you've done?"

"I've done nothing except refuse to marry a man all of England knows is morally repugnant. You would not make me marry him if you knew what he was truly like."

"You think I don't know?" Her father laughed. "You think I haven't known for years the rumors that surround him?"

Grace tried to speak but no words came out.

"Do you know how much he offered for you? Do you know how rich it would have made me? And I would have gotten rid of you at the same time."

Her father staggered to a small table like a man already drunk. He filled a glass from one of the crystal decanters there and took a long swallow. Then turned back to her with an angry, black look on his face.

"Get out! There is no room for you here anymore." He refilled his glass and took another swallow, his actions more controlled this time. "I am remarrying."

Grace couldn't believe this.

"Lady Constance Sharpley will be my wife. You don't know her. How could you when you spend all your time hiding in the country? But she knows you. Or knows you by reputation. Everyone remembers my oldest daughter who spent her London Season as a wallflower. Whose plain looks and sharp mind sent men fleeing instead of pursuing. Oh, yes. She knows you. Knows of your bookish, domineering ways. And my new countess wants you gone. She wants to come here to Warren Abbey and be mistress of her own home."

Grace couldn't hide her look of surprise.

"What, Grace? Did you think I would be content with you as my companion for the rest of my life? That I would let my spinster daughter hide away in the country because no one wanted her? That I would want you to nurse me in my old age so your life would have some semblance of worthiness in your otherwise dull existence?"

"No, Father. I never thought that. Never thought you would ever want me. Just as you've never wanted any of us."

"I wanted a son! An heir! And I intend to have one."

Grace felt a chill of dread engulf her. "I see."

"Do you? It would have been so perfect for you to marry Fentington. He would have taken you off my hands and given me a healthy profit in the bargain. And I was so sure you were still a virgin. I never imagined that you weren't. No one has ever shown an interest in you."

He spun around to face her. "Who have you been giving yourself to, Grace? One of the grooms? Surely no one of quality would want you, even if you gave your favors away freely."

Her legs buckled beneath her. "No. Surely no one of quality would want me."

"And you'd best pray he hasn't planted his seed in you. If you think you can come back here and foist your bastard off on me to support, you're sadly mistaken. Now get out before I have you thrown out!"

Grace stiffened her spine and lifted her chin. "Be assured, my lord, you can sleep well tonight knowing you have rid your home of all things unwanted and undesirable."

Grace turned around and forced her legs to carry her across the room. She reached out a trembling hand and opened the door, then closed it behind her without a backward glance.

Their butler was waiting in the hall. "George, have a wagon brought to the front."

"Now, my lady?"

"Yes. Now."

"Very well."

Grace made her way up the stairs, refusing to let a single tear fall. She'd realized when she gave away her virginity that her life would never be the same and had made up her mind to accept the repercussions, no matter what.

"Esther, have some trunks brought up, then come back to help me pack."

Grace ignored the shocked look on her maid's face and threw open the doors to her clothes closet and pulled out her gowns. She had no idea where she was going or how she would live, but she would get by. She had no choice.

Chapter 6

Raeborn took the steps to Madam Genevieve's two at a time. He'd waited the week as she'd demanded and cursed her every day for having the upper hand, for forcing him to bend to her will.

How had this happened? What possible reason could any woman have for wanting to give her virginity to a man she didn't know? To a man she'd never met?

The more he thought about that night the angrier he got. He'd been used. Singled out for some reason only Genevieve knew.

By the time he reached the front entrance, he was more inclined to kick the door off its hinges than to knock. Fortunately Jenkins didn't give him the choice. The door opened before he reached for the brass knocker, and the familiar butler stood back to let him enter.

"Where is she?"

The butler bowed respectfully, showing no sign that he realized Raeborn's temper was close to doing someone harm. "Good day, Your Grace. Madam Genevieve is waiting for you in the Gardenia—"

Vincent didn't wait for him to finish but stormed across the foyer and past the familiar half dozen sitting rooms. When he reached the Gardenia Room, the same room in which he'd met with her one week earlier, he threw open the door and entered.

"I've been waiting for you," she said when he halted in front of her. She pointed to a chair angled before the fireplace. "Would you care to sit?"

"Where is she? *Who* is she?"

Genevieve lifted the corners of her lips into something that resembled a smile but was not quite and walked past him to close the door.

Raeborn felt his temper snap. "I want her name, Genevieve! I want to know who I slept with. I want to know the name of the woman whose virginity I took under the assumption that she was one of your girls." He sucked in a deep breath that left an ache inside his chest. "Dammit! I want to know the name of the woman I could have left pregnant!"

Genevieve paused with her hand still on the closed door, then dropped it and walked over to a small serving cart against the wall. "Such a dominating air may serve you well in the House, Raeborn, or in your own home, but you know me well enough to realize it has no effect here." She poured them each a glass of wine and handed him one. "Please, let's sit down and discuss this rationally."

Raeborn took the wine, keeping his gaze locked with hers. A part of him wanted to throttle her. Another part trusted her enough to know that whatever her reason, the need to do what she did had been compelling enough to leave her no other choice. He understood her well enough to know her actions had been born of desperation.

He walked to the settee and waited for her to join him.

She stopped in front of him but did not sit. "I need to preface what I'm about to tell you by explaining that there was no hidden agenda behind what we did. In fact," she added, the corners of her mouth lifting slightly, "we both hoped you'd never notice you'd just made love to a virgin."

"Was that the reason you added something to my drink?"

"It was just to relax you. To keep you from being too aware of what was happening. It would have been totally effective on most men."

"Obviously I'm not most men," he added without humor.

"Obviously."

Genevieve sat on the edge of the settee, her outward appearance relaxed and composed. Only her clutched hands in her lap gave evidence that she was not.

He sat down and waited for her to begin.

"This is not easy for me, Raeborn. I gave a friend a promise and she will know I betrayed her."

"You should have known that would happen when you included me in your plan."

His voice contained none of his usual ease, but was hard and cold. His anger prevented him from trying to understand why Genevieve had used him. "First of all, I want to know her name."

Genevieve hesitated, then answered his question. "Her name is Grace. You don't need to know more."

Raeborn started to object, then stopped when he saw the determined look on Genevieve's face.

"She is my best friend, Raeborn. Probably my only friend. There is nothing I wouldn't do for her."

"You have already proved that. At my expense."

"And I would do it again."

He felt his temper erupt. "I just want to know why this Grace needed to play the whore for one night!"

Genevieve sucked in a deep breath and turned to face him squarely. He knew from the look in her eyes that if their roles were different and Genevieve were a man, they'd be facing each other over pistols in the morning. When she spoke, the tone of her voice proved it.

"Never..." She stopped to glare at him with more intensity. "*Never* put Grace in the same class as me. She doesn't even deserve to have her name whispered in the same breath with mine."

He stared at her serious expression, then nodded his head in acquiescence. "My apologies."

"Grace came to me because she was desperate. Her father was forcing her younger sister to marry a despicable man old enough to be her father. To keep her sister safe, Grace agreed to take her place."

"Marriage to the man would have been so terrible?"

Genevieve rose from the settee and stood in front of the window. "Yes. Every hour with him would have been hell on earth."

Raeborn watched Genevieve's shoulders shake with each shuddering breath. She turned and scorched him with a look of repulsion.

"His first wife died birthing his only child, a daughter. His second wife killed herself before she'd been married a full six months. The man is evil in the cruelest sense of the word. His sexual depravity and vile penchants make the devil appear saintly." She paced in agitation. "He is a man of some means and gives all who know him the impression of being ever so pious and righteous, while behind closed doors his actions are foul and perverted." She paused and turned her haunted face to the window. "He's an abomination to everything good. Lewd and despicable. Not fit to be called human."

He rose from the settee and stood behind her. Her whole body shook uncontrollably, and he wanted to place a comforting hand on her shoulder. But he was afraid she'd recoil from him if he reached out to her.

"She could have refused. She was of age."

"But her sister wasn't. Grace had to agree to his offer until her sister was safely married."

"Is she married now?"

"She was married two weeks ago." She paused, and Vincent saw her shoulders relax. They lifted when she took a deep breath. "On the day of the wedding, the man informed her that their betrothal would proceed without delay. There was only the simple matter of the papers to sign assuring him that she was a virgin before he would take the steps necessary to make her his bride."

"Assurance?"

"Yes. Her signed and witnessed assurance that the woman he was taking as his wife was a virgin. One couldn't expect a man so closely created in God's image to accept a tainted woman as his bride. A written oath vowing of her virginity was essential before she could be sacrificed on the altar of perversion."

Vincent felt a certain revulsion. "So to keep from marrying him she needed to lose her virginity."

"Grace knew that simply refusing him would do no good. It would only incur her father's wrath and make the man more determined to have her. He's relentless when he wants something and won't let anything get in his way. He is convinced he's been sent by God to punish women for their sins. To abuse and humiliate and beat them into submission until they repent for their immoral ways."

She turned to face him. "Grace knew this was her only choice. The man would never force marriage on her if she refused to swear that she was a virgin. Coming here, giving herself to you had been her choice. She made it freely."

"Why me?"

Genevieve smiled. "You were *my* choice. Who else could I have entrusted my most cherished friend to?"

Raeborn shrugged off the embarrassing compliment and walked across the room, needing to put some distance between them. A fire crackled in the grate, the flames licking upward in slow, mesmerizing movements. He spread his arms and braced his hands on the mantle.

"Does she know who I am?"

"No. Grace came to me with certain stipulations. One—that the man to whom she gave her virginity be a stranger to her."

"What else?"

Genevieve smiled. "That the man she slept with be older than she. Grace is twenty-nine and considers herself quite old. She didn't want the man she slept with to be younger."

Raeborn arched his eyebrows in a questioning gesture. "Anything else?"

"She was most emphatic in her demand that whomever I chose for her be unmarried. She didn't want to give herself to another woman's husband."

He stared into the fire. Finally he took a deep breath and pushed himself away from the mantle. "Where do I find her?"

"She does not want to be found, Raeborn."

"I don't care."

"She's not your responsibility. Leave her be."

"She became my responsibility when the two of you included me in your scheme."

"That was not our intent."

"That no longer matters. I have to know if she's carrying a babe."

He heard Genevieve suck in a breath. "It's only been one week. She can't even suspect that she might be."

"I need to make sure."

"And then what?"

He shook his head. "I will find a position for her on one of my estates. Someplace where I can be assured that she is cared for. As well as the babe—if there is one."

"A position?"

"Yes. What position does she hold now? Kitchen help? Upstairs maid? Ladies' maid? What particular talents does she have?"

He turned around and found Genevieve smiling at him. "I'm sure she will be excellent in whatever position you find for her, Your Grace. She's quite accomplished."

"Then I will find her something. Something she's used to doing. But nothing too strenuous in case she finds herself in a delicate condition."

"That's very kind of you," Genevieve said, refilling her glass with wine and taking a sip. "But I doubt she will accept a position in your household."

Raeborn thought he heard a hint of humor in Genevieve's voice, and it irritated him. "What more do you expect me to do, woman? I didn't ask for this problem to be thrust upon me. I don't want another woman to risk bearing my child, especially a woman I don't know and a child I can never claim."

"I understand," Genevieve whispered.

"Just tell me where I can find her and I'll make sure she's provided for. Maybe there won't be anything to worry about. Maybe I didn't get her with child."

But even as he said the words, his body broke out in a cold sweat and his stomach knotted painfully. He took several deep breaths and told himself this time it would not be so bad. At least she was not his wife. At least he could distance himself from her if she did find herself in difficulty. At least he would not have to live through her birthing pains, then her death. He would meet with her, offer her a position and a generous settlement, and never see her again.

"Where can I find her?"

Genevieve absently straightened the flowers in one of the bouquets sitting on a small table, removing wilted petals from the otherwise perfect blooms. Without glancing in his direction, she went over to a sideboard and picked up a pitcher, then added some water to the arrangements.

"I hear the Marquess and Marchioness of Wedgewood are hosting a dinner and musicale on Wednesday next."

Her switch in topics confused him. "Yes. I received an invitation this morning."

"How fortunate. Invitations to the marchioness's affairs are quite coveted." She set down her pitcher and locked her gaze with his. "I'd make sure to attend."

He nodded his understanding.

"Now if you'll excuse me, Raeborn, I'm expecting a caller."

"Of course."

Genevieve walked him to the front door and took his hand. "Don't be angry with her, Raeborn. There was no other choice for her."

Vincent hoped the expression on his face concealed his true feelings. What he felt was not anger as much as fear. And he knew it would not go away until he knew for sure she was not carrying his child.

He turned to bid Genevieve a final farewell and was surprised when she squeezed his hand.

"Don't be angry if she refuses your help, Raeborn. She has never had the luxury of having someone to rely on. I doubt she will find the thought appealing."

She held his hand a moment longer, then released it.

He couldn't let her words be the last between them. "Then she will have to get used to the idea. If she is carrying my child, she will have no choice but to accept my help," he said, and turned to walk down the steps.

* * *

The near week he had to wait before Lady Wedgewood's dinner seemed an eternity, but Wednesday finally came.

Vincent arrived early and scanned the halls of Wedgewood's town house, watching every maid and female servant helping with the marchioness's dinner and musicale. He wasn't interested in the guests who were in attendance, nor in who would provide the musical entertainment. He was only interested in observing the steady stream of female servants who came from the kitchen area with trays of food and drinks for the guests.

So far, none was the woman Genevieve had called Grace. The woman who'd offered him her virginity two weeks earlier.

When dinner was announced, Vincent conversed with one of the female guests as he escorted her into the formal dining room, but he couldn't remember one word she spoke. He was too busy scanning the area for anyone in Lady Wedgewood's employ who matched the woman he remembered, the woman with hair like golden silk, the woman with round, full breasts.

Vincent shook his head to clear it and took his place near the head of the long dining table. The memory of the woman Genevieve called Grace haunted his memory day and night. No matter how much he ordered his brain to forget her, he couldn't. Her searching gaze and tender touch refused to abandon him.

He reached for his glass of wine and took a healthy swallow.

The dowager Countess of Eversely was seated to his right, but he had a difficult time carrying on a conversation. Although he'd always enjoyed visiting with her, tonight he couldn't concentrate enough to pay her the attention she deserved. He was too busy watching every female servant.

But none of them was the woman who'd given him her body nearly two weeks earlier. The woman who'd clung to him when he entered her and cried out her release when she reached her climax.

Vincent swiped at the sheen of perspiration on his brow caused by the memories of her lying naked in his arms and attacked the braised beef tips on his plate with a vengeance. He couldn't allow himself to constantly relive the memories from that night. He couldn't allow the woman who'd given him her virginity to consume his thoughts the way she did. It wasn't normal. In all the years he'd gone to Genevieve's, he'd never given any of the women with whom he'd lain a second thought.

Yet he hadn't been able to think of anything or anyone except the delicate woman called Grace since that night.

Vincent reached for his glass of wine and took another swallow.

When the meal was over, he didn't accompany the men to the library to enjoy the customary brandy and cigars. Instead he loitered in the halls, searching for the small, blonde serving girl that Genevieve had promised would be here. She wasn't. She wasn't anyplace he searched. When he had looked in every conceivable place, he finally gave up his search and made his way to the music room. He'd resume looking for her when the performance was over.

He slipped into the music room through a side door and took the first empty chair against the wall. The room was crowded since the evening's entertainment had already begun, making it impossible to glimpse the performer. But Vincent recognized the selections immediately.

The pianist was in the middle of the first movement of Beethoven's *Moonlight Sonata.* He remembered someone remarking that one of Lady Wedgewood's sisters was quite accomplished and had agreed to play for them tonight.

If the performer was truly one of her sisters, she was indeed very good. She'd captured the haunting sadness of Beethoven's first movement to perfection. He would have to compliment her when she finished.

He took a deep breath and leaned back in his chair to listen. Her playing was flawless as she captured the drive and dynamic shifts of the second movement. When she finished, Vincent smiled. Beethoven would have approved of her interpretation of the first two movements. The real test of her talent, though, would come with the third.

Raeborn waited, then smiled in appreciation as her fingers flew over the keys. The lady was good. More than good. He was not an accomplished musician himself, but he recognized talent. And this lady had it in abundance. He would make sure to seek her out later. After he found Grace. After he gave the deceiver the set down she deserved.

He wondered what it would be like to see her again. To talk to her, a perfect stranger of the working class, after he'd shared such intimacies with her. He dreaded the thought. He wasn't used to making love to women who did not freely give their bodies to men as a means of earning a living. The thought of taking an innocent's virginity rankled him, and he became furious with both her and Genevieve all over again.

He listened to the music, the fast, ferocious frenzy of the last movement fitting his mood, paralleling his irritation. The minute Lady Wedgewood's sister finished, he was going to continue his search for the elusive maid. He couldn't stand to go another week worrying about her. Couldn't stand to have this loose end not taken care of.

The music intensified as the performer neared the end. The furor built inside him at the same rate. He would find her. Even if he had to go to Wedgewood and ask if he had someone in his employ by the name of Grace.

Raeborn anticipated the final note and sat forward in his chair, ready to make his exit. He would begin his search again before the guests headed for the door.

Lady Wedgewood's sister struck the final chord and the guests erupted in applause.

Vincent rose and turned. He wanted to catch at least a glimpse of the woman who possessed such amazing talent before he resumed his search.

The lady at the piano turned toward the guests and bowed her head. The blonde curls she'd tied with a ribbon at the back of her head fell over her shoulders.

Vincent froze, unable to move. Lady Wedgewood's sister was slender, with hair the color of burnished gold that captured the reflection of the candlelight. He remembered twining his fingers through hair that same color. Remembered seeing hair as thick and lustrous fanned out on the pillow as he loomed over her.

When she lifted her chin to look out at her admirers, he saw that her complexion was clear and satiny. He remembered touching that skin, running his fingers down her cheeks, pressing his lips to her face.

He stared at her, mesmerized by her beauty. She was the Grace he'd been searching for. He didn't dare blink for fear that he'd lose sight of her.

As if her gaze were drawn to him, she turned. Their gazes locked.

Recognition was instant. Her fear palpable.

The air rushed from his body and he couldn't breathe. Her reaction was similar.

The color drained from her face and she reached out a hand to steady herself against the piano. Her breasts fell and rose, then fell again as she gasped for air.

He stared at her, struggling to recover from the shock.

She held his gaze for several seconds longer, then turned toward the nearest exit and bolted from the room.

Chapter 7

Grace ran down the hallway, desperate to reach the stairway before he came around the corner. She couldn't breathe. Her heart thundered in her breast and her legs barely held beneath her. He was here. Heaven help her. He'd seen her. Recognized her.

She picked up her skirts to allow quicker movement. If she could make it across the foyer she could run upstairs and lock herself in her room.

Why, oh why, had she let her sister talk her into playing tonight? She should have known there was the slightest possibility the man Hannah had given her was a member of the *ton*. Someone who ran in the same circles as her sister and Wedgewood. Oh, why hadn't she realized this possibility sooner?

Every muscle in her body trembled. What if he caught her? How could she ever face him after what they'd done?

She ran across the foyer and reached to clasp the railing on the bottom step. Nothing had turned out the way she'd intended. She'd known it was possible that her father would put her out but hadn't really believed it would come to that. Just as she hadn't considered she'd have to ask her sister if she might stay with her until she decided what she would do. And she never considered she'd come face-to-face with the man to whom she'd given her body. Face-to-face with the stranger with whom she'd lain and done the things she had. Face-to-face with the man who'd touched her until she cried out to him.

Her face burned with embarrassment, and she raced up the steps as fast as she could. She would rather die than have to face him again.

"Stop!"

Grace froze with her hand on the railing and her foot reaching for the next step. She swallowed a small cry of desperation and squeezed shut her eyes. Heaven help her, she couldn't turn around. She couldn't look him in the eyes. She couldn't.

Gasping a shuddering breath, Grace placed her foot on the next step and pulled her body upward. She prayed her feet would carry her away from him. Prayed he'd let her go.

"I. Said. Stop."

Grace stopped. For several agonizing seconds she stood with her back to him. Her chest heaved and her lungs burned, partly from exertion. Mostly from fear. She'd been aware of the power that emanated from every part of him the night she'd lain with him. Knew that even though he was the most gentle and considerate of lovers, there was a formidable force that hovered about him. He was a man to fear. A man to be wary of. A man used to dominating everyone around him.

She sucked in a deep, fortifying breath and turned to face him.

Her heart jolted in her breast. He was the most magnificent example of masculinity she'd ever seen. And tonight, dressed in his formal black jacket and white satin cravat, he was breathtaking. The most handsome man she'd ever seen. And the most angry.

He stood with his arms stiff at his sides, his hands clenched into two white-knuckled fists. His long, muscular legs were braced wide, his broad shoulders raised, his chest expanded. Grace knew there was only the thinnest filament of control keeping the air he held inside from erupting in violent fury.

She tried to forget how beautiful he'd been naked. Tried to forget the masculine power he'd emitted. Tried not to think of how it had felt when he'd lain naked atop her. When he'd entered her, filled her. Taken her on a journey so incredible she still ached from the beauty of it. Instead, she looked him in the eyes and faced him bravely.

Her heart plummeted to the pit of her stomach. Her gaze locked onto the fiercest scowl imaginable, a look filled with fury and regret.

She couldn't do this. Couldn't battle him without losing.

She turned away from him, every muscle in her body screaming to escape. To race up the stairs and never stop running.

"Do not even consider it," he said, his voice a low, deadly growl.

She swallowed hard and conceded. On trembling legs she turned toward him.

Grace had never done anything so difficult in her life. Not even waiting for him that night at Hannah's had been this hard. Or enduring her father's wrath. Or being forced to leave her home, knowing she'd never be assured of a roof over her head again. None of these had required as much courage as it took to take that first step toward the man waiting for her at the bottom of the stairs. A man whose livid expression held more fury than she'd ever seen before.

Grace squared her shoulders and took a tentative step toward him. His gaze did not leave her, but held her in a grip so tight she feared she'd suffocate. This was not going to be easy. But not much of her life had been since her mother had died and she'd been left to raise her sisters and protect them from her father's greed and disregard.

One step after another, she reached the bottom. She would face this problem the same as she had every other—head-on, and alone.

When she reached the foot of the staircase, she stepped past him and slowed, not sure what he wanted her to do. His hand touched her back and guided her to go to the left, to the room her brother-in-law used as a study. She lifted her chin and walked defiantly down the hall.

"I don't think Wedgewood will mind us using his study to talk privately," he said, throwing open the door. "I'm sure he'd prefer that we not publicly discuss what transpired between us where half of London society can overhear our conversation."

Her face burned but she refused to be intimidated by his caustic remarks. "Yes, I'm sure he would."

With her head held high, she swept past him and entered the room. The fireplace cast the only light in the wood-paneled room. Grace lit a taper from the flames and walked to light the lamp sitting on her brother-in-law's desk. She prayed the man watching her didn't notice how her hands trembled. Prayed he didn't realize how frightened she was.

Prayed he didn't notice her jump when the door slammed shut behind her.

Although her hand shook almost uncontrollably, she attempted to light a second lamp that sat on a small side table. She would light them all. The brightness would let him know she didn't intend to hide in the shadows.

She nearly screamed when his hand touched hers and he took the taper from her.

"Let me."

Grace stepped back to avoid being so close to him. She didn't want to be reminded of his height or the width of his shoulders or how he fit so perfectly beside her.

"Do you want them all lit?" he said, lighting a third lamp and setting it on the corner of the desk.

"Yes."

He turned his head and cast a glance over his shoulder. A mocking gaze locked with hers. "I seem to remember you preferred the darkness the last time we were together."

Her breath caught. "You're not going to make this easy, are you?"

The look on his face turned dark, daunting. "You don't deserve it to be easy."

Grace stood before the fire and let the warmth seep into her. She knew there wasn't a chill in the room, but she couldn't stop her body from shaking. Couldn't suppress the deep-rooted trembling that gripped her very soul.

One by one he lit the lamps, moving about the room with the stealth and wariness of a hunter stalking its prey. When he spoke, his voice startled her.

"Do you think we should begin by introducing ourselves?" he asked when he'd lit the last lamp and set it on a table by the door. "I know after what we've shared, a formal introduction is hardly of much consequence, but—"

"Stop it!"

Grace reached out her hand and gripped the edge of the mantle. Every nerve in her body screamed from the tension that stretched between them. "Sarcasm will not erase what happened," she said, clasping her hands in front of her. She faced him squarely. "I am the Marchioness of Wedgewood's sister Grace."

He frowned. "Your family name?"

"Warren."

"Then your father would be…?"

"The Earl of Portsmont."

"And you would be…*Lady* Grace."

"Yes."

"Bloody hell."

He turned his back to her and stood behind Wedgewood's mammoth desk, staring into the darkness beyond the terrace doors. His fingers clutched the door handle as if he were preparing to throw open the door and walk through hell itself if it took him away from her.

"Do you know who I am?" he asked without turning around to face her.

"No. But it's not necessary that I know your name."

He spun around and leveled her with the most intimidating look she'd ever seen. "Oh, it's necessary, my lady. It's very necessary. I am Vincent Germaine, Duke of Raeborn."

Grace's knees gave out beneath her. Raeborn. The Duke of Raeborn. She couldn't believe Hannah had picked Raeborn to take her virginity. Even her secluded life in the country hadn't prevented her from hearing about the renowned Duke of Raeborn. She knew the important position he held in government. How influential he was not only as a political leader in the House, but also as an advisor to the queen on occasion. And she'd heard the sad tale of the two wives he'd lost in childbirth.

He took a step closer to her. "How is it we've never met?"

Grace realized she'd been staring and moved her gaze to a spot just to the left of his broad shoulders. "I have only been to London a few times in the past few years, Your Grace. And then not to involve myself with the social season."

"Why not?"

His questions made her uncomfortable, but she couldn't think of a good reason not to answer him. "I am the oldest of seven daughters. My mother died giving birth to my youngest sister, Anne. I promised my mother I would see to their upbringing and make sure they all made matches of their choosing. My responsibilities gave me time for little else."

"What about your father? Didn't he involve himself in raising his daughters?"

"We were not his heirs, Your Grace. You especially can understand the difference in importance between a daughter and a son. Multiply that by seven."

The duke took a step toward her. "Tell me why you found it necessary to lose your virginity to a stranger."

Grace sucked in a painful gasp of air. She would not allow him to intimidate her. She didn't regret what she'd done and wouldn't let him make her doubt her decision. "In order to save my youngest sister from marrying a truly horrible man, I agreed to take her place, knowing the man wouldn't want me once he found out I wasn't a…virgin."

"So you let me take care of that little matter for you?"

She looked to the floor. "Yes."

"Did your plan work?"

"Yes," she whispered, unable to look directly at him.

"So what are your intentions now?"

"Intentions?"

"Yes." The duke took another step toward her. "What do you intend to do now? Go back to the country where you can live in seclusion the rest of your life?"

"No." She could not tell him her father had evicted her from his house. Tell him she was now at the mercy of the six sisters she'd raised.

"Get caught up in the whirlwind of London's social life and search for a husband?"

Her gaze flew to his face. "I am far past the marrying age. I have no intention of competing for a husband with young debutantes fresh out of the schoolroom."

"Do you expect me to marry you then?"

The floor dropped from beneath her. "No! I have no intention of ever marrying. I am quite content to be alone."

"Then what is it you expect me to do?"

"You?" She stared at him in disbelief. "Nothing, Your Grace. Other than the role you played that one night, you aren't involved in this."

"And you, my lady, are either unbelievably naive or a fool. And I doubt you are a fool. Desperate, perhaps. But not a fool."

Grace decided she needed to get this over with as quickly as possible. If it was an apology he wanted, she would give it to him and he could leave her without giving her a second thought. "I'm sure you are disturbed by—"

"Disturbed? I think you do not have the vaguest idea how disturbed I am."

Grace took a fortifying breath and started again. "Very well. I know you're angry with me—"

"The word is *furious*."

She swallowed past the lump in her throat. "Very well, I know you're furious. I appreciate your feelings. I apologize for any inconvenience I caused, but I was desperate and needed you to help me."

"And now you expect me to say thank you for an enjoyable evening and walk away?"

She lifted her chin even though her cheeks burned as if on fire. "Yes."

The corners of his lips lifted into a smile that turned the expression on his face even more daunting. "You should know that's hardly possible."

"Your Grace." She stepped closer to him to give her words more emphasis. "To avoid an unimaginable marriage I made a decision to give up my virginity. I would do it again without hesitation. I expected nothing from my actions other than to escape a life with a man I detested. It was not my intent then, nor is it my intent now, to demand anything from you. I most assuredly did not intend to trap you into assuming responsibility for me."

"What did you think I would do?"

Grace shrugged her shoulders. "To be honest, I gave you little thought. I expected you would treat me as you did any other of Madam Genevieve's women. I expected you to spend the night with me and forget me."

"That is hardly possible knowing that the woman I slept with was a virgin."

Grace swallowed. "I regret you realized that. Genevieve said she would give you—"

"Yes. I know. She expected the potion she gave me to mask the fact that you had never lain with a man before."

Grace lowered her gaze to the floor. A niggling confusion stirred within her. His being here was not a complete coincidence. She should have known even Hannah couldn't stand up to him. Well, it didn't matter. She was through talking. Through trying to explain why she'd been so desperate to sleep with him. Through letting him think he was responsible for her because of one night.

"I would appreciate it, Your Grace, if you left me now. I apologize for deceiving you, but I had no choice. I hoped you would wake up the next day and not give me a second thought. I assumed you would not care to discover my identity or seek me out. I cannot imagine why you have. I deeply regret that you found me."

Grace held her ground, lifting her head in a show of determination. "I intend to forget what happened between us, and I ask that you do the same."

"You can do that?"

"Yes," she lied. "As far as I'm concerned, that night never happened."

"What if you're with child?"

The room spun around her and Grace reached out a hand to the wall to steady herself. "I'm not."

"Are you sure?"

She gasped for air. "Of course. It takes more than once to conceive."

He laughed. "That belief has made mothers out of more young women than not."

She turned her face away from him.

"Have you resumed your monthly courses since we made love?"

Grace felt her cheeks burn hot.

"Have you?"

"No. But it isn't time."

"How much longer until you know for sure?"

Grace shook her head. "I don't want to talk about this with you."

"You wouldn't have to if you hadn't tricked me into your bed."

His words were meant to hurt and they did. "I've already apologized, Your Grace. Please, leave and forget we met."

"How much longer?"

She fisted her hands in frustration at his mortifyingly personal questions. "I don't know. I'm not as...predictable as some women."

"Bloody hell."

He'd whispered the words, but that didn't make them any less dangerous. The way he shot his fingers through his thick, dark hair emphasized it.

"Please leave, Your Grace. You are not responsible for me. I will not let you think you are."

"And if you find you're *enceinte*?"

She clutched her hands around her middle. "I'm sure I'm not."

"And I have no intention of taking the risk that the next Raeborn heir might be born illegitimate."

The air caught in her chest. "I would never let that happen," she whispered, her whole body trembling. For the first time she realized what it might mean if she had conceived the night they'd been together. She felt another wave of fear greater than any she'd felt before. She lowered her gaze to the design on the carpet. "I would tell you if I discovered I was carrying your child."

"And then what? We'd shock society with a rushed wedding when they'd never once seen the two of us together?"

Wedding!

Grace felt a noose tighten around her neck. "There is no need to fear just yet, Your Grace. I'm sure your worry is for naught."

The duke closed his eyes and looked away as if he did not believe her. As if the thought of taking her for a wife wasn't pleasant. Grace tried not to let the hurt show. She had never been as pretty as her sisters. She'd been ordinary and plain, with only her thick, golden hair and large, dark eyes to recommend her. She could tell from the disappointment on the duke's face that those attributes weren't enough.

She wanted to escape his scrutiny but forced herself to stay still.

"Are you staying at your father's town house here in London?"

His question took her by surprise. "No. I am staying here with my sister and her husband. They were gracious enough to open their home to me while I was in town."

"Very well. I'll call on you tomorrow and we can talk more. Now we'd best return to the musicale before we are missed. You go first. I'll come later. After I enter, I'll escort you to get something to drink. Without a doubt our association will be noticed. Tomorrow afternoon we'll join the five o'clock parade through Hyde Park. That will cause more talk.

"You can give me a list of the social engagements you plan to attend during the next week or two and I'll adjust my calendar accordingly. We will have to be seen together often to avoid questions should the need for a hasty wedding arise."

Grace staggered back a step. "Surely all this isn't necessary," she whispered, the noose tightening even more.

"Pray your monthly visitor arrives soon, my lady. Otherwise the risks you took may force you into a marriage even worse than the one you thought to escape."

Grace clutched her hands to her middle, fearful she might be ill.

"Are you ready to pretend to all of London that the thought of being courted by the Duke of Raeborn doesn't frighten you to death?"

Her gaze darted to his face. "Why should being courted by you frighten me?" She studied the formidable frown deepening on his forehead.

The corners of Raeborn's mouth lifted slightly, but not enough to be called a smile. "You *have* been in the country and away from the gossip mills too long, my lady. Never fear, though. It won't take long for someone to enlighten you to the fact that I long outlive my wives."

Grace started to object but stopped when she took in the expression on his face. Surely he didn't think he was responsible for the deaths of his wives. They had both died in childbirth. As did many women. That was hardly his fault.

He didn't give her time to argue with him, but walked across the room and placed his hand on the knob. "Shall we begin?"

Grace hesitated a moment, then followed him on legs that threatened not to hold her. When she reached him she paused long enough to catch a glimpse of the man she'd deceived. A man she'd hoped would not notice he'd made love to a virgin. A man she'd hoped would not care if he did.

She wanted to say something to him. Needed to say something, but all that came from her mouth was "I'm sorry."

Her admission softened his features. "As am I," he answered. His expression told her he meant it. Before she could move, he placed a finger beneath her chin and tilted her face up to his. "A smile would perhaps make our ruse a little more believable."

Grace tried to smile, then swallowed hard and walked past him. She reached the hallway, where she was alone, and paused. For some reason she couldn't explain, she placed a trembling hand on her stomach and held it there. How could she not want there to be a babe inside her? She'd ached her whole life to have a house filled with babes. Been desperate to have a home of her own and a husband who loved her. She'd wanted what each of her sisters had.

But not like this. Not having forced herself on a man who did not want her. Did not even like her.

Not living the rest of her life with a man she'd deceived.

Chapter 8

He'd just come from spending an afternoon with her. From their ride through Hyde Park. From their first outing together. If their goal had been to surprise and shock the members of society, then the outing had been a rousing success. It seemed nearly everyone was out enjoying the warm day, even though it wasn't yet spring. And his companion, Lady Grace Warren, was noticed by each and every one of them.

Raeborn placed his hat and gloves in Carver's waiting hands and walked across the marble foyer toward his study. He stepped into the quiet room and closed the door behind him.

Soft rays of sunshine sifted through the windows, casting filtered shadows that stretched out across the floor. They nearly reached from one side of the room to the other. Warmth from the sunlight touched his cheeks, caressed him with the softness of a woman's hand. As her hand had done when he'd lain with her before he knew who she was.

He drew his hand across his face, wanting to erase the memory. Yet in contrast, wanting to hold on to the feeling and never forget the emotions she'd awakened. He knew why his emotions were so at war with each other. Knew why the turmoil churning inside him was such a struggle.

She had done it. She had given him cause to hope when he'd convinced himself he was long past hoping. Given him cause to believe he'd received another chance to have what he'd always wanted in life. A wife. Children. A reason for existing.

He pushed his jacket from his shoulders and hung it over the back of the chair, then sat down behind his desk. He leaned his head back against the cushions like a battle-weary soldier and closed his eyes. He needed to block out the stares, the looks of disbelief he'd seen on everyone's faces, both last night when he'd made a point of paying court to Lady Grace at the Wedgewood musicale, and again this afternoon on their ride through Hyde Park.

He knew by the time he walked through the Earl of Pendleton's doors tonight, everyone would have heard of Raeborn's quest for another bride.

He gave an angry tug to his cravat and bolted to his feet. Maybe he hadn't gotten her with child. Maybe in a day or two she'd tell him there was no need to worry. That her errant courses had begun.

Huge beads of perspiration formed on his forehead. Oh, how he prayed she'd tell him that. How he prayed he wouldn't have to go through another woman's pregnancy. Especially Grace Warren's. She seemed so fragile. So delicate.

He thought of the woman with whom he'd spent the afternoon. Of course there'd been a certain degree of tension between them, but he couldn't say he hadn't enjoyed himself. In fact, the two of them got on quite well. There never seemed to be a lull in their conversation except when he stopped their carriage so they could talk to some curious passerby who wanted to get a closer look at the Duke of Raeborn and the lady he sought to wed. The way she stiffened at his side told him she was uncomfortable with the attention being with him attracted.

But when they were alone she held her own. He already knew she was extremely talented. Now he knew she had the intelligence to match. Talking to her was not like talking to some immature, addlebrained ingenue. She was levelheaded as well as up on all the current political events. She had an opinion on every topic they discussed. Raeborn smiled. And she didn't back down when her opinion didn't match his.

For just a flash, he thought of what it would be like to court a woman again, to take a wife, to have someone waiting for him when he came home, someone to talk to and laugh with and sleep next to. To have someone who would bear his children and perhaps even learn to care for him. To have someone to grow old with.

But these were the same thoughts he'd had while courting his first two wives. Two innocent women who'd died trying to give him the children he wanted. The heir he needed.

Raeborn rubbed at his jaw and let the bright sunshine wash over him. No. It would have been best if he hadn't spilled his seed inside her. Best if she told him tonight or perhaps tomorrow that she wasn't carrying a babe.

A part of him prayed she would.

Another part of him, a part he didn't let himself acknowledge very often, prayed she wouldn't. That God would give him another chance.

* * *

"Are you awake, Grace?"

Grace heard the soft knock on the door and waited for Caroline to come in.

"I thought maybe you'd be resting for tonight."

"No. I was reading." Grace picked up the closed book on her lap and opened it. She knew Caroline saw through her lie but was thankful when she didn't comment on it.

"These just came for you." Caroline held out a beautiful bouquet of flowers. "They're from the Duke of Raeborn. That was very thoughtful of him, don't you think?"

Grace rose from her chair by the window and took the flowers. "Yes. Very."

"You must have made a favorable impression on him last night. Or were the two of you acquainted before?" Caroline asked. The tone of her voice told Grace she knew they weren't. Or at least they hadn't been before last night. Caroline was as surprised as everyone else when she noticed them both gone, then observed them coming back minutes apart.

Grace had seen the look Caroline had given her. Recognized the worry and concern because she'd been alone with Raeborn. She knew she hadn't been very convincing when Caroline questioned her later. Knew Caroline didn't believe her when she told her she'd gotten overly warm and needed a breath of fresh air and Raeborn had followed her merely to make his compliments on the music and see that she was all right.

"The duke is certainly being considerate. I think he's quite smitten with you."

Grace set the flowers down on the corner of a small writing desk. "Perhaps."

"Are you saying you're not as taken with him?"

Grace saw the questioning look on Caroline's face and turned her attention back to the flowers.

"Are you averse to his attentions, Grace?"

"Of course not. What makes you think that?"

"I don't know. It's just that you seem a little tense around him. Almost as if he's forcing his attentions on you. I can't imagine Raeborn doing so, but is he, Grace?"

"No. Of course not."

"Then what is it?"

Oh, how Grace wanted to tell Caroline. How she wanted to share at least a part of the burden that terrified her every hour of the day and kept her awake at night. How she wanted to talk to her sister, to tell her the duke was not smitten with her. That she'd deceived him and this show of being enamored of her was all an act. That he felt nothing but disdain for her and was putting on a brave front because she may have trapped him into a marriage he didn't want. "It's nothing."

Caroline closed the small distance between them and took Grace's hands and held them. Grace suddenly felt like the younger sister. Like the one being taken care of instead of the other way around. The feeling was totally alien to her.

"Sit down with me," Caroline said, pulling Grace over to a small settee angled before the fireplace. "I want to talk to you."

They sat and Caroline turned to face her. "When I married Thomas, I came to him with nothing to my name. Father didn't provide a dowry for any of us, as you well know. But I was the luckiest of women because Thomas's family was wealthy enough that they didn't care about money. In fact, they paid the amount Father greedily demanded for me without question."

"I know," Grace said, remembering how frightened Caroline had been that Thomas's father would refuse to pay what their father demanded and she and Thomas wouldn't be able to marry.

"On our wedding day, Thomas's father took me aside and gave me this. He said it was his wedding present to me."

Caroline reached into a pocket of her gown and pulled out a piece of paper. She handed it to Grace. "I want you to have it."

"What is it?"

"It's the deed to a small country manor. It's quite nice and only about an hour's ride from here. And it's in my name."

Grace stared at the paper in her hands. "No, Linny. I can't take this."

"Yes, you can. I want you to have it." Caroline reached for Grace's hands and held them tighter. "Thomas's father said he wanted to make sure if something ever happened to Thomas, that I would never have to rely on Father again. I won't tell you his opinion of Father, but he wanted to make sure I never had to go back and live under his roof."

Grace brought the paper to her heart and fought to keep her tears from spilling down her cheeks.

"It's yours, Grace. For as long as you live. I want you to know you don't have to give up your independence if you don't want to. Although I can't think of a finer man than Raeborn, I don't want you to feel forced to marry him because you have no place else to go."

"Oh, Caroline," she said, throwing her arms around her sister and hugging her tight. "I love you. I couldn't ask for a better sister. But I'm not letting Raeborn court me because he can provide me with a roof over my head. Maybe I should," she said, covering her embarrassment with choked laughter. "Otherwise I'll be a plague and bother to all of you for the rest of my life."

"You'd never be a bother, Grace. We each of us owe you more than we can ever repay for what you've done for us. Thomas said to tell you you're welcome to stay with us for as long as you like. And Josie is terribly upset because you came here first instead of going to her. And Francie and Sarah and Mary each sent word they're expecting you to visit them next."

Grace smiled through her tears.

"If it's not the concern over having a place to live, what is it? Surely it's not Raeborn? I can see where you could come to care for him. He's an exceptional man, Grace. And it's obvious he's interested in you."

Grace looked away from Caroline. How could she tell her Raeborn's interest would die the second he found out she wasn't carrying his child? "I never thought anyone would consider me, and now..."

"And why wouldn't they consider you?"

"You know that as well as I. Just look at me, Linny."

"I am. There's not a thing about you not to like. Obviously His Grace feels the same. I know he can be rather intimidating at times, but—" Caroline paused. "Are you afraid of him, Grace?"

"No. Of course not. It's just that..."

"Surely you haven't listened to the gossip about him?"

Grace turned her head to look at Caroline. "What gossip?"

"That he's cursed because his first two wives died in childbirth."

Grace laughed. "Of course not. If anything, he has my sympathy. It's tragic losing one wife. But to have to go through that loss twice? And the heirs he was hoping for. Surely he knows he was not responsible for their deaths. We all know the risks in having children. No, that's not it."

"Then what is it, Grace?"

Grace fought to keep from placing her hand on her stomach. "It's nothing, Linny. I'm just nervous, I guess. The scene with Father and Fentington still gives me nightmares."

"I wish I had been there to help you," Caroline said. "I wish I could have heard what you told him. It would have been worth all the treasures in the world to see him squirm when you told him you knew what he was. What he'd done to his wife. That everyone knew she'd taken her own life rather than spend another day with him."

"You wouldn't say that if you had seen him. The glare in his eyes still terrifies me. And to know Father knew the kind of man he was and still intended to sell me to him for money."

"We've always known that about Father. What I can't believe is that Fentington gave up on you so easily. That you didn't need some leverage to escape him."

"I'm just thankful he did."

Grace couldn't look her sister in the eye. Didn't want her to know what it had taken to save herself from having to marry him. Didn't want her to know she had deceived Raeborn.

"Don't worry, Grace. Fentington can't hurt you as long as you're with us. And Father has no one left to barter and sell. We're all free from both of them."

Grace hoped that was true. Hoped Fentington had spoken his threats in anger and would not do something to make her pay for deceiving him. But Caroline was right. She was safe here. Safe—except from the Duke of Raeborn.

"Now," Caroline said, getting up from the settee, "I'd better leave so you can get ready for tonight. Raeborn will no doubt be there and you'll want to look your best."

Before Caroline left, Grace reached for her hand and gave her back the deed. "Linny, keep this for me," she said, folding Caroline's fingers around the paper. "I'll know where it is if I ever need it."

"Don't forget. It's yours if ever you have need of it," Caroline said, then walked out of the room.

Grace stared at the closed door, her vision blurred with tears. She couldn't explain the gratitude that consumed her. The joy of knowing she wouldn't have to suffer through the embarrassment of seeking a husband. The comfort of having a place to live so she wouldn't be a burden to her sisters. There was no doubt in her mind it would only be a matter of days until her natural cycle resumed and the Duke of Raeborn could drop his pursuit of her. Then she would have to seriously consider what she wanted to do with the rest of her life.

She sat back down on the settee and hugged a pillow to her chest. Last night she'd secretly calculated how long after their wedding nights it had taken each of her sisters to conceive. It had taken Caroline three months, Josie four, Francie barely two, Sarah three, and Mary four.

Annie hadn't been married a month yet, so she was still a question. That proved none of her sisters had conceived on their wedding night, so the odds were that she hadn't either—even though the night she'd spent with the duke hadn't been her wedding night. All she had to do was wait the week or so until nature proved it.

Then maybe she would take Caroline up on her offer and live in quiet solitude in the country. It was not as if she were without the ability to support herself. She could hire herself out as a tutor and music instructor. The income she'd earn would not make her wealthy, but at least she would be able to support herself and not have to rely on a husband or her sisters to take care of her.

Grace rose from the cushions, telling herself she had nothing to fear. Telling herself she should be happy, that a great weight had been lifted from her shoulders. Yet there was a niggling sadness that would not go away. A sadness because she would have to give up the dream she'd cherished her whole life. The dream of a home made warm and inviting because of the love shared between a husband and wife. The dream of a house filled with children's laughter.

The cost of her deception would indeed be high.

* * *

Grace stood to the right of the staircase of the Pendleton ballroom visiting with a small circle of friends. Caroline was next to her on one side and another sister, Josie, was on the other. She tried to keep her mind focused on the conversations going on around her but found her thoughts wandering. Found she could think of only one thing. Of only one person.

She knew the minute he arrived. Knew the moment he stood at the top of the stairs. Knew he was there even before he was announced.

The room seemed smaller. The air warmer.

She told herself she wouldn't turn around. Wouldn't look into those ebony eyes or feast on his noble features. Told herself she wouldn't notice the perfect cut of his clothing or his broad shoulders or muscled thighs. Told herself she wouldn't remember his naked flesh pressed against hers, her hands running along the corded muscles that bounded across his shoulders and down his arms. But she did.

She turned. His gaze locked with hers, his eyes honing in on her with a possessiveness she found disconcerting. Even though he didn't move from where he stood, his dominance swept down the steps and across the room like a dense fog, making its way to where she waited, wrapping around her until she felt as much a part of him as she had the night she'd lain with him.

Her stomach clenched nervously. Long, unyielding fingers gripped within her chest, squeezing until she couldn't breathe. Until the room seemed to spin around her. It would be so much easier if he didn't affect her as he did. If she could forget what that one night with him had been like. If a miracle had happened ten years ago and he had noticed her then. If she didn't know he was drawn to her only because she'd deceived him. Only because he *had* to until he knew she wasn't carrying his child.

"Are you all right, Grace?" Caroline asked, touching her gloved hand to Grace's arm.

Grace sucked in a breath of surprise and pasted a smile on her face. "Of course. I was just lost in thought."

Before Caroline could comment further, her gaze lifted over Grace's shoulder. Grace knew from the flirtatious smiles of the ladies around her and the parting of their small circle that he was there, behind her. She could feel the heat from his body, feel the power that emanated from him. A breath hitched in her chest when she turned to look at him.

"Good evening, Lady Grace. Ladies," he said as a general greeting to the others.

"Your Grace."

For a few moments Raeborn made pleasant conversation as if everyone in the room hadn't noticed where he went upon arriving. Hadn't noticed which lady he'd targeted as the object of his attentions. He couldn't have been more obvious if he'd hung a banner and hired trumpeters to announce his intentions.

"They're getting ready to start the next set, Lady Grace. Would you do me the honor of this dance?"

Grace smiled and took his proffered hand, knowing it was what was expected of her. She went with him and felt everyone staring after them. Knew if she looked, there would be disbelieving expressions on their faces. Knew it was impossible for anyone to understand why the Duke of Raeborn was courting her.

She had nothing to recommend her, no huge dowry, no well-respected family name. Even youth and a pretty face worked against her. Not to mention that everyone assumed since the duke hadn't shown interest in anyone during the five years since his last wife had died in childbirth, he was not interested in taking another wife.

So why her?

A wave of panic consumed her. Surely someone would realize she'd done something to force such a magnificent catch to court her. Her heart pounded in her breast. They may not know to what lengths she'd gone, but it would not take them long to figure out she'd done something to trap him. Why else would the influential Duke of Raeborn give her a second look? She'd even heard it whispered that the duke's cousin had proclaimed his shock because the Duke of Raeborn had sworn he had no intention of ever remarrying.

"You look exceptionally lovely tonight, my lady," he said, leading her to the dance floor. He took her into his arms.

She wished the dance were not a waltz. Wished she could keep at least some distance between them. But that was impossible. He held her close and carried her with him across the floor. A shiver washed over her.

"Is something wrong?"

She shook her head. "No. Of course not."

"Then perhaps you would explain the look on your face and why you're trembling in my arms."

She tried to erase any expression from her face that hinted at her fear and lifted her mouth in what she prayed was a sincere smile. From the arched lift of his brows she knew she'd failed.

He tucked her closer to him and twirled her in three rapid circles, then led her out the open double doors and onto the terrace. He didn't stop until they'd walked down the three small steps and out into the garden.

He placed his hands high on her arms and turned her to face him. "Now what is it?" he said, placing a finger beneath her chin and tilting her head upward.

She turned away from him. "It's nothing."

"Yes, it is. You're trembling. Tell me. What's bothering you?"

Grace took a deep breath and stepped away from him. "You don't have to do this."

"Do what?"

"Make such an effort. People are making too much of the attention you are paying me."

"That makes you uncomfortable?"

"Yes. They are assuming you're serious. That you would actually consider me for your duchess."

"But of course you know differently."

"Yes." She looked away from him. "I would much rather have them shocked by a hasty marriage than suffer through their smirking looks when they realize you're no longer interested in me."

"Do you anticipate that day coming?"

She spun on him. "Of course I do."

He sucked in a breath. "Have you begun—?"

Grace felt her cheeks burn. "No. But it's only a matter of time before I will. It is highly unlikely I could have conceived after only…once."

Raeborn lifted his lips in a smile that held no humor. "Perhaps that will be the price you must pay for your deception."

Grace shivered. Her blood turned cold. She would be glad when this was over. Glad when she could tell him she wasn't carrying his babe and he could give up this charade.

The weight of what she'd done was suddenly more than she could stand up under. The guilt and embarrassment nearly strangled her. She had thought she could survive their sham a little longer, but she couldn't. She couldn't bear to have him look at her, touch her, dance with her—even smile at her—when she knew it was the last thing he wanted to do. When she knew the only reason he even noticed her was because she'd deceived him and he was forced to pay attention to her. When she knew there was an underlying anger boiling beneath the surface at how she'd tricked him.

"Please, return to the ballroom, Your Grace. I'll be in shortly."

She turned away from him and took several steps down the path, intentionally placing enough distance between them to regain what little self-control she had left. She couldn't stop her body from trembling. She prayed he'd realize she needed to be alone, that she needed him to leave her be. She heard him move and held her breath.

Just let him be gone.

She clutched her hands around her middle and pressed her lips tight to stop the whimper that threatened to escape. It was best to end this now. Before they were embroiled with each other any more than they already were. Before anyone assumed their feelings for each other were real and she'd have to survive the looks of pity when he no longer sought her out. Hadn't they already given society enough to gossip about? There would be more when her system righted itself and there was no longer a need for him to play this deceiving role.

She squeezed her eyes shut, willing him to leave her. She started when he stepped up behind her and clasped his fingers around her upper arms. Her pulse raced in her breast, her flesh burned where he touched her. Then he did the unthinkable. He pulled her up against him and held her.

Her back was pressed to his chest, his warm breath touching the exposed flesh at her neck and shoulders. He wrapped his arms around her and locked his fingers together at her waist.

"Just take several deep breaths and relax," he whispered in her ear. "There's no sense in upsetting yourself until we are sure of anything, one way or another."

His voice affected her like a calming balm that soothed even the places deep inside her that ached from a fear that wouldn't go away.

She gasped for air, her whole body shuddering. As if he realized the turmoil raging inside her, he turned her in his arms and brought her close to him.

His arms wrapped around her comforted her, while his hand moved up and down her back. She felt his soothing heat radiate through her and leaned closer to him as if he alone could support her.

"How touching. I hope I'm not interrupting anything, Your Grace."

Grace stiffened and Raeborn's hands stopped, holding her so she wouldn't lose her balance when he separated himself from her. He turned around to face the intruder, yet positioned himself so Grace would be shielded.

She recognized the voice, and shards of alarm shot through her. Sharp needle pricks stabbed at her flesh as her panic increased, recognizing the voice as belonging to someone she feared.

"I'd heard the rumors that you were in pursuit of another wife, Raeborn, but could hardly believe it when I heard whom you had chosen. I had to ascertain for myself that the rumors were true. I must say I'm surprised."

"And why is that, Lord Fentington?"

Grace lifted her gaze and looked at Baron Fentington. Seeing him caused a gasp of fear she couldn't stifle.

Raeborn moved closer to her, pulling her protectively to his side. A look of confusion appeared on his face. Then a slow, comprehending look of understanding.

He knew. Raeborn knew Fentington was the reason she'd given him her virginity.

The expression on his face turned deadly, his eyes black with anger. His arm tightened around her, holding her in a viselike grip. She could feel the fury building close beneath the surface. A fury she feared would erupt with deadly consequence. She was suddenly more afraid than she'd been the day she faced Fentington in her father's study.

She was terrified of what Raeborn might do to protect her honor.

She knew Fentington was capable of anything, that he'd gloat in telling the *ton* Grace wasn't a virgin, and use what he knew to embarrass Raeborn. And Raeborn would be left with no choice but to defend her honor.

Fentington took a step toward them. "Let us just say that I have privileged information concerning Lady Grace."

Raeborn lifted his shoulders. "I'm sure that anything you may have heard can only be compliments of the highest degree."

Grace swayed on her feet. Raeborn looked down at her and smiled.

"And if they are not?"

Raeborn slowly shifted his gaze to Fentington. When he spoke, his voice was low, the lazy drawl rife with warning. "Then I would be very careful if I were you, my lord. I have developed a special fondness for the lady and would hate to have to call you out for making any disparaging remarks about her."

"I assure you, Your Grace, anything I said would of course be nothing but the truth and said expressly for your benefit. To save yourself from—how can I delicately put this?—a future embarrassment."

Raeborn held out an arm to push her behind him. Grace felt the first true warning sign. The second was the low, deadly hiss in Raeborn's voice when he spoke.

"Be careful, Fentington."

With a great show of piety, Fentington lowered his head in reverence. "Believe me, Raeborn, when I tell you I take no great pleasure in telling you what I must. But it is my Christian duty."

Grace felt her knees buckle when Fentington lifted his head and focused a sneering glare directly at her. She could feel Raeborn's anger building. Knew he would not hesitate to call out the baron.

This was all her fault. She was the cause of everything. If she didn't do something soon, she had no doubt Raeborn would put himself in danger to defend her honor.

"Please leave us, Lord Fentington," Grace said, stepping forward. "I take great exception to your presence—as well as your accusations—and wish you gone."

Fentington laughed. "I'm sure you do, but I would be remiss if I let His Grace's fondness for you develop further without telling him what I know."

"No."

"Oh, yes, my lady." He turned his attention back to Raeborn. "There are perhaps a few details of Lady Grace's—let's see..." Fentington placed a long, narrow finger to the side of his face as if deciding on the perfect word to use, "...*character* that you may want to investigate before you develop a more serious fondness for her."

Raeborn pulled her back beside him. "I'm warning you, Fentington."

Fentington smiled. "Believe me, Your Grace, when I tell you that no one was more shocked than I to learn the truth about Lady Grace."

"Enough," Raeborn growled. "Unless your purpose in telling me this is for tonight to be your last night on this earth. If you want to live to see tomorrow, I suggest you remove yourself from my sight. Otherwise you leave me no choice but to issue a challenge to meet at dawn in Cravenshaw's meadow."

Grace felt the earth move beneath her feet. "Your Grace, no." She started to say more but was stifled to silence when the Duke of Raeborn looked down on her with the blackest glare she'd ever seen.

Fentington looked even more shocked at the turn of events. "But surely Your Grace would—"

Before Fentington could react, Raeborn grabbed the baron's cravat, lifting the impeccably dressed man nearly off the ground. "I suggest you do not say another word. There has never been one hint of scandal associated with the lady, and it is only your perverse mind that seeks to destroy her. And everyone knows your reason for doing so. It is because she wisely rejected your offer of marriage and you are not man enough to accept her rejection without retaliation."

"That's not true."

"And one can hardly blame her. There is not one member of society who is not aware of your cruelty and immoral tendencies. Unfortunately, they have all chosen to look the other way rather than acknowledge such abhorrent behavior. But no longer. If so much as one word concerning the lady comes out of your foul mouth to besmirch her good character, I will not hesitate to expose every skeleton in your lecherous past to all of England. Is that understood?"

Raeborn released Fentington, who staggered to gather his balance. His hands were fisted tightly at his sides, and even in the moonlight Grace could see the veins that stuck out on his neck. She'd never seen such blatant hatred, such evil intent.

"You'll regret this," Fentington said, his voice a low growl that only hinted at a deeper violence. He took a step closer and pointed an accusing finger at Grace. "I won't forget."

Then he spun on his heels and walked away, his angry retreat forcing a half-dozen onlookers off the narrow pathway.

For a long moment no one moved, then, with only a look, Raeborn commanded the small gathering to go back into the ballroom. They left, their heads huddled as they shared muted whispers.

Grace worried her lower lip. The thought of what had just happened caused her stomach to churn unmercifully. She had narrowly missed having a duel fought over her. Being the cause of a man's injury or death. She had no doubt that Raeborn would have issued Fentington a challenge. Fentington had backed down this once. But that did not mean he wouldn't find some other way to retaliate. Some other way to get back at her for what she'd done. And Raeborn too. He'd caused him the greatest blow by publicly humiliating him.

Grace wrapped her arms around her middle and hugged herself. She couldn't stop shaking. Could hardly find the strength to stand on her feet. She was never so thankful in all her life as when Raeborn stepped close and wrapped his arms around her.

"It's over now, Grace," he whispered, one hand moving slowly over her back while the other cradled her head against his chest. "Don't worry about Fentington. He'll never bother you again."

Grace wrapped her arms around his waist and listened to the steady thrumming of his heart in her ear. For the first time in her life, she felt safe. Felt there was someone she could lean on. Someone who could take care of her instead of the other way around. The feeling was wonderful. It was also frightening. It wasn't safe to rely on him the way she wanted to. It would make facing the members of society that much more difficult once they knew.

She had no doubt that before the ball was over, the scene between Fentington and Raeborn would be replayed a dozen different ways. And there was one fact of which Grace was certain. Everyone would know she'd been the cause. The *ton* would know the argument had been over her.

More questions would be raised as to why the Duke of Raeborn was interested in someone with a questionable past.

Chapter 9

Another week passed and she had yet to tell him she was not increasing. Raeborn knew now it was news he would not be hearing. It had been nearly a full month since he'd lain with her.

He took a deep breath. There were some aspects of a man's life over which he had no control. Vincent knew this was one of them. He told himself if the choice had been his, he would have kept the promise he'd made after Angeline's death to never marry again. He'd have lived with the regret of knowing the next Raeborn heir would not come from his loins, but he would have done it. Because he refused to put another woman at risk.

But God saw fit to take such a decision out of his hands. Vincent didn't know whether to shout for joy or weep with despair.

He reached for a glass off a tray from a passing footman and looked to the top of the stairway, anticipating her arrival at Baron Covington's ball. He knew the look on her face when she appeared would be the same as it had been last night at Lady Plumbdale's soiree, or the night before at the Countess of Mentery's musicale. Or the day before when he'd escorted her on a ride through the park, or the night before that when they'd attended the opera—an anxious look brimming with nervous anticipation. Of guilt. And a hint of terror.

He yearned for the day when this anxiety would be in the past.

He was laying the groundwork as best he could and had, so far, been successful. Every member of society took note of the attention he paid her, and her name was linked with his more every day. It was as he intended it to be. The way it must be.

He wanted to laugh out loud when he recalled their last conversation. The subtle hints she'd made telling him that she was convinced she had not conceived. With her cheeks brimming red from embarrassment, she told him she was positive her courses would resume. But he knew differently.

He knew she was deluding herself, pretending it was impossible for the actions of one night to have such permanent consequences. Knew she had conceived as surely as he knew his own name. Knew that giving her more time would only cause her needless worry and perhaps even harm the babe.

He had no intention of taking such a risk. The babe would come early the way it was. There was no need to give society any more grist for their gossip mill than they would have when the babe was born and they counted backward to the day of their wedding. A babe born a month early was bound to cause a certain amount of speculation. A babe born more than two months early resulted in blatant proof.

He already had a special license in his possession. He would give her one more week. If the situation wasn't resolved by then, they would marry, whether she wanted to or not.

He looked to the top of the stairway and saw her. She wore an emerald-green dress tonight with a lower décolletage than she usually wore. Her neck was long and graceful, adorned simply with a single strand of pearls. She made a stunning picture, with her head held high and a slight smile lifting her lips.

A strange warmth spread through him, swirling in the pit of his stomach and moving to his loins. He couldn't stop the smile that touched his lips when her gaze scanned the room and stopped when it reached his.

She had the most fascinating eyes he'd ever seen. Huge and dark with the sparkle of intelligence and life. Her golden hair was pulled loosely to the top of her head, then allowed to cascade in rich, loose curls down the back. A few shimmering tendrils framed her face, the rosy glow from her cheeks making her the most appealing woman in the room.

He smiled. He knew even if he told her what he thought of her appearance she'd deny it was so. That quality made her even more beautiful. She truly did not see herself for the beauty she was.

Vincent walked across the room to meet her when she reached the foot of the stairs. He knew the whole room was focused on his action—focused on her reaction. The thought did not displease him. It was all part of the act. The charade the two of them were playing to convince all of society they were enamored of each other. The charade they were playing to convince each other.

He bowed low when he reached her and kissed her hand. "Lady Grace."

"Your Grace."

"Lady Wedgewood. Wedgewood," he said, greeting Grace's sister and brother-in-law.

He turned his attention back to Grace and she avoided his gaze for just a moment. But it was long enough for him to realize she still had no news for him. She still could not tell him she was not carrying his child.

"Your Grace," the Marchioness of Wedgewood said, drawing Vincent's gaze away from the shadows beneath Grace's eyes. "I'm planning a small dinner party a week from tonight to celebrate the return of my youngest sister, Lady Anne, from her honeymoon. Would you do us the honor of attending?"

Vincent bowed politely. "I'd be delighted."

"Excellent," Lady Wedgewood said, her smile sincere. "I'll send an invitation by messenger tomorrow."

His gaze met Grace's for just a moment before the Marquess of Wedgewood included him in a conversation he was having with three or four other men who'd just arrived. Vincent kept half his attention tuned to what the men were saying while keeping an eye on Grace at the same time. She was pale, and if he was any judge, she'd thickened around the middle in the last month. A niggling worry churned deep inside him.

He stepped closer to her. "Excuse me, my lady, but would you care to accompany me outside for a breath of fresh air?"

A frown creased her forehead, her expression almost one of surprise. Then a smile lifted her lips as if she suddenly remembered the role she was to play. Vincent held out his arm and she took it.

The terrace was empty when they reached it, but he led her down one of the lighted paths, not wanting to take a chance of being overheard. A small, vine-covered gazebo sat in the center of the garden. He led her there.

They stepped up the stairs and he followed her to a bench. She sat down and he stood in front of her, resting the fingers of one hand on her shoulder. "Are you all right?"

"Yes, fine. I am just tired, that's all."

"Are you ill in the mornings yet?"

She jerked away from him and bolted to her feet. "No!"

Vincent stepped back to let her rush past him.

She walked to the other side of the gazebo and stopped with her back to him. She clutched her arms around her middle in a stance of self-protection and stared out into the darkness as if there were something she might see.

His heart ached to go to her, to hold her, to comfort her. But he knew she still needed time. She still needed to come to terms with what was happening to her. To them.

He saw her shoulders quiver and heard her breath shudder. He couldn't take her torment any longer. He walked up behind her and turned her into his arms.

"It's all right, Grace. There's nothing to be done about it now."

"I'm still not certain. I'm quite irregular. I…I…"

"Shh," he whispered. He held her close and cradled her head against his chest. She trembled in his arms and he knew she was struggling to keep the tears from building.

"Would it be so terrible to carry my name and bear my child?"

She pulled away from him and swept one gloved finger across her cheeks before leaning against the wooden railing. She kept her back to him, her shoulders rigid and her chin high. "Let me ask you, Your Grace," she said, her pain-filled gaze locked with his. "Would you have cast me even a second glance had we met under normal circumstances?"

"I would like to think I would have."

She smiled. "The perfect answer. Just as every overture you've made in the last weeks has been perfect—the flowers, the notes, the afternoon rides, the warm smiles when we're in public. Not only have you made me feel like the most sought-after female in all of London, but you've convinced all of society that you truly wish me for your bride."

"What would you have had me do?"

She absently rubbed her fingers over the wooden railing. "I've left you little choice, haven't I?"

He didn't answer. He couldn't. How could he tell her how angry he'd been? How furious, knowing she'd trapped him into marrying her? How terrified he was, knowing he'd probably gotten her with child? Knowing she was forcing him to face his worst nightmare for a third time. He was so bloody terrified, there were times when he thought he would be ill.

And yet, a very small part of him realized her deception had offered him another chance to have an heir. A risk he would never have taken on his own.

She looked at him over her shoulder. "To save myself, I have ruined you. Perhaps there was even someone else you—"

She spun around and her hands flew to her throat. Her eyes grew wide and there was a look of pure panic on her face. "Was there someone else? Was there someone you thought to marry? Someone with whom you considered yourself in love?"

"No. There was no one else. And you have not ruined me."

He heard her sigh. "Haven't I? What would you call it?"

Her hands twisted in front of her and Vincent felt the anxiety building. He closed the distance between them and with his fingers clasped on her upper arms, he brought her closer to him. "I think you are worrying far more than is good for you." He placed a finger beneath her chin and tilted her face upward, then brushed her cheek with the backs of his fingers. "Far more than I want you to."

With that, he leaned down and kissed her.

* * *

Grace knew the minute he held her he was going to kiss her. A commanding voice deep inside her whispered he was only kissing her because it was expected of him. That a simple kiss in the moonlight was the next step in their courtship. That the kiss was an obligatory gesture that meant nothing more to him than the flowers he'd sent or the notes he'd written. A part of her wanted to turn her head away from him so he'd know she didn't expect him to show his affections when there wasn't an audience to impress.

But a more commanding voice wouldn't let her. A part of her was so desperate for him to kiss her that she ached with wanting. That same part of her was desperate to feel his arms around her and his lips touching hers—the way he'd held her and kissed her that night at Madam Genevieve's. She wanted to relive that moment so badly she could hardly restrain herself.

And a part of her was terrified it wouldn't be the same. That now that he knew who she was and what she'd done to him, his anger and disappointment would show in the way he touched her. The way he kissed her.

She stiffened, not exactly pulling away from him, yet not yielding either.

"Don't be afraid, Grace," he whispered, cupping her face in his hands and rubbing his thumbs in gentle circles against her cheeks. His fingers reached around to the nape of her neck and held her securely.

She breathed a heavy sigh that he must have taken for submission and his lips came down and covered hers again.

The kiss was soft, gentle, teasing, as he moved his lips over hers. And she kissed him back. Tentative at first, then with greater passion. It was all the encouragement he needed.

With his own deep sigh, he wrapped his arms around her and opened his mouth atop hers.

Oh, yes. This is what she remembered. The mating of two souls, the blending of two people's breath, the clashing of lips. Grace wrapped her arms around his neck and pulled him closer. His kisses deepened, the effect heady, sucking her under into a spinning whirlpool of uncontrolled emotion. He deepened his kiss, demanding she do the same. And she did.

His tongue touched her lips, running sensually over each one, then boldly entering her mouth as if in search of a prize, as if on a quest. Grace splayed her fingers on the back of his head and held him tight, keeping him close to her while his tongue invaded her mouth. She met him boldly, reaching out to him, seeking, searching, wanting. Finding.

The mating of their tongues was an explosion of raw emotions. An earthy moan whispered in the silence and she knew it was hers.

His mouth moved over hers, each kiss more intense than the last, each meeting of just this one part of their bodies almost more than she could take. And then his kiss deepened.

Grace clung to him because it was all she was capable of doing. Her legs were not strong enough to hold her, her knees no longer steady enough to support her. She held on to him and kissed him back with a desperation she'd never felt before. With a need so consuming she couldn't believe it was possible to survive without what he offered her. And she nearly died when he broke away from her.

His lips stilled atop hers, then he lifted his head, separating himself from her. She stifled a cry, his absence almost painful. But he did not release her. With a heavy sigh, he pulled her against him and held her until their breathing returned to normal. For a long time neither of them moved.

"I think it's time we returned," he finally said. "People will talk if we stay out much longer."

He held out his arm and she took it and walked with him back to the house.

"Are you all right?" he asked when they stepped into the warm ballroom.

She wanted to flippantly answer that of course she was, but she wasn't sure. She only managed a nod.

"Stay here and I'll get us something to drink. I'll be right back."

She nodded again and he left her. She watched him cross the ballroom floor, every magnificent inch of him exuding power and grace. His broad shoulders exemplified a dominant stature and his regal stance demanded respect and admiration. She couldn't lift her gaze from him.

"He's quite a striking figure, isn't he?"

Grace turned to face a very tall, very handsome stranger whose smiling eyes matched the smile on his face. She was instantly drawn to him but didn't know why, except that he had Vincent's dark hair and ebony eyes.

"Please, forgive me for startling you, my lady."

Grace took in several deep breaths. "You didn't, really. I just didn't know anyone was there."

"Allow me to introduce myself. I am Kevin Germaine. Raeborn's cousin."

Grace couldn't hide her surprise as Germaine bowed low, then lifted her hand to his lips. When he raised his gaze back to her face his eyes contained an openness that connected her to him.

"Ah," he said, tilting his head to the side in a relaxed gesture. "I see His Grace has been remiss in talking about his family."

"An oversight I will be sure to bring to his attention." Grace made the statement with sincerity, but suddenly realized how little she knew about Vincent. How little she'd asked him about his family and his past. "Did you say you were cousins?"

"Yes. My father and Raeborn's father were brothers. My father died when I was sixteen, leaving Raeborn my guardian."

"Your guardian?"

"Yes. My father wisely put His Grace in charge of my inheritance as well as my upbringing. I can't tell you the impact Raeborn has had on my future."

Grace thought she saw a glimmer of something dark in Germaine's gaze, but when she looked again it was gone and she realized she must have imagined it. "And does this arrangement meet with your approval?"

"Why would it not, my lady? I can't imagine a more conscientious trustee than Raeborn. Anyone more in control. I can hardly envision the life I would have if Raeborn weren't there to oversee the running of my inheritance."

"Then you and Raeborn must be very close."

Germaine smiled. "I like to think so. I am his only living relative, which is why I am disappointed he did not tell me about you. Or you about me."

"I share your disappointment," she smiled in return.

"I was surprised to discover quite by accident that he'd begun his search for a wife again. You can't imagine how shocked I was."

"Shocked?" Grace said, feeling a nervous twitch deep in her stomach.

"Why, yes. Especially considering the tragedy of losing not one, but his two previous wives. And his heirs with them. I am immensely relieved to see he changed his mind and doesn't intend to abide by his vow to never marry again."

Grace lowered her gaze. Did people know of this vow? Bring it to mind each time they saw her with Raeborn?

"Remaining alone would have been such a waste. He was quite devoted to them both, and when he didn't seek companionship again after he'd lost his dear Angeline,

I was afraid perhaps he actually believed the ridiculous rumors that he was cursed never to have an heir."

Grace felt her face grow pale. "Theirs was a love match?" she asked, dreading the answer.

Germaine smiled. "Yes. I believe it was. But that was in the past and this is the present. Anyway, I'm inordinately pleased to see he paid no attention to such gossip," Kevin Germaine continued. "I'm even more pleased to see he had such impeccable taste as to choose someone with such elegance and beauty."

Grace's heart pounded in her breast. She knew she should leave Raeborn's past buried, but she couldn't. She wanted to know more, and she knew Raeborn would never divulge that part of his past. "Thank you, sir. But surely you realized His Grace would eventually marry again."

"Actually I didn't believe he would."

"But why?" Grace said, trying to quiet the little voice warning her to leave Raeborn's past buried.

"Perhaps he does not think the risk worth the loss. I only know he swore most adamantly after the death of his last wife that he would never take another. That he would never consider fathering another child." Germaine's smile broadened. "You must be quite special, my lady. Not once since the beautiful Angeline died has his name even been linked with anyone."

Grace clutched her hands at her sides, trying to hold steady while the room spun around her.

"And may I add that he couldn't have made a more perfect choice. I can see the two of you will suit each other admirably."

Painful stabs of guilt weighed heavily against her chest. She couldn't let Germaine think so. Deceiving the *ton* was one thing, but deceiving Raeborn's cousin quite another. "Thank you, sir. I'm glad you think so, even though your remarks are quite precipitous. Raeborn and I are just friends."

The look on Germaine's face told her he didn't believe her, but she was thankful he didn't say so. "Nevertheless, Mr. Germaine, I am glad to make your acquaintance. I should have realized by looking that you were related to Raeborn. Your coloring is the same and you have many of the same features."

Kevin Germaine smiled broadly. "I will take that as a compliment, my lady. I assume that is because our fathers were brothers."

"Twins, actually," Raeborn said from behind her.

Grace turned to see him standing there with two glasses in his hands.

"Twins?" she said, trying to cover her unease.

"Yes. They run in our family on occasion."

He handed her one of the glasses, and when she took it he stepped closer to her. Grace wanted to separate herself from him. Wanted to put enough distance between them that she didn't feel as if his nearness were a blanket wrapped around her.

She understood so much more now. She knew the cause of the underlying fury she sensed each time he talked of marrying. He'd had no intention of ever taking another wife. He hadn't wanted to marry again. Hadn't wanted another child even though he had no heir.

The room swayed around her and she lifted her glass and took a quick swallow of the cool liquid he'd brought her.

"I didn't realize you were here," Raeborn said to his cousin, his eyes holding a special understanding. "It's a pleasure to see you. It's been several weeks."

"Yes, well. I've been busy."

"So I've heard. And making admirable progress."

For several long seconds the two men simply stared at each other. Although Grace wasn't sure what had transpired between them, she knew it was something. And it was important. Vincent's cousin was the first to break the silence.

"I suppose I should have realized you would receive a daily accounting," Germaine said, ignoring the compliment, and then focused his attention on her.

"Raeborn. I can't tell you how disappointed I am that you did not tell me you had met someone so charming."

"Then I must apologize. I have indeed." Raeborn turned his gaze to her and Grace knew it was her cue to play her part again. She smiled.

"And I think there is nothing I would like more right now than to dance with such a beautiful lady." He offered her his hand. "If you will excuse us."

"Of course."

Raeborn took the glass from her and handed it to a passing footman, then led her to the dance floor. The orchestra was just beginning a waltz, and he pulled her into his arms and expertly twirled her around the floor.

"You dance beautifully," he said, making conversation. "You cannot imagine how I appreciate dancing with someone who does not tromp on my toes."

Grace started, then laughed. "That is because I had six sisters I was required to teach to dance. It gave me plenty of practice."

"Who taught you?"

"My mother. She loved to dance."

"It shows. How old were you when she died?"

"Twelve."

"Was she ill?"

"No. She died giving birth to Anne."

The air suddenly chilled and Grace felt Raeborn's muscles tense beneath her hands. When she looked up, his face was devoid of expression. "Is something wrong, Your Grace?"

"No," he answered, but she could see there was. And she knew what it was. For a long time he did not speak, but led her through the steps as effortlessly as if they were second nature to him. When he did pick up the conversation, his words were short and clipped.

"What did my cousin have to say, Grace?"

"Nothing. Only that he wished to make my acquaintance and was disappointed that you had not done the honor of introducing us yourself."

"That is all?"

Grace felt her face pale. How could she tell him all that Kevin Germaine had told her? How could she tell him that now she knew why he didn't want her for a wife? Didn't want to go through a woman's pregnancy? Didn't want to risk losing another heir?

"What more could there be?"

His brows lifted. "Nothing."

He kept his gaze focused on her as if he knew she wasn't telling him everything. She desperately wanted to be separated from him. To be somewhere far away where she could think. Where she could be by herself. Perhaps that was all she needed. A few days away from everyone and everything. Perhaps if he weren't standing watch over her, if she didn't have to continuously play the role he'd assigned her, her body would come back to its senses and this whole nightmare would be over.

When they finished their dance, he took her to join Caroline. She bade him good night, then indicated she was tired and wanted to go home. Caroline quickly agreed. After wishing their host and hostess farewell, they walked out into the cool spring evening.

The minute the nighttime air hit her, her mind suddenly cleared and she knew without a doubt what she had to do.

* * *

"Are you still up, Linny?" Grace whispered after knocking on her sister's dressing room door.

Caroline's lady's maid opened the door.

She heard Caroline's voice from inside. "Come in, Grace. Is something wrong?"

"No," Grace said, stepping into the room. The maid left the room, closing the door behind her. "I just needed to talk to you."

Caroline rose from her chair in front of a mirrored table and sat down beside Grace on the floral settee angled before the fireplace. "What is it, Grace?"

"I need a favor, Linny."

"Of course. Anything."

"I would like to take you up on your offer to let me stay at your manor house for a few days."

"Now?"

"Yes. For only a week or so." Grace rose from the settee and walked to the other side of the room where Caroline's desk sat in front of the window. "I'll be back in time for your dinner a week from tonight. Would you mind?"

"Of course not. Is something wrong, Grace?"

"No. I just need to be by myself for a few days. And since you offered, I thought..."

"Of course, Grace. You can take one of the servants with you. There's only Herman and Maudie that live in, so if you want—"

Grace shook her head. "No. I'll be fine. I really do need to be alone."

"Very well," Caroline said, rising to her feet.

Grace couldn't bring herself to look at her sister. Instead, she absently ran her finger along the edge of the desk. "Would you do me one more favor?"

"If I can."

"Please don't tell anyone where I've gone."

"Even the Duke of Raeborn?"

Grace shut her eyes, trying to block out Vincent's face. His kiss. The anger he was sure to feel when he found out she'd gone.

"Yes. Even the Duke of Raeborn."

"Grace, is something—"

"Please, Linny. Don't worry. Everything's fine. I just need some time to myself. You know how I am. I've never been one to enjoy London and the endless round of parties and balls. I've always been content to stay in the country and live a more quiet life."

"And if he asks?"

"Tell him I was called away unexpectedly. That I'll be back in time for your dinner next Friday."

"I doubt he'll accept that without question."

"Perhaps not. But by the time he finds out I'm gone, it will be too late for him to do anything about it. So it doesn't really matter."

Caroline was quiet a moment, then Grace heard her breathe a heavy sigh. "When did you want to leave?"

"In the morning. Early."

"Very well. I'll have a carriage ready."

Grace reached out to give her sister a tight hug. "Thank you, Linny. Good night."

"Good night, Grace."

Grace went to her room and put enough clothes to last a week into a small trunk. When she finished, she slipped into a nightgown and slid beneath the covers.

She closed her eyes with a smile on her face. This was the first night she felt a sense of real peace since she'd come face-to-face with the man to whom she'd given her virginity. She was sure all she needed was a few days away from everything and her situation would resolve. She could finally tell him with certainty that she wasn't expecting.

Grace felt better than she had in weeks.

Until she woke up in the morning and barely made it across the room to a chamber pot before she was ill.

Chapter 10

❦

Vincent let the heavy brass knocker fall against the front door and waited for the Marchioness of Wedgewood's butler to open the door. After last night, he had decided it was time to inform Grace of his plans. Time to inform her they would marry within the week.

He rubbed a hand across his jaw. He wasn't sure how she'd take the news, but after watching her last night, he knew it was time. Even if she wasn't sure whether or not she was increasing, he was. It was as if he'd known it from the start. From the moment he'd taken her virginity, he'd known he'd planted a babe in her womb.

Bloody hell, but he wasn't sure he could go through this again. She was so damn fragile. More delicately built than either of his first two wives.

He fought a wave of anger and frustration as he stepped through the open door a butler held for him.

"I'd like to see Lady Grace," he said, handing his hat and gloves to the navy-liveried man.

"I'm afraid Lady Grace is out, Your Grace."

Vincent stopped short. "Do you know where she is?"

"I'm afraid I don't, Your Grace. But Lady Wedgewood is in the morning room. She's about to have tea. She's expecting you."

An uncomfortable lump formed in the pit of his stomach.

The butler didn't wait for his acknowledgment, but led the way to the back of the house. With a soft knock, he opened the doors and announced the Duke of Raeborn.

"Your Grace," Lady Wedgewood said, extending her hand in greeting.

Vincent walked across the room and bowed over the marchioness's hand, kissing it formally.

"Please be seated, Your Grace."

Vincent sat in the chair opposite the marchioness and waited. There was a tenseness in the room, a feeling of anxiety. As if his presence were part of a play, a well-rehearsed play familiar to all the characters except him.

His chair was positioned at an angle, far enough from the settee on which she sat so his closeness was not too intimate, yet near enough for easy conversation. For easy interrogation. It was obvious she'd been expecting him.

A small nervous warning churned deep in his gut. Something was wrong.

Lady Wedgewood leaned forward to the edge of the settee and daintily poured two cups of tea. "Cream and sugar?"

"Just cream."

Vincent watched as she poured cream into two cups. If he wasn't mistaken, her hand trembled slightly. Another wave of unease jolted inside him. "I have come to see Lady Grace," he said, keeping all emotion out of his voice.

"I'm afraid Grace isn't here at the moment."

Lady Wedgewood held out a cup and saucer then sat back against the cushion when he took it from her. Not once did her gaze meet his, and this time there was no doubt her hands shook.

"Where is she?"

Lady Wedgewood breathed a deep sigh, then took a small sip of her tea. "I'm not at liberty to tell you that, Your Grace."

"Why not?"

She looked him in the eyes. "I promised Grace I wouldn't."

Vincent tried to dampen the fury building inside him but knew the effort was useless. "When did she leave?"

"I'm not sure that is important, Your Grace."

"When?" he repeated.

"Early this morning."

"Did she give a reason for wanting to go away?"

"She said she needed to be alone for a few days. Grace isn't accustomed to London life like you and I and occasionally prefers solitude."

"It is imperative that I speak with her. Please, tell me where she's gone."

"I'm afraid that's impossible. Grace was quite emphatic in her instructions. She wants to be left alone."

Vincent bolted from his chair. "And I don't want her to be alone right now."

He heard the sharp gasp from Lady Wedgewood. "With all due respect, Your Grace, I hardly see where you have the right to determine what decisions my sister makes. Nor is it your concern where she goes. Have you once considered *you* might be the reason Grace felt the need to leave London and have a few days to herself?"

Vincent saw the anger in Lady Wedgewood's eyes and heard the determination in her voice. He knew he would never find out where Grace had gone simply by asking.

"What hold do you have on my sister? What pressure are you putting on her?"

Vincent rose and walked to the window. He stood with his back to her, his shoulders rigid and his hands clasped behind his back.

"I don't know what it is," she continued, her voice as harsh as he imagined it had ever been, "but I've felt for some time now there is something not quite right between you and Grace. As her sister, I feel it my responsibility to protect her in every way possible. I will not see her hurt."

"And I would never do anything intentionally to hurt her," he answered without turning around.

"Then what is between you that has upset her? Because she *is* upset. I have known so for some weeks now."

"I need to speak with her, Lady Wedgewood. Please, tell me where she has gone."

"I'm afraid nothing you have to say can possibly be so important it cannot wait. She promised she would be back in time for the dinner I am hosting next Friday night to welcome our youngest sister back from her honeymoon."

Vincent shook his head. "I cannot give her that much time."

The air crackled with tension. He knew he'd alienated Grace's sister even more.

"I'm afraid you'll have to. I can think of nothing so important that she cannot have the week she wants."

The perfectly manicured garden beyond the window where he stood escaped his notice. Vincent looked but saw none of the early splendid springtime flowers that would soon be in bloom. Nor did he notice two squirrels scampering from tree to tree as they chased each other. He saw nothing except Grace's pale complexion, the dark circles beneath her eyes, the desperation when she looked at him. It should be obvious to her by now whether or not she was increasing. And if she was, he could not let her face it alone.

He turned. "I will ask you once more to tell me where she's gone."

"I'm sorry. As I've told you before, nothing can be so important that you need to bother her. You will simply have to wait until she returns in a week."

He dropped his chin to his chest and breathed a deep sigh, not eager to tell Lady Wedgewood what he suspected. He knew Grace hadn't spoken her fears either. But she'd left him no choice.

"There is something important enough." Vincent faced Grace's sister with all the regal bearing he'd been taught from the time he was old enough to walk. "There is the very distinct possibility your sister is carrying my child."

The cup and saucer in Lady Wedgewood's hand fell to the floor. Tea darkened her skirt. All color left her cheeks as both hands flew to her mouth to stifle her cry.

Vincent took one step closer to her, ignoring the scattered china lying at her feet. "If that is indeed the case, I don't want Grace to be alone right now. Also, to avoid talk, it is imperative we marry as soon as possible. I have already obtained a special license and have made arrangements with Reverend Carrington to keep Friday afternoon free of any interruptions."

The Marchioness of Wedgewood swallowed several times before she was able to speak. When she did, her voice was shallow and strained. “It’s not possible. Grace can’t be—”

Vincent held up his hand. “Suffice it to say, my lady, that there is a very good possibility.”

Lady Wedgewood seemed to sway.

“I do not divulge this information lightly, my lady. If there were any other way to gain the information I seek without exposing an embarrassment I am sure Grace intended to keep private, I would have done so.”

Lady Wedgewood clenched her hands in her lap. She was visibly shaken. “I didn’t know,” she said. “Grace didn’t even hint that…”

“I think she is still expecting a miracle of sorts. I’m afraid it will not come.”

The marchioness drew in a harsh breath, then leveled him with a very serious stare. “Are you hoping for a miracle, Your Grace?”

Vincent lifted his eyebrows. “I am a very practical man, Lady Wedgewood. I have never believed in miracles.”

“I see,” she whispered, her hands clutched so tightly her knuckles turned white.

“We will therefore marry as soon as possible. Next Friday at the latest. I am sure Grace would appreciate it if her entire family were in attendance for such a special occasion. If it meets with your approval, perhaps you would consent to holding the ceremony here, and the dinner you had planned for that evening can be a celebration of sorts.”

“Of course.”

"Now if you will tell me where I can find your sister, I'll be on my way."

The Marchioness of Wedgewood wiped a stray tear from her cheek, then told him where Grace had gone.

* * *

Vincent pushed his mount over the soggy English countryside, ignoring the lack of sunshine and the heavy mist that came down harder with each passing mile. He was chilled to the bone. She should be thankful. Perhaps by the time he reached her the cold rain would cool his blazing temper.

But more than likely, it would only serve to irritate him further and inflame the anger growing inside him. Why the bloody hell had she left? What possible good would come from running away? He would never in a million years understand the female mind. Never understand what she thought to accomplish by avoiding him.

Vincent lowered his head over his horse's neck to protect himself from the falling rain and berated himself a thousand times over for not anticipating that she would flee. But estate business had consumed his entire morning and most of the afternoon, and he'd been forced to send his apologies and miss their scheduled ride. It wasn't until he'd gone to Wedgewood's town house much later that he found out she'd gone.

He tried not to think of how angry he'd become when he realized she'd left him. Just as he forced himself to remember every reason he'd given himself to never search for a wife again. And he wouldn't have. Except that she'd forced him to.

He thought of her, thought of the night she'd lain beneath him, given herself to him, and knew it was a memory that would have to last a lifetime. Once this babe was safely delivered—and dear God, but he prayed it would be—he would never lie with her again. Would never risk getting her with child again.

Just as he would never risk loving her. For the past month he'd courted her, danced with her, and talked to her. He'd laughed with her, held her, and made the mistake once of kissing her. He knew it would be ever so easy to fall in love with her. But that was one emotion he would never allow himself to feel again. He'd barely survived the loss twice. He wouldn't go through the pain again.

Vincent pushed his horse faster. He was soaked to the bone, and the sooner he got there the sooner he would be warm and dry. And the sooner he could get this confrontation over.

He pulled his horse to a sudden stop and turned around when he realized he'd gone past the lane Lady Wedgewood told him would lead to the country manor where Grace had gone. He sat as straight in his saddle as the pouring rain would allow, then pulled on the reins and turned his horse around.

His horse had only taken a few steps when Vincent was jolted by a painful stitch in his side. A second later, a muffled shot echoed through the air. It took another moment for him to realize he'd been shot. A moment more until real fear consumed him.

Vincent clutched his hand to his side and looked to the right, to a small copse of trees. His eye caught a movement in the shadows, but he saw nothing except a white blur moving through the trees. He looked again, but it was gone. Vanished as if it had never been there.

He tried to take a deep breath, but white-hot shards of pain spiraled through his chest, then shot down his arms to the tips of his fingers. He battled the overwhelming pain that consumed him, then after a momentary hesitation, he bent low and kicked his mount into a run.

Another shot rang through the air. It took every ounce of his strength to hold on to the saddle. Every ounce of stamina to keep from falling to the ground.

Vincent clutched his hand to his side and blood seeped through his fingers. Pain as hot as a burning poker consumed him.

The sky spun around him and he realized he was in danger of losing consciousness. He barely made it up the pebbled lane to the front of the manor house before his world went black and the earth came up to meet him.

* * *

"My lady, come quickly!"

Grace rose from the bed where she'd been resting and rushed across the room she'd taken as her own. For a moment the room spun precariously, and she reached out to steady herself. The feeling didn't last long but was followed by a rush of panic. She knew dizziness was just another symptom of what she could no longer deny was wrong with her.

How could she ever face him now? What choice did he have but to marry her, to take her along with the child she was carrying?

A painful weight pressed against her chest. Every single waking hour she'd prayed she hadn't conceived. Prayed she wouldn't have to spend the rest of her life with a man who didn't want her. With a man she'd deceived from the beginning.

A fine sheen of perspiration broke out on her forehead. She was glad she was here and not in London. Glad she would at least have a few days to come to terms with what she now knew was fact before she had to face him. Before she had to look at the resignation in his eyes. His resolve to do what was right even though he didn't want to.

"My lady, hurry!"

She ran across the room and opened the door, confused at the anxiety she heard in Mr. Featherly's voice.

Grace didn't know them well, Herman and Maudie Featherly, but from the minute she'd arrived, their relaxed calmness had blanketed her like a soothing balm. She felt more in control of her life than she had since she'd seen Raeborn standing in the back of Caroline's music room and knew she'd been discovered.

She rushed to the top of the stairs and looked down. Her heart leaped in her breast.

"Vincent?" she uttered, her voice a strangled choke.

"My lady. We found him in the drive. He's been injured."

Grace rushed down to meet them. "Vincent?" She brushed his wet hair from his forehead. "Where are you hurt?"

"It's his side, my lady," Herman volunteered.

Grace looked down at the blood staining his shirt and soaking through his jacket.

"Grace..."

"Shh, Your Grace. Don't talk. We have to get you to a bed."

"I…I…"

He didn't get anything else out before a cough wracked his body and he doubled over in pain. Herman nearly lost his grip and staggered beneath Vincent's weight.

"Don't talk, Vincent. Can you make it up the stairs?"

"Yes…But I have something…to…"

"Hush. You can tell me later. We need to stop this bleeding."

He reached out his hand to clasp her fingers, squeezing hard.

"No," he said on a gasp. "Promise me…you won't… leave."

"No, Your Grace. I won't leave you."

"Promise…me."

"I promise."

Step by step they climbed upward, Raeborn helping as much as he could, but the loss of blood was taking its toll. He could barely lift his feet, and more than once his knees buckled and the four of them nearly went down.

When they reached the top, Grace ran ahead and opened the door to the room next to hers. She rushed inside and pulled down the covers on the bed.

"Put him here, Mr. Featherly. Maudie, please bring some water and bandages. And a needle and thread."

"And I'll bring that bottle of brandy Herman's been keeping in the cupboard." The housekeeper scurried from the room as fast as her short, plump legs would carry her.

Herman lowered Vincent to the bed, steadying him with one hand while pushing his jacket off his shoulders with the other. "We'd best remove his shirt to see what damage has been done," he said, removing Vincent's clothing while Grace grabbed a towel from the stand and wet it.

When Vincent was naked from the waist up, Herman laid him down and pulled off his boots. "You'd best turn around, my lady, while I remove the rest of His Grace's clothing. We need to get these wet things off him and warm him up before he takes a chill."

Grace kept her back to the bed until Herman was finished, then turned around and placed a cloth on Vincent's forehead to wipe away the perspiration.

"Press that cloth here," Herman said to Grace, pointing to the spot where blood still seeped from the larger of two wounds. A bullet had torn through his side, but whether it had nicked or cracked a rib, she couldn't tell. Two wounds showed the deadly missile's path, one clean and not bleeding terribly, the other a ragged, bloody mess.

Raeborn sucked in a harsh breath when she pushed against the long, jagged tear in his flesh, then dropped his head back against the pillow and closed his eyes. The muscles in his jaw tensed as he clenched his teeth against the pain.

"The bullet didn't do as much damage as it could have, Your Grace." Herman lifted the cloth to examine the wound more closely. "But you've lost a lot of blood. We'll need to stitch you up."

Grace kept her hand pressed against Vincent's side, all the while trying to focus her gaze on something other than his face and naked torso. On something other than what was covered by the thin sheet pulled low on his waist. She couldn't. He was just as she remembered from the night she'd lain with him. Just as magnificently muscled as she remembered from when she'd held him and run her hands over his lean, taut flesh. Her body turned uncomfortably warm with the memories.

His flesh was dark by nature, and clinging drops of rainwater still beaded on his chest and shoulders. With her free hand she reached for a dry towel and wiped the wetness from his face. His eyes slowly opened and he looked at her. His gaze was filled with pain.

"Maudie will be here in a moment," she whispered, brushing the soft cloth over his flesh. "You'll be better soon."

"Promise you'll…not leave…my side."

"I promise," she said, drying as much of him as she could without getting too close to the wound.

Grace turned her gaze to the open door when Maudie rushed in, a tray with warm water and ointments and salves in her hands. She had a half-full bottle tucked under her arm.

"Here, my lady," she said, handing Grace the bottle and a glass. "Have His Grace drink a glass of this before we start."

Grace put some of the liquid in the glass, then lifted Vincent's head and put the glass to his lips. He took two huge swallows, then dropped his head back to the pillow.

"That's enough," he rasped. "Let's just get this over with."

Grace went around to the other side of the bed so Maudie had plenty of room to clean the wounds and do the stitching, and Vincent's gaze followed her as if he were afraid she'd lied to him and intended to flee the second she could.

"I'm just going to clean the wounds first, Your Grace," Maudie said. "I'll use some of Herman's fine brandy to make sure the wounds don't get infected."

Grace couldn't bring herself to watch what the housekeeper was doing. Instead, she kept her gaze locked with his.

"I'll be sure to replace your brandy," Vincent said, his breathing more labored, his complexion a pasty white. He kept his eyes still focused on her.

"I'll hold you to that, Your Grace," Herman said in an attempt at humor.

There was a slight pause, then Maudie spoke. "This is going to sting something fierce, Your Grace."

"I anticipate…as much," Vincent gasped. "Fine brandy… is bound to…do that."

"That it is," Maudie answered. She barely finished the words, "I'm sorry, Your Grace," before she poured a goodly dose of brandy over the wounds.

Vincent's body flinched, but other than the tightening of his grip around Grace's fingers, he showed no reaction.

"It will be over soon," she whispered as Maudie poured another dose of brandy onto the raw, gaping flesh.

A heavy film of perspiration covered Vincent's pale complexion. The combination of exertion and pain was taking its toll, and Grace knew he was close to losing consciousness. Although she knew it would be a blessing, she also knew how much he would fight it. The grim determination in his eyes and the rigid set of his mouth told her he'd stay conscious for every agonizing moment of it.

"There, Your Grace," Maudie said, threading the needle. "The worst is over."

Vincent sank back into the covers and breathed heavily.

"I'll try to be gentle. I'm a fair hand at needlework but can't say it'll win any prizes," she said, settling back down on the side of the bed. "But it'll heal nice and proper. That I can promise."

"I have…every confidence…in you," Vincent told her, still focused on Grace's face.

Maudie gave him a warm smile, then stuck the needle through his flesh.

"What happened, Vincent?" Grace asked, partly to keep his mind occupied so he wouldn't feel the pricks of the needle. But more because she couldn't imagine how he could have been shot. "Do you think it was a hunter?"

Vincent broke eye contact for the first time. He moved his gaze to where Herman stood holding a lamp so Maudie could see better.

Herman cleared his throat. "There ain't no hunters 'round here, my lady. Not this close to the manor house."

The air caught in Grace's chest. "Vincent?"

The Duke of Raeborn closed his eyes. "You'll not… leave the house…unless I am with you. Do you understand, Grace?"

Grace watched Maudie's nimble fingers work the needle in and out of the flesh of Vincent's side while her mind tried to read the meaning behind such a demand.

"Yes, but surely—"

Raeborn's eyes snapped open and the hand she'd been holding shot upward, palm out, stopping her from finishing her sentence. "Do you?"

She swallowed hard. "Yes, Your Grace."

He breathed a heavy sigh, then closed his eyes again. Grace saw the determination and the pain etched on his face and prayed Maudie would finish soon.

"Keep an eye out, Mr. Featherly," he said through clenched teeth. "Don't let anyone in."

"No, Your Grace. You can count on me."

A thousand questions raced through her mind, and the staggering implication of Vincent's orders frightened her. She'd have to think on that later, but right now she only wanted this to be over so he could rest.

"All finished," Maudie said, snipping the last thread. "Give His Grace another swallow of brandy. I imagine he needs it."

Grace lifted the glass to his lips and let him drink, then lowered his head back to the pillow and pulled the covers up to his chin. He watched her through pain-filled eyes.

"Don't leave me, Grace."

"I won't."

He closed his eyes and slept.

Grace brushed her fingers through his hair, lifting a stray lock from his forehead. Herman and Maudie gathered the blood-soaked cloth and Vincent's clothes and quit the room, leaving her alone with him.

Grace stood at the side of the bed and watched the rise and fall of his chest. Even asleep he was the most magnificently handsome man she'd ever seen. Every feature of his sculptured face was perfectly formed—his wide forehead, thick eyebrows, high cheekbones, and rugged jaw. She shifted her gaze to his lips. They were just soft enough that when he kissed her she melted against him, yet firm enough to carry her to a world totally unknown to her before she'd lain with him.

She remembered the color of his eyes, so dark and deep and penetrating she was sometimes afraid when she looked at him, yet so warm and comforting she could lose herself in the depths of them. He was perfection to her plainness. He was a replica of the kind of man she'd always dreamed of finding, of marrying.

But that was when she still had dreams. Before the weight of protecting her sisters from their father's greed had destroyed any hope she'd had for her future. When she still believed someone could look beyond her very ordinary outside covering and see something special inside. And want to spend his life with her.

Instead, she'd deceived a man, and now he had no choice but to take her as his wife.

Grace pushed a chair close to the bed and sat down. His hand lay atop the covers, his long, graceful fingers clutching at the material as if he fought the pain even in his sleep. She reached out to touch him, to take some of the pain onto herself—then stopped.

Holding him, binding herself to him even more, was not wise and she knew it. She knew to come to care for him would only bring her pain. But she knew with that same certainty that it was already too late. She'd passed the point of protecting her heart. It had happened because of her deceit, on the night she'd given him her body. On the most glorious night of her life.

Grace held his hand in hers, entwined his fingers with hers, placed her palm snugly against his. A warm heat so intensely alive it stole her breath raced up her arm, through her breast, then dropped as it swirled in the pit of her stomach.

She closed her eyes and prayed she could live without the part of her heart he possessed but did not want.

Chapter 11

Vincent opened his eyes just a slit at first and tried to remember where he was. He moved, then tried to remember why he hurt so damn bad.

The room was unfamiliar, the burgundy roses on the wallpaper unlike any room in his house, the forest-green draperies completely foreign to him. He closed his eyes again, then breathed in a deep rush of air through his nose. His side burned like hell and his head throbbed as if he'd been on an all-night drunk. He pried his eyelids open a little more and moved his head to look around the room. And saw her.

She lay curled in a cushioned wing chair, her legs tucked beneath her and a dark quilt under her chin. Her eyes were closed, and more than once while he watched, her shoulders lifted and fell when she took a deep breath and released it.

Her wheat-colored hair was tied at the nape of her neck by a pink ribbon. Sometime during the night she'd changed out of the blood-splattered gown she'd worn while she tried to stanch his bleeding.

She shifted in her sleep and the quilt fell over one shoulder. She wore a nightgown with a very proper robe fastened high at her neck. She was less exposed than when she wore one of the ball gowns that were in fashion now, but knowing she was no doubt naked beneath the nightgown affected him more than he wanted it to. Visions of how she'd looked the first night he'd met her refused to go away.

As if she realized he was awake, she opened her ebony eyes. "Good morning, Your Grace."

Her voice was little more than a whisper and he wondered if she realized how sensual it sounded. "Good morning."

She pulled the quilt up higher beneath her chin and leaned forward. Her hand reached out and she placed her fingers first against his forehead, then against his cheek. He didn't let his gaze move from her face and was blessed with a warm smile.

"You're not hot. That's good. Would you like some water?"

"Yes."

She moved to fill a glass with water but had to release the quilt in order to use her hands. He saw her cheeks darken before she turned her back to him and placed the quilt over the chair. She paused.

"I suppose you think it's silly to be modest in front of you after what we've..." She turned to the small table beside the bed and filled a glass with shaking hands. "I didn't intend to fall asleep and thought to be dressed before you woke."

"It's all right, Grace."

She lowered the glass to his lips. He drank a few swallows, then lowered his head.

"How do you feel?" she asked.

"Like hell."

"I don't wonder." She sat back in the chair. "Did you see who shot you?"

He decided to ignore her and change the subject. "Why did you run away?"

A frown creased her forehead followed by a look of understanding. "You did. You saw him. Who was it?"

"Surely you must have known I would come after you."

"You're not going to answer me, are you?"

"No. Why did you run?"

She rose and walked to the grate to place another log on the dwindling fire. She took an inordinate amount of time. Her delaying tactic only stretched his already fragile temper.

"Don't ignore me, Grace. I'm not in the mood to play games."

He heard her harsh sigh from across the room; then she turned and faced him squarely.

"I needed to be away, Your Grace. I needed time to be by myself where I could think."

"About what?"

"Surely you know what I had to think over," she said, the expression on her face one of incredulity.

"I'm not sure there is much for you to think over. It is much more the time to take action."

She paled, her face losing all color.

"No. Not yet," she whispered.

"Why? Is the idea of marrying so terrifying?"

"To me or to you?"

Her words affected him like none others could. "I'm not sure what you've heard, Grace, but—"

With their penetrating gazes locked, she held out her hand to stop him. "I know you do not want to marry. I know when you lost your last wife you vowed never to marry again. Even abandoned the need for an heir. Did you love her that much?"

Vincent felt as if the air had been knocked out of his lungs. "She was very special. Both my wives were."

"Then we will hope it is not too late."

"I think you already know it is."

"No. I don't."

Vincent pressed his head deeper into the pillow and closed his eyes. "Why did you come here, Grace?"

Confusion was evident in her voice. "I've already explained that."

"No, why *here*?"

"Caroline offered me the use of her home for a few days. I knew it was not occupied, and it was not all that far from London."

"Why didn't you go home?"

Vincent turned his head to watch her fidget with the ribbons on her robe. "Do you know what I heard the night before I came here while I was at one of my clubs?"

She shook her head.

"I heard your father remarried."

He did not get the reaction he thought. She remained passive, almost as if the news didn't affect her. "Did you know he was going to?"

"He mentioned he might."

"When?"

"Before I left to go to Linny's."

"Don't you think it strange a father would marry without any of his children in attendance?"

She smiled, but the smile rang far from true. "You don't know my father, do you?"

Vincent shook his head.

"You are fortunate."

"You don't have a home to go to. Do you, Grace?"

She flinched, then faced him with her hands clenched at her sides. "I have six homes to go to, Your Grace. And this one too, if I so wish to stay here."

"But they would not be a home of your own."

"Why are you doing this?"

"Because you need to face your situation without blinders. You need to admit it is more than possible you are carrying my child. And I will not allow it to be born outside the bonds of marriage. You need to face the fact that you have no place else to go. You have no home to go to without being a burden on your family. This marriage may not be what you want, but you don't have a choice."

"And what choice do you have? To take another wife you do not want? One you do not love?"

"I don't see where that matters now. It is the only choice you have left me."

Vincent watched the color drain from her face and wished he could take back his words. But it was too late.

She clutched her hands in the gathers of her robe. "Perhaps it is not too late. Perhaps there isn't a child and I am just…"

Her face was completely devoid of color now and he watched as she swallowed fast, then reached out to steady herself against the chair. Vincent tried to sit, tried to reach for her, but the stitch in his side stopped him. He had no choice but to lie there and watch while she clamped her hand over her mouth and ran from the room.

* * *

"What are you doing out of bed?"

Grace rushed across the room and anchored her hands around Vincent's middle, making sure to avoid his side where the stitches were. A sheen of perspiration glistened across his forehead as he stood with his hands propped against the wall to hold himself upright. He was dressed in pants and a shirt. His boots were on the floor, ready to be put on his feet.

"It's only been two days since you were injured. You shouldn't be up yet."

"How long have you been ill in the mornings?"

The air caught in her throat.

"How long?"

She lowered him to the edge of the bed and reached over to pour him a cup of tea. "Three days."

"It's early yet, then."

Grace handed him the tea, then walked over to the window and looked out at nothing. "I'm sorry."

"Don't be sorry. Don't *ever* be sorry."

She dropped her head back on her shoulders and blinked to keep the tears at bay. "Can I say the same to you?"

When he didn't answer, she asked the question that had been bothering her since he arrived. "How did you find me?"

"Lady Wedgewood told me."

Grace shook her head. "No. I asked her not to. She wouldn't have told you unless—" Grace's gaze darted to where he sat. "You didn't!"

"Tell your sister you are with child? Yes. It's not as if any of them will not realize it the moment we return with the special license in my hands."

"You already have the license?"

"We will marry Friday afternoon. Lady Wedgewood has agreed to let us hold the ceremony in her home and has promised to inform all your sisters so they are there. I didn't think you would want your father to attend."

She couldn't keep from trembling. "No," she whispered, holding on to the nearest stable object. "Just my sisters."

"Grace?"

"Yes."

"Come here." He reached out his hand and pointed to the place beside him on the bed. "Sit here."

She hesitated, then sat next to him. He turned toward her.

"Give me your hands."

She held out her trembling hands and he took them in his. "I know this is not easy for you."

She opened her mouth to speak, but he stopped her with a look. "No, it is not easy for me either," he hurried to add. "But we will both make the best of it. We will come to know each other and what we want from the other. There is nothing you will lack for your comfort. I am a man of means and everything I possess will be yours for the asking."

"And in return? What is there for me to give? I don't come with a dowry. Nor am I the beauty society expects you to choose. I am rather plain and nondescript, and everyone will know when I am delivered early of the child that I trapped you into marrying me."

He smiled. "No. They will assume, and rightly so, that I was so captivated by your charm I could not control my passion. They will expect me to marry quietly. This is, after all, my third marriage."

She hesitated a moment, then added, "I would not have done anything differently." She looked deep into his eyes, hoping to see at least a small sign that said he understood. Praying she would see a glimmer that told her he was glad she hadn't. She didn't. There was only a sadness there, a haunting resignation that told her he would accept the lot that was forced on him because she'd given him no other choice. A fleeting look of fear and despair. "I could not have married Fentington."

"No. You could not have."

"But I regret what I have done to you."

"You have done nothing to me. You are the one who will be left to pay the price."

"Or reap the rewards."

He smiled. It was a sad smile, yet he put on a noble front. She knew she should not be affected by him, knew it put her heart in greater danger, but her body warmed at his nearness. Her flesh burned where his leg brushed against her thigh. Her arm, from her shoulders to the tips of her fingers, tingled from the warmth of his hands holding hers.

She studied his face, the soft furrows that indented his forehead, the high cheekbones, and the strong, rugged cut of his jaw. Then she lowered her gaze to his mouth. To the lips that had kissed her. An eruption of fiery heat soared through her insides, plummeting to the pit of her stomach, then moved lower yet, to the very core of her. To the place he'd awakened the night of their lovemaking.

Her cheeks blazed hot and she turned away from him, praying he couldn't read her thoughts. But she knew he did. And she suddenly realized how easy it would be to fall in love with him.

In that moment she made a vow. She vowed that she would never give him cause to regret what she'd forced him to do. She would be the best wife she could be, the best companion, the best listener, the best mother, and the best friend. She would give him a house filled with children and laughter and love. And she would be there when he needed her.

She did not expect love. Not at first. Perhaps never. But she would not let that matter. He had already done more for her than she could ever repay.

She looked at his hands lying in her lap, still holding hers. She lifted his fingers to her lips, then held them to her cheek.

"I will forever be grateful," she whispered. "And I promise I will spend every day from now on making sure you never regret taking me as your wife."

"As I will pray you never regret having me for your husband."

She lifted her head and looked at him, her eyes filled with emotion. She couldn't find the words to ease the worry she saw on his face.

"Have you eaten yet?" she asked, releasing his hands and standing in front of him.

"No. I was attempting to dress and go down to join you."

"Would you like me to bring up a tray?"

"No. But I will need help with my boots. Perhaps Herman—"

Grace picked up his boots, silencing him when she slipped the first one onto his foot.

"You make an excellent valet," he said when she finished.

"Thank you." She held out her hand to help him up. When he was on his feet, she walked beside him, letting him lean against her as they made their way out of the room and down the stairs.

"You are doing quite well," she said when they reached the dining room. "But don't tire yourself."

He pulled out a chair for her. "I'm fine, Grace. It was little more than a scratch."

She poured them each a cup of tea while Vincent ate the food Maudie had placed on the table. "When we're finished," he said, putting more coddled eggs on his plate, "we'll tour the house so I build my strength."

She paused with her cup midway to her mouth and arched her eyebrows.

"And then," he said, ignoring her concern, "I will have you play for me. You are wonderful, you know."

Grace felt her cheeks warm.

They ate in companionable silence, then toured the house. Vincent was noticeably tired when they stopped, and he relaxed on the settee while she played a Haydn piece she'd always loved.

This is how their lives would be. The two of them together, quiet, content, a special sort of love steadily growing between them. Grace smiled as her fingers ran over the keys. All would be well. She was confident it would be.

Chapter 12

He paced the hallway outside her bedroom, trying with every ounce of his being to block her muffled moans. Sweat beaded on his forehead, then ran down his face and into his eyes. He wanted to run but there was no place for him to go. No place where her agonizing pleas for help would not follow him.

He stiffened his shoulders and walked to the end of the hall, his carriage every inch a duke's even though inside he hardly felt like one. He'd known it would be this way. He'd gone through this before. Had always known it would be like the last time. And the time before.

Great waves of terror washed over him, the panic building inside him nearly bringing him to his knees. He couldn't go through this again. Couldn't survive it.

His legs trembled beneath him. His stomach churned until he feared he'd be ill. A painful weight pressed against his chest, stealing the air from his body. He couldn't stand by while another woman lost her life trying to give him an heir. Not again.

He clamped his hands over his ears to stop her cries of agony. The guilt was too much to bear, the regrets too consuming. He sucked in a razor-sharp breath of air. No. Not again. He would not allow her to die too.

He ran down the hall and threw open the door. His gaze flew to the other side of the room where she lay in bed, her face deathly gray, distorted with pain. Her sweat-drenched hair was plastered to her scalp, and before he could reach her she arched her fragile body as another spasm gripped her.

With trembling hands, he clasped his fingers around hers, thinking he could hold her to him and protect her. But he knew it was too late.

Death already had hold of her, was already pulling her from his grasp. The fear ravaging his body was so palpable he couldn't breathe. She was dying and he couldn't save her. And he didn't want to live without her.

He dropped his head back onto his shoulder and cried to the heavens.

"Grace!"

Vincent threw back the covers and bolted from the bed, his sweat-drenched body burning with a fiery heat he doubted would ever cool. He raced to the open window and let the nighttime March air wash over him.

The moon was full and directly overhead, meaning it was after midnight, perhaps one or two in the morning. Bloody hell, he could swear he'd been living his nightmare for at least ten hours.

His heart thundered in his chest and his legs felt so weak they buckled beneath him. He braced his hands on either side of the window and hung his head between his outstretched arms and gasped for air.

Damn! Damn it to hell! Damn her!

He couldn't do this. He couldn't spend every day of the next seven months and more with her, getting to know her, learning to care for her. Coming to love her. Watching her body grow big with his child, with the heir he longed to have. Then have her die in his arms and the babe with her. He couldn't do it. He wasn't strong enough to go through it again.

Cold sweat poured from his body and he jabbed his hands into his hair, struggling against the fear that pummeled him like a tidal wave in a raging storm. He squeezed his eyes shut tight, then opened them, praying his nightmare would go away.

Something moved in the distance. Someone. His heart began a steady drumming, beating faster and faster until he feared it might leap from his chest.

A man moved below his window. The thin form slouched low and kept to the shadows as he ran from the front of the manor house down the long drive to the lane. He wore a long, dark cloak over white breeches and jacket and a wide hat that covered most of his features. Before he reached the lane, he turned to look back. Then he lifted himself up on his white mount and rode away.

Vincent felt a greater fear than he thought was possible. He knew only one man with such a penchant for white. One man whose threats could cause harm.

He raced across the room, pulling on his breeches and boots before he went out the door.

He ignored the stitch in his side and slipped his loose shirt over his shoulders as he ran down the hallway toward the stairs. He froze halfway down the staircase as the faint whiff of smoke assaulted his nose. He shifted his gaze to the entrance and saw flames licking up the outside of the house from the two windows on either side of the door. He turned and vaulted back up the stairs.

"Grace!"

Vincent threw open the door and raced across the room. "Wake up, Grace."

Her eyes popped open and she shook her head as she struggled to waken. "Vincent? What is it?"

"There's a fire," he said, shoving her slippers onto her feet. "Here, put this on." He handed her the robe lying across the foot of the bed then grabbed another blanket and threw it around her shoulders. "Hurry. Come with me."

He wrapped his arm around her waist and propelled her to the stairs, keeping a tight grip on her as they made their way to the bottom. Heavy smoke seeped under the door, the acrid smell assaulting his nose. "Go to the back. We can't get out the front."

He pushed her forward. When they reached the rear of the house he yelled to wake Herman and Maudie. Before he and Grace reached the kitchen area, the two servants were rushing from their quarters.

"There's a fire in the front of the house," Vincent said, rushing for the door.

They had to get out before the smoke got too bad. He reached for the door and pushed. It was locked.

"Where's the key, Herman?"

"There ain't no key, Your Grace. This door ain't never been locked."

"Keep the women back," Vincent said, throwing a log from the fireplace through the only window in the room. He pushed a chair near the opening and crawled up. "Hopefully the door has only been wedged shut and I can get it open."

Vincent shoved himself through the opening and dropped to the ground. A heavy bench had been lodged under the latch. He pushed it away, then pulled open the door.

"Are you all right?" he said, rushing Grace from the house and taking her into his arms.

"Yes. I'm fine."

"Sit with Lady Grace on that bench, Maudie," he ordered, giving Grace a quick kiss on the forehead, "and don't either of you move. We have to get that fire out before the house burns. Fill some buckets, Herman."

He raced around the side of the house with Herman at his side.

It didn't take long to extinguish the blaze. Thankfully he'd seen it soon enough. If he hadn't, they could have burned to death. Especially Grace and he. The fire was set to cut off any escape down the stairs. They would have been trapped up above.

"Vincent?"

Vincent spun around to see Grace standing behind him, hugging the blanket he'd wrapped tightly around her shoulders. "It's over now, Grace. Are you unharmed? Is the baby…?"

He watched as one of Grace's hands moved to her stomach.

"The baby's fine."

Vincent couldn't believe the relief he felt.

She took a step toward him. "What happened?"

"Nothing." He crossed the rest of the distance to where she stood and pulled her into his arms. She flattened her hands against his chest and pushed away from him.

"Don't lie to me. What's happening? First you are shot, then someone sets fire to the house where you're sleeping. Do you know who it is?"

He tried to pull her back against him but she stepped out of his reach. "Did you see something? You must have discovered the fire soon after it started. It hasn't done too much damage. What did you see?"

Vincent shook his head, but she held out her hand to stop his denial.

"What!" she demanded a second time.

"I saw a man ride away on a white mount just after I was shot. I saw him again tonight."

"A white mount? Who do you know who has a white horse? Perhaps it is someone who—"

Vincent saw the color drain from her face and stepped close to her to hold her. "It's him," she whispered, and he felt her sway in his arms.

"I can't swear to it, Grace. I didn't see his face."

"It has to be. Fentington's known for his penchant for white. His white horse, white carriage, white clothes."

"Perhaps it's just coincidence."

"You know it's not. He means to kill you because you embarrassed him at the Pendleton ball. I thought he'd forgotten about it because he didn't attend any functions after that."

"He wasn't invited."

Grace looked up at him in surprise. "Wasn't invited?"

"The *ton* have finally decided to put their stamp of disapproval on his sexual perversions. Fentington has been removed from everyone's guest list."

"He blames you, Vincent. He blames us both."

Vincent wrapped his arms around Grace's shoulders and pulled her close to him. "We'll leave for London in the morning."

"And then what?"

"We'll marry as planned. You'll have my name to protect you. I'll take care of Fentington."

Vincent ignored the concern on her face and led her back into the house. "Maudie has the windows open down here and the smell isn't too strong any more. We'll sit in the study until the house is aired."

They walked together to the study, but when they entered the room, Vincent couldn't let her sit alone on the long, floral settee. She looked so small and frightened. So fragile. Instead, he walked to a brown-leather wing chair.

"Come here," he whispered and held out his arms for her. Without hesitation, she walked into his arms. He sat, then pulled her to his lap. She breathed one heavy sigh before she curled up in his lap and turned her face into his chest.

Vincent tucked the blanket beneath her chin and held her, promising God that if He spared her life and delivered the child from her safely, he'd never put her at risk again.

He rested his chin on the top of her head and felt a wave of desire. He ran his hands across her shoulders and down her arms. He sifted his fingers through her thick, golden hair and caressed the taut muscles at her neck and back. Then he lowered his gaze and looked into her eyes—into the wealth of emotion he'd fought so valiantly to ignore. And he knew the battle was lost.

He lowered his head and kissed her with all the desperation he'd struggled against since he'd met her. Since he'd first touched her. Since he'd lain with her.

He pressed his lips against hers and kissed her again, then deepened his kiss when she wrapped her arms around his neck and turned into him.

He was desperate to have her. Frantic to possess her. Desperate to keep her safe.

Such possessiveness was a feeling he'd sworn he'd never feel again. It went against his vow to do everything in his power to protect himself—to protect his heart.

He kissed her again, then nestled her close to him and rested his chin against the top of her head. He could not look at her but stared straight ahead. He did not want her to see the raw desire in his eyes. Didn't want to see her red, swollen lips and ache to kiss them again. He knew he'd already committed a grievous error and did not want to compound it with emotions that were irreversible.

He knew he'd already come to care for her more than was wise. More than his heart could withstand if he lost her.

Chapter 13

Grace would rather have taken a beating than return to London and face Caroline. And by now all of her other sisters knew too.

She turned her head and focused on the scenery out the carriage window. Watching the green hills and verdant meadows was better than thinking about the scene to come when they arrived. Much better than watching the grim expression on Raeborn's face darken.

She'd been ill again this morning, just as they were preparing to leave. She could almost cut the worry emanating from him with a knife. She took a deep breath and prayed she'd make it to London without having to stop.

"Are you feeling all right?"

Grace swallowed hard in an effort to calm her queasy stomach. "I'm sorry I delayed our leaving."

"It doesn't matter. Sickness is part of a pregnancy. It will probably last at least a few more weeks."

Grace smiled. "My sister Josie was ill the whole term with her first. She's married to Viscount Carmody, and we all thought by the time the babe was born we'd hear she'd been charged with murder."

Raeborn looked at her from beneath furrowed brows, and Grace thought how endearingly handsome he was this morning. How such a simple gesture made her heart race. "She made her poor husband suffer unmercifully. He even threatened to move in with Caroline and Wedgewood until it was over. Thank heaven her next two babes were much kinder to their mother. With the last, she wasn't ill in the least."

He frowned. "How many children does she have?"

"Three. Although I anticipate news of a fourth soon. It's just a feeling I have."

"Are they all daughters, then?"

"No. They're all sons."

Raeborn's frown deepened. "If the viscount already has three sons, why would she consent to risking her life to give him a fourth?"

Grace wanted to laugh, but one look at the expression on his face told her he was deadly serious. For a heartbeat her blood ran cold. "Most women don't look at bearing children as a risk, Your Grace. They consider children a blessing. Don't you?"

His gaze turned hard, his expression haunted. "No. Perhaps I did once. Before I knew what was at stake."

The air left her body. She knew she should let the matter drop, but she couldn't. "Not every woman dies in childbirth, Your Grace."

His face paled in the warm England sunshine and he gave a start as if she'd spoken sacrilege. "No, not all. But even one is too many." He hesitated as if he wanted to say more on the subject, but decided against it, then added, "When we reach London I'll send for my physician."

"That's not necessary. I'm fine. Besides, my sisters will all be there tomorrow. I'll get more mothering than either you or I want."

"Nevertheless, I think—"

"Vincent, please," she said, more forcefully than she'd intended. She closed her eyes and clenched her fists, willing her stomach to calm. "At least wait until after we are married. Please. There's no need to let someone outside the family know before we've even spoken our vows."

He nodded politely, making her wish this whole nightmare were over. Making her wish she would wake up in the morning and find a reprieve from impending motherhood. Making her wish just once she'd look at him and not see regret in his gaze.

"As you wish."

She breathed a relieved sigh. "Thank you. Vincent, what are you going to do about...Fentington?"

"I will handle the matter, Grace. You have nothing to fear from him."

"It's not me I'm afraid for. It's you. The man isn't rational. There's a part of his mind that is not right."

"It doesn't matter. What's done is done and I'll take care of it."

Grace knew the subject was closed. She leaned back against the seat, praying nothing would happen to Vincent. The attacks had been her fault. She was the one Fentington wanted to punish. Raeborn was only the innocent victim Fentington thought Grace had despoiled with her wicked ways.

The carriage rumbled along the narrow road with Herman atop. They had to be nearly halfway there. Grace would be glad when they were home. No matter how often she tried to take in deep breaths as Maudie told her, her stomach still lurched and rolled.

"We're reaching Waverly crossroads, Your Grace," Herman hollered from above. "Did you want me to stop so you and the lady can stretch your legs?"

Raeborn gave her a concerned glance, then answered, "Yes, Herman."

Grace breathed a sigh of relief when Herman stopped the carriage and Vincent helped her out. When her feet reached the dirt pathway, he extended her his hand and they leisurely walked down the road. Herman followed with the carriage a discreet distance behind.

"Tell me when you tire," Vincent said, holding her close so she wouldn't stumble.

"Probably not until we reach London," she said, making an effort to smile. "I don't make a very good hothouse flower, Your Grace. I've never been one to sit indoors and embroider."

"Only to play the piano."

"Yes. Only to play. It is my one true passion."

"You will enjoy the music room, then, at Raeborn Estates. The piano there is one of the finest."

"Is that where we will go after the wedding?"

"Eventually. But we'll stay in London as long as possible."

He must have felt her hesitation because he stopped and looked down at her. "I have arranged for our wedding announcement to come out in the *Times* tomorrow morning. I'm sure it will cause quite a stir, but it is customary for polite society to give the bride and groom a two-week grace period before callers begin to arrive, so we should miss the majority of the gossip. And we will at least have that amount of time to accustom ourselves to married life."

He placed his hand beneath her elbow and they continued walking. "Then, when the two weeks are up, we will impose on one of your sisters, perhaps Lady Caroline or Lady Josalyn, to host a ball to introduce you as my duchess. After that, we will adhere to the customs of a London Season that will be in full force—a select ball here and there, the opera, private dinners, soirees, musicales. Anything where we will be seen together. And, of course, there will be sessions in the House that I must attend. We won't go to the country until your confinement forces us to. That will keep the talk to a minimum as long as possible."

Grace stared at him in amazement as they continued to walk down the road. "You've thought of everything, Your Grace."

"I've merely endeavored to hold down the speculation as to our rushed marriage. Nothing more."

A painful weight pressed against her chest. She had done this to him. He was detaching himself from her and from the life she'd forced on him by immersing himself in the details of their wedding and their future together as if they were details of a business arrangement. As if keeping busy with less important matters could push to the background the facts he could not control—that he was being forced to marry when he'd vowed never again to do so. That he had to marry a woman he didn't love, didn't even know. That he was being forced to go through another woman's pregnancy and live with the fear that she might die birthing his heir.

She stopped and turned to face him squarely. She suddenly realized she could not continue this path of guilt. Such emotions were not good for her or healthy for the babe. What was done was done. She could not survive until the birth of her babe always feeling as if she needed to apologize. It was far too late for apologies. There was too much of life ahead of them to live with the regret that was smothering them.

"While we still have a moment alone, Your Grace, I would like to ask a favor."

"Yes."

"I would ask that you no longer worry about me, Your Grace. I am carrying a child, not suffering from a fatal disease."

His eyes widened, his surprise obvious.

"For the next few months I will do everything in my power to cause you as little worry as possible. And I will make you this promise here and now. I have no intention of dying while bringing your heir into the world. So you have no need to worry on that score."

Grace didn't wait to see his reaction, but turned toward the carriage, leaving Raeborn and his dark worries behind her. The days—perhaps weeks, perhaps months—ahead promised to be very long indeed.

* * *

Grace stood beside the open window in the room where she'd always slept when she stayed with Caroline. A soft, gentle breeze lifted the delicate chintz curtains, billowing them toward her as she stood in the darkening room. The afternoon was nearly gone, the hours after she and Raeborn arrived having been taken up in serious discussion with Caroline concerning the details of their upcoming nuptials.

Thankfully, everything was taken care of. Her other sisters had been notified of her sudden wedding and would descend on Wedgewood's town house before the ceremony tomorrow morning. A mountain of food had been prepared, extra servants hired, flowers ordered. And a lavish wedding breakfast was planned for after the ceremony.

Champagne had been ordered, the best silver and china laid out. And netting flounces hung as decoration in the town house ballroom to make it as festive as possible. Caroline had worked miracles in a matter of days. As if this were a most joyous occasion.

Grace wasn't sure she'd survive the ordeal.

Since they'd arrived, she and Raeborn had continued with the ruse they'd begun weeks ago to convince everyone they were truly happy. They smiled at each other, looked at each other often, and when they toured the ballroom, Raeborn remained at her side. But she could tell from the look on Caroline's face that she wasn't convinced. An underlying current of explosive tension permeated the room, the atmosphere rife with unease. And all Caroline's hostility was aimed at Raeborn. He would have to be blind not to notice the barbed glances.

Of course Linny would assume Raeborn had taken advantage of her. All her sisters would assume the same, believing Grace would never willingly give her body to a man she hardly knew after living such a virtuous life for thirty years.

When they found out the truth, they'd be terribly disappointed in her.

Grace wanted to curl up in a corner and hide. How could she ever expect anyone to understand? And yet she couldn't let her sisters believe Raeborn had done anything dishonorable.

She dropped her face to her hands and fought the tears that threatened to fall. She started at the soft knock on the door and hastily dried the tears from her cheeks. "Come in."

The door opened and Caroline stood there, her face harboring all the unanswered questions Grace knew Linny wanted to ask. The look in her eyes, though—the expression of pity and sorrow—was hardest to bear.

The two sisters stared at each other, neither knowing what to say, how to begin. Grace tried first. "Linny, I…I…"

She couldn't finish her sentence. Couldn't bring herself to admit what she'd done. How could she expect Caroline to understand? "I'm…I'm…"

She couldn't. She clamped her hand over her mouth to stifle an anguished moan. No matter how desperate she was to keep the tears from falling, she couldn't do it. They ran in raging torrents down her cheeks.

Before she took her first breath, Caroline crossed the room and pulled her into her arms.

"It's all right, Grace. Everything will be all right."

"No, it won't. It's too late."

Caroline gave her another hug, then led Grace to the settee. They sat facing each other and Caroline pressed a handkerchief into Grace's trembling hands.

"Now I understand why you were so hesitant to associate yourself with Raeborn. Why you've been so upset of late. Why didn't you tell me what he'd done to you?"

"Oh, Caroline. He hasn't done anything."

Caroline fisted her hands and pounded one of them against her thigh. "Oh, he's done something all right. He told me you were expecting his child. I knew right away he'd taken advantage of you." Linny's eyes opened wide in shock. "Did he force you, Grace?"

Grace grabbed Caroline's hands and shook her head. "No, Caroline. You don't understand. None of this is Raeborn's fault. It was me. I was the one who took advantage of him. I'm at fault. Not him."

"Don't try to protect him, Grace. It's obvious what kind of man he is, even though I never thought it of him. I always thought him a gentleman, honorable, of noble character."

"He is. He is all of those and more. It was me. I was the one who forced him."

"It's no use, Grace. We all know better."

Tears streamed down Grace's cheeks again, her sobs coming in huge, painful gasps. "It was me!" she cried out, her whole body shuddering. "I deceived him!"

Caroline stared at Grace as if weighing whether or not to believe her. "What are you saying?"

"Baron Fentington made an offer for Anne's hand like he had for each of you before. Father accepted his offer. The only way I could save her was to agree to marry Fentington myself." Grace swallowed. "He didn't want me at first, of course, because I'm so long in the tooth, but I convinced him I would make him a perfect wife."

"Oh, Grace. Why didn't you come to me? We would have done something."

Grace took a shuddering breath and wiped her nose with her handkerchief. "I had a plan. I knew Fentington would only accept a bride who was a virgin. But he wanted my assurance."

"What assurance?"

"Before he would hand over one pound of the price Father demanded for me, I was to sign a paper swearing I was a virgin." She hesitated. "I knew he'd never marry me once he found out I wasn't."

Grace ignored the horrified look on Linny's face.

"I went to Hannah."

"To Madam Genevieve? To her brothel?"

"Yes. She agreed to find someone who met my qualifications—someone who wasn't married, someone I didn't know, and someone older than my thirty years. She picked Raeborn."

Grace rose from the settee when she heard Linny's horrified gasp and paced the room like a caged tiger. "I didn't once think I would conceive, Linny. Honest, I didn't. I only wanted to escape marriage to the baron. Losing my virginity was not that important to me. I am thirty years old, far past a marriageable age. No one has ever cast me more than a passing glance. And I come with no dowry. Hardly a catch in any man's opinion. I thought when it was…over, I could go back and live out my life at home with no one the wiser."

"But Father didn't want you interfering with his new wife."

Grace shook her head. "No. So I came here. But I still didn't think…" She clutched her hands to her stomach. To where Raeborn's baby grew.

"Raeborn realized I was a virgin that night, and his deep sense of honor wouldn't let him give up until he found me. Until he was certain I hadn't conceived."

"I see."

Grace spun around to face her. "No, you don't. Oh, Linny. He doesn't want to marry me, but he has no choice. I deceived him, used him to save myself from Fentington. Now I've trapped him into a marriage he doesn't want. And even worse. He's terrified of losing another wife in childbirth."

Caroline didn't move for several seconds. Finally she lifted her gaze to Grace's. "And are you? Are you terrified of birthing his babe?"

"Were you terrified of giving birth to Thomas's babes?"

Caroline smiled. "No. Anxious, perhaps. Desperate to have it over, especially when I grew large as a cow. But never terrified."

"Oh, Linny. I never thought to get married, let alone have children of my own. I never thought I could be so happy yet miserable at the same time. How can I ever expect Raeborn to forgive me after what I've done?"

Caroline rose and walked to her sister. She reached for Grace's hands and held them. "He will. Not all marriages begin as love matches, yet for the most part they turn out quite well. You will just have to take that extra step. Show Raeborn that you intend to work at making your marriage a success."

"I'm not sure I know how, Linny."

"Of course you do. You and Raeborn have done an excellent job of convincing half the *ton* you are enamored of each other already."

"But that was for show, an act."

"I'm sure not all of it was. Tell me you don't have feelings for him, Grace."

Grace tried to answer but couldn't.

"It's obvious you do. Just as it is obvious Raeborn has feelings for you. Don't let those feelings diminish. Build on them. Let them grow into something more than fondness."

"You make it sound so easy."

"It's not, but making it happen can be a lot of fun."

There was a twinkle in her sister's eyes and Grace felt her cheeks grow hot. Caroline laughed, then pulled Grace into her arms and hugged her tight. "Oh my, Grace. I do believe I'm going to have to be extra polite to Raeborn at dinner tonight. I did throw him some awfully hostile glares while we were taking tea."

"I noticed."

"I won't even tell you some of the plans your sisters dreamed up to torture him for what we thought he'd done to you."

Grace felt the blood drain from her face. "Oh, Caroline, no. You have to convince them he wasn't to blame. That it was my fault. But they can't know what I've done. I couldn't bear it. Only you, Linny. Only you."

"Grace, don't." Caroline hugged her again. "You're upsetting yourself for nothing. No one will know except me. I'll commandeer each of them upstairs as they arrive and tell them to keep their hostile glares and death threats under lock and key."

Grace was nearly frantic. "They mustn't think badly of Raeborn. They mustn't."

"They won't. By the time I'm done, they'll think him the most intelligent man alive for having the good sense and foresight to choose the most wonderful woman on the face of the earth for his wife. I'll just convince them the two of you were so enamored of each other that you couldn't help yourselves. You just got the baby before the ring."

"Oh, Caroline," Grace cried, covering her mouth with her hands.

"I'm sorry, Grace. But I'm afraid they already know the reason for your precipitous marriage. It's best if they believe your uncontrollable attraction for each other was mutual."

Grace breathed a heavy sigh. The weight that pressed painfully against her breast nearly choked her.

"You need to rest, Grace. Raeborn will be extremely upset if you get too tired. He wanted to come up himself to check on you but I told him he'd already done enough and I'd see to you now."

"Oh, Linny!"

"I know. But I still thought he'd...Well, I'll have to apologize for that too."

"He's just concerned, Linny. It's as if everything I do is a reminder of something that happened before. He knows more about childbearing than I do."

Caroline smiled. "It'll be all right, Grace. You just rest now and I'll send a maid up to help you change. Try to sleep. I'll wake you in plenty of time for dinner."

Chapter 14

It was nearly time for the ceremony to begin.

"Are you ready, Grace?"

Grace turned from the bedroom window and faced her six sisters. Each wore a dubious expression. Expectant. Confused. She realized it probably wasn't the first time she'd been asked that question, but she had been so lost in thought she'd missed hearing it. The smile she put on her face felt strangely out of place and insincere.

"Of course." She tried to keep her voice light, but from the serious look on Caroline's face, she hadn't done a very good job.

"Then we'd best hurry," her sister Josie said, ushering everyone toward the door. "If your groom is like every other groom in history, he's a nervous wreck down there and anxious to get this over with."

Her sisters all laughed and started talking about their own weddings as they made their way to leave.

Grace couldn't let them go without saying something to them, without at least acknowledging that, even though no one had been forward enough to openly discuss it, they all knew the reason for her rushed wedding. She wanted to apologize for the comments she knew they would all hear when her baby was born early.

"Wait."

In unison they turned, then stepped back into the room. Josie closed the door behind them.

Grace wasn't sure what she wanted to say. She stood there several long seconds before she could talk. "I know my marriage has come as a surprise, to say the least. Maybe I even shocked or disappointed some of you."

She held out her hand when all her sisters rushed to assure her she hadn't disappointed them.

"I don't blame you. It isn't how I would have preferred to start my married life. It's not how Raeborn preferred we start it either. But…" She struggled to keep the smile on her face. "I can't undo what's already done."

"It's all right, Grace," Mary, the most serious and tender-hearted of her sisters, said. "We know how much you sacrificed for us. How many years you ignored what you wanted so each of us could make perfect matches. You're just making up for some of the time you lost."

"That's right," Francine said, rushing over to give Grace a hug. "Don't give society's tongues a thought. By the time your babe is born, the whole of England will be so happy for you and Raeborn they won't think to count months."

"I just don't want you to think badly of Raeborn. What happened…" Grace clutched her hands into fists at her sides and willed herself to continue. "What happened was not his fault. He…wasn't to blame."

"We know how it is," Sarah said, two dark circles deepening on her cheeks. "All of London saw how the two of you looked at each other. It's obvious how much in love the two of you are."

"Yes," her sisters all chimed in, and their vote of confidence was almost her undoing.

"I love you," Grace said, her voice shaky and her eyes brimming with tears. "All of you."

En masse, her sisters rushed over to surround her. Each gave her a tight squeeze, careful not to muss her wedding dress.

"I think we'd best go downstairs now," Sarah said, wiping a tear from her own and one from Grace's cheek. "His Grace looked a little uncomfortable the last time I checked on him."

Grace's stomach churned. Of course Raeborn was uncomfortable. How else did she expect him to feel? Being here, marrying again, was the last thing he wanted to do. She knew he had to feel as if there were a gun pointed to his head. Her deception had given him no choice but to marry again even though he'd vowed not to. If not for the baby…

Grace brought her hand up to cover her stomach where a new life grew. Her breath caught.

"Are you all right, Grace?" Caroline asked.

"Yes. I'm fine. Let's go down."

They all moved to the door, only Caroline holding back to give Grace's hand a gentle squeeze. "Everything will be fine, Grace."

"Will it?" Grace asked when everyone had quit the room and she and Caroline were alone.

"Of course. It's just your nerves rushing in to give you doubts."

"He doesn't want to get married. To protect himself, he's built a great wall around his heart. I'm not sure I know how to breach it."

"You breach it the only way a woman can. With your heart. With your love."

"And if he doesn't want my love?"

Caroline smiled. "How can he not? Raeborn more than anyone has been starved for love—both the giving and the receiving of it—longer than any human should have to. He'll accept your love in time. He'll revel in it."

"I wish I were as confident as you," Grace said on a sigh.

"Just remember," Caroline continued. "The roles the two of you played until now were not real. You were acting out a charade, trying to fool everyone into believing you were enamored of each other. The charade must stop today. It cannot continue into your marriage bed."

Grace felt her cheeks redden. Caroline didn't give her a chance to feel embarrassed. She grasped her by the upper arms and looked her in the eyes.

"There can be no pretending in a marriage, Grace. The passion you share in private must be real. It will be the basis for your lives together. Lay the groundwork for your marriage quickly and solidly. Give Raeborn no reason to doubt your feelings for him or your resolve to make your marriage work. And don't be afraid to give him your heart. Now," she said, giving Grace one last hug, "we'd best go down before everyone returns for us."

Grace wore a smile as she and Caroline went down the stairs. When they reached the door to the room where she would say her vows, her footsteps faltered. As did her courage. Her heart thudded in her breast while a little voice inside her head pounded out the words, *If not for the baby…*

Grace took a deep breath and stepped into the room. Her eyes scanned the small group, her gaze focusing on the other side where the men were gathered.

Raeborn stood in the center next to the fireplace, his elbow propped against the mantle in a seemingly relaxed pose. She knew he wasn't. Knew today he was forcing himself to pretend composure and happiness more than ever before. She saw beneath the facade.

His expression was granite hard, his features chiseled. He was conversing with Caroline's husband, the Marquess of Wedgewood, and Josie's husband, Viscount Carmody. Even though a smile crossed his face, she saw it did not reach his eyes. Then he looked up and saw her.

His words stopped midsentence. The drink he was lifting to his lips froze midway to his mouth, and he stood for a moment in stoic silence, then placed the glass on the corner of a table nearby and walked toward her. But…

He remembered to smile a second too late.

Grace took a deep breath and forced herself to stay steady on her feet. Every instinct for survival told her to run. Every muscle stretched taut in readiness to flee. Suddenly it was too late. He was there, standing just inches in front of her.

He towered above her, exuding that overpowering dominance she'd come to associate with his presence. She'd give anything to know his thoughts. Anything to see something other than the regal detachment she'd glimpsed occasionally when they were alone. Anything to recognize even the most minute degree of emotion. But she saw nothing. Only a widening of the gap between them.

Exhibiting a show of perfect decorum, he took her hands in his and held them.

A spiraling rush of molten heat surged from her fingertips to even the remotest parts of her body. Her heart pounded in her breast, and deep inside her a thousand butterflies took wing. His touch did that to her.

Even though she'd warned herself over and over not to let it happen, not to risk too much of her heart to a man whose love was far beyond her reach, she'd done it anyway.

"You look beautiful, Grace."

She forced a smile. "Thank you, Your Grace."

"Vincent."

"Vincent," she repeated. "I'd hoped we'd have a moment alone today," she whispered soft enough so only he could hear her. "There was much I wanted to say to you."

"Such as?"

She stuttered, suddenly unable to speak. "I…I know this is not what you wished for your future."

His eyebrows arched high and for just a fleeting moment Grace saw through an opening that exposed his true feelings. What she saw chilled her to her bones. She hesitated, giving him time, praying he'd deny her words. He didn't. She took a breath and continued.

"I want you to know I will always do everything in my power to be the best wife I can be."

He bowed politely, acknowledging her vow. "And I will try my utmost to be your husband."

She staggered at his words.

I will try my utmost to be your husband.

A heavy weight fell to the pit of her stomach. A dark premonition sucked the air from her lungs. Her stomach rolled and she took in several deep breaths. *I will try my utmost to—*

"Are you all right?"

"Y…Yes. Fine."

With an unreadable look in his eyes, he offered her his arm and led her to the front of the room where the minister stood. Her six sisters gathered with their husbands at their sides. Only one other guest was present, Raeborn's cousin, Kevin Germaine.

Raeborn looped her arm through his with a proprietary air and held her steady. He stood as immovable as a chiseled statue while the minister conducted the service. His answers were firm and concise. He promised to keep her for richer and poorer in a voice filled with assurance. He hesitated only slightly over the promise to keep her in sickness and health, although she was sure no one present heard his misstep. Or that anyone guessed what Grace knew for a fact. That the man who had just promised to love her for all time already regretted his words. The man who had just taken her as his wife only did so because she'd given him no other choice.

Then it was her turn. The minister said the words and she wondered for just a moment what would happen if she said no. If she refused.

The room grew uncomfortably warm and Grace closed her eyes for a second, praying that when she opened them her world would no longer be spinning around her. But it did not happen. The world was as it had been before, and the words that had haunted her were there with no solution. *If not for the baby…*

She knew she had no choice.

"I do."

The minister smiled. "I now pronounce you man and wife."

It was over. Raeborn turned her toward him and lowered his head. He was going to kiss her. She knew it before his lips touched hers. She wanted him to. Wanted to feel a small reminder of the intimacy they'd already shared.

His lips were firm and warm, almost exactly as they had been the last time he'd kissed her. And yet totally different. There was no feeling in this kiss, no emotion. Only a perfunctory gesture that caused an emptiness Grace couldn't explain.

And just as quickly, he lifted his mouth from hers.

She stared at him in surprise, but he wasn't watching her. His gaze was concentrated on the small crowd gathering around them.

"Congratulations!" her sisters all chimed together, each taking their turn to hug her tightly.

As if on cue, servants entered the room carrying glasses of champagne on trays, and each of her brothers-in-law toasted the Duke and Duchess of Raeborn's health and happiness.

Grace took one small sip and fought the roiling of her stomach. From then on she only pretended to drink, and as often as she could, found something solid to lean against to support herself.

"Your Grace," a strange voice said from behind her. "Let me congratulate you on your marriage."

Grace turned to find herself facing Kevin Germaine. Vincent was suddenly at her side, his hand possessively around her waist. He wore a pleased look, the look he'd perfected whenever they were in public.

"Raeborn," Germaine said, lifting his glass in salute. "You have no idea how surprised I was to receive an invitation to your wedding. And how delighted."

A smile lit Germaine's handsome face, and Grace looked up to see the expression her husband wore. The practiced look was still in place, and Grace wished for just a second to be able to know what he truly felt. Surely now he no longer needed the pretense.

"I can't believe you've married. That you took the step again. I'm very happy for you."

"Thank you, Kevin."

"And terribly happy for you, Your Grace," he said, nodding in Grace's direction.

"Thank you, Mr. Germaine. I'm glad you could come."

"I'm honored you thought to invite me. I wouldn't have missed it for the world. You can't imagine the buzz your announcement caused among the *ton.* There's not a club, salon, or sitting room in all of London that was not in total shock and disbelief this morning. Of course everyone boasts having a suspicion the two of you intended to marry. They all noticed your closeness of late. They are just surprised you married secretly. And by special license."

Grace knew her cheeks had turned a fiery red, and she looked at the floor.

Vincent pulled her closer. "Our marriage was hardly secret. It was quite public," he said, casting a gaze at the large family he'd just inherited. "As for the special license, you can see we're far too happy to suffer through a prolonged engagement."

"Well, you certainly took everyone by surprise. It's not often anyone can get the better of society's expert gossipmongers. But you certainly did. I'm happy for you both, though. Truly happy."

"Thank you," they said in unison, then Germaine stepped back as Grace's sisters gathered around them to offer more good wishes.

Grace went through the motions, smiling at the appropriate times, laughing with what she knew was forced gaiety, and accepting Vincent's attentions with all the warmth and elation a bride should show her new husband.

Under different circumstances, it would have been the perfect celebration.

After an appropriate time, they moved to the formal dining room and sat down to the wedding breakfast that was originally intended to be a luncheon to welcome Anne home from her honeymoon. Grace did little more than shove her food around on her plate as she tried to keep her lack of appetite from Vincent. The way he watched her made it impossible.

"Are you well?"

She looked up at him and smiled. "Of course. Just not overly hungry."

He placed his hand on top of hers, a gesture noticed by everyone and commented on by more than one of her sisters with a teasing remark.

He laughed. The first time she'd heard him laugh in weeks, and a stabbing warmth rushed through her. Oh, how she wished his laughter was genuine. How she wished his actions were real and the look on his face sincere. But she knew none of it was. It was all an act. Just as the last month and more had been an act.

When the meal was finished, the men adjourned to Wedgewood's study and Grace and her sisters shared a cup of tea before she went upstairs for a few minutes of privacy before leaving.

Grace entered her room and closed the door behind her. A part of her was eager to start her new life. A part of her wasn't ready to face the challenge. A part of her wasn't sure she knew how.

She sat on a chair and let Linny's words come back to her. "Don't give him a choice to turn away from you, but bind yourself to him from the start."

Grace repeated Linny's advice over and over until the words were indelibly etched in her memory. In time, she felt as if a great weight had been lifted from her. The answer had been within her grasp all this time but her fears had gotten in the way. She knew exactly what Linny meant, knew exactly what she had to do.

She rose with a smile on her face. This may not have been how she'd have chosen to start her married life, but she owed it to Raeborn to be a wife with whom he could be happy and content.

She vowed she would be everything he wanted in a wife. Because she already cared for him a great deal. And because she was carrying his child.

Could anything be more wonderful?

* * *

"Welcome to your new home, Your Grace."

Grace took her husband's hand and stepped to the ground. She looked up and for the first time saw the house where she would live.

Raeborn House was one of the most impressive homes in London. Her heart swelled with pride.

"Does your new home meet with your approval?"

She looked up and met Vincent's serious gaze. He truly cared what she thought of his home.

"It's beautiful, Vincent."

His gaze softened. "I'm glad you like it. It will be our home for—"

He paused as if he wasn't sure how to finish. Grace finished for him. "For the rest of our lives."

He nodded. "Yes, the rest of our lives."

The way he spoke those words caused her whole body to turn strangely warm. Spiraling spikes of emotion soared to every extremity the moment he touched her. She trembled.

"Are you cold?"

He wrapped his arm around her shoulder and held her closer to him. "No, I'm fine." But she wasn't fine. His nearness was like a fiery blaze, warming her. She was burning from the inside out.

"It's been a long, exhausting day. I'll have some warm tea brought to you before you go to bed."

"Thank you. That would be lovely."

They walked up the steps and through the open door. Even though it was quite late, the whole staff was dressed and waiting.

Her stomach churned. At first she was nervous to meet the servants. But any qualms she had vanished the minute she saw the broad smiles on their faces.

"Carver," Raeborn said to the butler, "may I present Her Grace, the Duchess of Raeborn."

Carver bowed politely. "Your Grace."

"It's a pleasure to meet you, Carver."

"Your staff, Your Grace," the butler said.

With Raeborn at her side, Grace went down the long line of servants, with Carver introducing each of them. She made an effort to speak to each of them individually. When Carver finished, the staff bade her good night and went to their quarters, probably glad to lay their heads on their pillows.

"If there's anything you need, you have only to ask. The staff is at your disposal." Raeborn tucked her hand through the crook of his arm and walked with her to the long, curving stairway. "It has been a while since they've had a mistress to oversee them, but they are all longtime employees and very loyal."

"I'm sure everything will be perfect, Vincent," she said as they walked up the stairs. Grace turned her head and looked back behind them to the rich oak woodwork and the ornate vases adorning the massive foyer. "Your house is beautiful."

"Thank you. But it's your home now. Tomorrow I'll take you on a tour. I think you will be especially pleased at the gardens. Hennely seems to have the ability to turn even the homeliest plants green."

"I look forward to it."

They reached a room at the end of the hall and he stopped. "This is your suite of rooms, Grace."

"*My* suite?"

"Yes. My rooms are next door. There's an adjoining sitting room."

Grace felt a cold chill race through her body.

He looked to the side as if he couldn't meet her gaze. "I will be nearby if you have need of me."

"I see," she whispered, struggling to find her voice.

"I've taken the liberty of asking Alice to serve as your lady's maid. Carver recommended her. If she isn't to your liking—"

"I'm sure she will be fine."

"Very well. Good night then, Grace."

"Are you coming to bed now?"

"No. I've got work to see to before I can sleep. I'll be in my study."

"I see."

He gently pulled her toward him and kissed her chastely on the forehead. "Good night," he said again, then opened the door to her room and stepped back for her to enter.

Grace walked into her new room on legs that weren't quite steady beneath her. Surely he did not mean he intended to separate himself from her? Surely he did not mean theirs was to be a marriage in name only?

Grace didn't see the pretty young maid standing beside the bed until she spoke. Her tumultuous thoughts were too confused by the way Vincent intended to start their marriage.

Grace changed from the gown she'd worn for her wedding into a beautiful satin nightgown Anne had given her especially for this night, then sat on the cushioned stool before a mirrored table and let Alice comb out her hair.

The little maid chatted nervously while doing her work, but Grace hardly heard a word she said. Her thoughts were too occupied with her husband who'd gone back downstairs. With her husband who'd left his wife on their wedding night.

"Will there be anything else, Your Grace?" Alice asked, standing behind her with a pensive smile on her face.

"No. Thank you, Alice. That will be all. I appreciate your help."

Alice opened the door just as an upstairs maid named Jane came with a tray. "His Grace thought you'd like some hot tea before you went to sleep."

Grace looked at the tray and for a second wanted to send the plump little maid back downstairs to tell His Grace that what his wife wanted was her husband to come up to her. Instead, she motioned for the maid to set down the tray.

"Please tell His Grace thank you."

"Yes, Your Grace. I'll be sure to tell him."

Grace stared at the pot of tea long after the servants left. The tea service was of fine china, and Grace rubbed her finger over the delicate gold-leaf design on the cups while her anger and disappointment grew stronger.

How did he think they could have a marriage if they never shared the same bed? How did he think they could grow closer if he separated himself from her?

She walked to the window and looked out in the darkness, seeing nothing.

How on earth could she breach the wall he intended there to be between the two of them?

Linny's words came back to her. "You breach it with patience and with love."

Grace sat in the burgundy velvet wing chair next to the dying fire and waited, praying he'd change his mind and come to her eventually.

Several hours later she heard him climb the stairs. Then she heard the soft thud of the door when he closed it.

Her heart pounded in anticipation. She waited, praying the door connecting their rooms would open. Praying he wouldn't leave her alone on their wedding night. Praying he didn't intend for theirs to be a loveless marriage. Praying…

Grace sat in the darkness long after the last ember in the fireplace had died. Her head ached, her temper grew increasingly more fitful, and her heart ached as it never had before.

She took a shuddering breath as Linny's advice slapped her full force in the face. *You breach the wall he erects with patience and love…and don't give him a chance to turn away from you.*

Grace dropped her blanket to the floor and walked to the door that connected their rooms. She understood with clarity how much she would truly lose if she gave him the chance to turn away from her.

Chapter 15

Vincent stood at his bedroom window, looking out into the darkness below. The street outside was quiet, the last of society's partygoers having gone home long ago. His wedding day was finally over. And somehow he'd survived.

Bloody hell, he never thought he'd have to go through another wedding day.

He remembered every detail of it, from the time he stepped into Wedgewood's town house this morning. He'd thought to have a moment alone with Grace. A moment to prepare her for how their personal lives would be instead of seeing the surprise, even disappointment, on her face tonight when he'd walked her to her rooms—and left her.

But there hadn't been an opportunity to talk to her. Lady Caroline gave the excuse that Grace was busy getting ready for her wedding, but he knew that wasn't entirely truthful. He knew she was ill. Ill from the babe he'd planted inside her. Like she'd been ill every morning when they'd been in the country, even though she'd tried to hide it from him.

Vincent fought a rush of panic that nearly took him to his knees. He'd never been part of a family like this. A family burgeoning with life and love and laughter. Their numbers alone were staggering. Their exuberance astounding. He'd grown up alone, an only child. To this day he had only one living relative. Grace grew up in a crowd, and they had descended on Wedgewood's town house like a band of merrymaking revelers. En masse. Her entire family. Her six sisters and their husbands.

Lady Caroline and Wedgewood were, of course, already there. Then Lady Josalyn arrived with her husband, Viscount Carmody. And Lady Francine and her husband, the Earl of Baldwin. And Lady Sarah and her husband, Baron Hensley. And Lady Mary and her husband, the Earl of Adledge. And finally Lady Anne and her husband, Wexley.

Thankfully the children—good God, eleven of them, and if he were any judge there would be more by Christmas—were immediately closeted upstairs with a regiment of nurses and nannies. How was it possible for them to be so cavalier when it came to producing children? How could each of these men risk his wife in childbirth again and again?

At first he thought perhaps their marriages weren't based on love or any emotion resembling it. But that hadn't been the case. The affection between each sister and her spouse was plain to see, even surprising at times in the looks they gave each other, the smiles, the familiarity with which they touched.

Vincent wiped a sheen of perspiration from his brow. They didn't know the risks. They hadn't experienced the devastating heartbreak of losing someone you cared for. Of knowing you were to blame.

He closed his eyes and willed Angeline's heart-shaped smiling face and Lorraine's somber, porcelain features to appear. He wouldn't forget them or repeat his mistakes in this marriage. It was too late to prevent a third pregnancy, but it wasn't too late to protect his heart.

A heavy pressure weighed painfully against his chest, stopping his lungs from taking in air. Oh, how he wanted her. How he'd wanted her since the night he'd trapped her in Wedgewood's study, her eyes wide with fright, her breasts rapidly rising and falling as she gasped for air. No matter how hard he tried, he couldn't erase how he'd felt when he held her and touched her and buried himself deep inside her as he'd done on their first meeting. Or how he ached to hold her in his arms even now and kiss her until neither of them could breathe.

He braced his hands on either side of the window and leaned his forehead against the cool glass. If only he'd never had her. If only he didn't know what loving her was like. He was burning inside, on fire from flames he had no hope of extinguishing except in her arms.

He dragged his hand across his face, praying the gesture might wipe any thought of her from his mind. He breathed a heavy sigh, then walked to the fireplace and placed another log on the dying embers. The door opened and a faint light crept across the floorboards. Vincent jerked upright and turned. "Grace?"

He reached for a dressing gown and put it on to cover his nakedness. "Is something wrong?"

"May I come in?"

"Of course. Is there something you need?"

"Yes." She stepped into the room and closed the door behind her.

He waited where he was. After a slight pause, she walked toward him, her back and shoulders straight, her satin gown shimmering around her legs. He locked his hands behind his back to keep from reaching out to her. To keep from pulling her into his arms and holding her. To keep from covering her mouth with his own.

"What is it? What do you need?"

She lifted her chin and answered, "You."

* * *

Grace stood close to him, so close she could feel the heat from his body. So close she could smell the fresh scent of soap he'd used to bathe. So close she could hear the breath he sucked into his lungs when she answered him.

Her heart thrummed with excitement, with fear. The blood raced through her veins with such speed that every part of her body came alive with need. She clutched her fists in the material at her sides to keep from reaching for him.

"What do you need?" he asked again, as if he hadn't understood her. As if he chose not to understand her.

"Is this where you intend to sleep for the rest of our marriage?"

His shoulders lifted. "This is my room. Yes."

"And is the room next to yours where I am to sleep?"

"Yes."

"Do you ever intend to come to my room? To my bed?"

A frown covered his face, his features turning almost angry. "What is this, Grace? It is nearly three in the morning.

Surely your questions can wait until some other time. At least until tomorrow."

"No, Your Grace. I think it best we put everything out in the open so there will be no misunderstandings."

Grace fought the urge to walk away from him. Fought the urge to lower her eyes so she didn't have to look into his ironclad gaze. "Please answer me, Your Grace. Do you ever intend to sleep in my bed?"

His chest rose and fell with each labored breath. But he remained silent.

"Is this my punishment, Your Grace?" she said, her voice sounding hollow to her ears. "Is this how I am to suffer for deceiving you?"

She lost her courage and stared at the burning logs. "Do you intend to parade me through the *ton*, keeping up with our charade? Do you intend for us to continue playing our parts as if we had a perfect marriage?"

She knew her voice held an accusatory tone. Knew the words had not come out as a question but as a criticism. She did not care. She was fighting for her very existence.

"How long do you intend for us to pretend our infatuation was so all-consuming that we could not be bothered with a courtship or lengthy betrothal but married mere weeks after we met? And by special license?"

She turned from the fire and caught his gaze with hers. "A month, perhaps? Longer?"

"Grace, I—"

"Then what, Vincent? Do you intend for us to return home each evening and for me to allow you to politely kiss me on the cheek, then tuck me into bed and not bother with me until it is time for our next performance? Do you envision us walking up the stairs each evening, arm in arm like the loving couple we have pretended to be for the day and evening? And do you intend to bid me a polite good night before you close the door behind me so you can forget I exist?"

"Grace, that's not—"

"I cannot live like that, Vincent. I will not." Grace swiped her hand through the air. "I would undo what I did if I could, but it is too late. I cannot turn back the hands of time. I can't—"

"Enough! What is it you want from me?"

She took a step toward him so he had no choice but to look her in the eyes. "I want you to be a husband to me."

"You don't know what you're asking."

Grace stood her ground. "I do. I know how much it hurt you to lose your first wife and your babe with her. I know how much harder it was to lose a second wife with another babe, then go on living while your heart was breaking. I know the vow you made afterward never to marry again."

His eyebrows furrowed. "How did you—"

"Your cousin told me while profusely congratulating me on stealing your heart and forcing you to take the risk you'd vowed never to take again."

"Then you know—"

She shook her head. "I know nothing except that I am taking just as big a risk as you. Can you guarantee me you will not walk out onto the street and get run down by a team of horses before our child is born? Can you promise me Fentington will not attempt to harm you again? And this time succeed?" She tried to keep the tears at bay, but they swam in her eyes. "Do you know the guilt I live with each day, knowing he blames you for what *I* did?" Grace hugged her middle tighter. "Do you know the guilt I live with each day, knowing the bullet you took was because of me?"

"No. That was not your fault."

"Yes. Just as forcing you to marry again is my fault. I would give the world to have thought of another way to escape Fentington. One that did not involve you. One that did not put you in danger. But I could not. I didn't expect you to ever find me. I didn't expect you would ever want to."

Her tears ran freely now. He reached out to pull her to him, but she twisted out of his grasp and slashed the air between them with her hand. "I do not want to live my life like this, Vincent. I don't want a chasm of fear between us that can never be bridged. I don't want our marriage to be an empty shell with no substance. Please, don't leave me alone with my regrets."

She watched the haunted look in his eyes grow darker and felt her world fall away from her. "I don't expect you to ever love me," she said, her words no louder than a whisper. "Not after what I did to you, how I deceived you. But please, don't condemn us to a bitter existence. Don't make me pay for deceiving you every day for the rest of my life."

He stood as if rooted to the floor. Finally Grace heard and saw the ragged sigh that lifted his shoulders.

"I do not blame you for what you did to escape Fentington. You had little choice. And anything Fentington did after that is not your fault, Grace. He is deranged. He does not think like you and I. You are not responsible for his attempt on my life."

"Then what is it? Is it so impossible for you to want me as your wife? Is it so hard to hold me like you did that night at Madam Genevieve's before you knew who I was? Is it so impossible to make love to me?"

"No," he cried out, and Grace could hear the pain in his voice. "But it would be impossible to give you up once I did. I cannot go through that again."

His words struck her with the force of a battering ram. He'd laid his fear out before her like an open wound, raw and festering. An infected sore that tormented his very soul.

"You will not have to give me up, Vincent. I promise. You will not lose me like you did Angeline and Lorraine."

"You can't make such a promise," he said, his voice teeming with regret.

"I can." Grace reached for his hand and placed it low on her stomach. "I am going to give you this babe I have growing inside me. And a dozen more besides. Together we will love them and care for them and watch them grow into adulthood."

His agonizing moan held the untold heartache and sorrow of his painful past.

"Love me, Vincent."

She waited, praying he'd lift his arms and hold her. Praying she could break through the barrier he'd erected between them and love her. "Don't condemn us to living our lives alone. I can't survive the emptiness you intend for our marriage."

She turned into him, standing so close her body was pressed against his. Waves of need and want rushed through her, every part of her yearning for his touch. It was always like this. Every time she was near him. "Please. Love me."

With a low growl of surrender, he wrapped his arms around her and pulled her against him. His mouth came down on hers, kissing her with the force of a man dying of thirst, desperate for a last drink of water. His lips crushed hers, then opened, his demands obvious.

Grace followed his lead. She clung to his shoulders and opened her mouth, granting him entrance.

Their mating was explosive. Again and again he kissed her, ground his lips against hers, giving to her, taking from her until she could no longer breathe. But breathing no longer mattered. She didn't need any air other than the air she and Vincent shared. She didn't need anything except to be held in his arms.

She lifted her arms, winding them around his neck, pulling him closer to her.

"I should have known it was impossible to keep away from you," he whispered against her mouth.

"Impossible. From the first," she whispered.

He moved his kisses to her cheek and down the side of her neck. Grace burned with desire, her body heating until she feared it would burst into flames.

Vincent's hands moved over her flesh, over the sensitive skin down her back, then pulled her closer.

She moaned into the silent darkness and pushed her fingers through his thick, dark hair.

He lifted his mouth from her neck and brought it back to her own, deepening his kisses until her legs felt weak beneath her. Her heart thundered in her breast like a runaway team of horses while his hands worked their magic, skimming up her sides and curving inward.

A soft moan escaped from deep within her and her head fell back to her shoulders. His fingers were relentless in their ministrations. She could no longer think.

"Vincent..."

Her breaths came out in ragged gasps, her body trembling with a frantic need she'd never felt before. A desperation she didn't think was possible.

She was barely conscious of her gown being lifted over her head, of the nighttime air hitting her flesh. She welcomed the coolness. Her body seemed on fire. Then he touched her. Flesh on flesh. His fingers and hands moving over her skin, finding their way down her stomach to where their babe rested.

Grace clung to his shoulders when her body turned limp. She struggled to stay upright.

"I need you," he said, and lifted her in his arms and carried her to the bed.

Grace pulled him toward her. She needed him too. The way she'd never needed anyone in her life.

* * *

For a long time after their lovemaking, neither of them moved away from the other, but lay in the shadowed moonlight, their arms and legs entwined, their bodies still joined. She moved her hands over his flesh, over the pulsing muscles at his shoulders and arms.

"Are you all right?" he asked, propping himself on his elbows and looking down at her.

Tiny worry lines etched his face and she smiled as she brushed back a lock of dark hair that had fallen over his brow.

"I'm perfect. You were perfect."

She wrapped her arms around him and held him close. She cradled his wondrous weight, stroking his damp flesh and marveling at the sensations she'd just experienced. Tears streamed from her eyes, tears of emotion. Tears of love.

"You're going to force me to risk it all, aren't you?" he said, turning to his side and taking her with him. He nestled her close to him and pulled a cover over them.

"What kind of life would we have if I didn't?"

Grace lay against him with her head tucked beneath his chin. He kissed the top of her head, then stroked her flesh with light, gentle movements, running his fingers up and down her arms, then over her back. Her body warmed at his touch and she knew there was little she wouldn't give up for it to be like this forever.

"I'm not sure I have the courage, Grace. I've…"

He hesitated and Grace knew how difficult it was for him to find the words. How difficult it was to admit how frightened he was.

"I know what you've lost. But I have enough courage for both of us." She placed her palm against his cheek and held him steady so he was forced to look at her. "Promise that you will never doubt me. That you will know I will never leave you."

There was a sadness in his eyes, a hint of regret. A depth of emotion that tore at her insides. She could see it. His struggle to protect his heart. Yes, it would take all her courage. And her patience. And her love.

Grace twined her fingers around his neck and brought his lips down to hers. The feel of him against her sent fiery pokers spiraling through her, warming her body from the top of her head to the tips of her toes, then circling and spinning until all the roiling sensations collided.

He kissed her with a tenderness that filled her with emotion, then deepened his kiss when she opened her mouth to take him in. "Love me, Vincent."

"Are you sure?" he whispered against her mouth as his hands moved over her body.

She smiled. "Trust me."

He kissed her once more. "You've left me little choice, wife."

Chapter 16

Vincent had been right. The *ton* gave them exactly two weeks privacy before intruding on the newlyweds. Not one soul bothered them for a full fourteen days. And they were the most glorious two weeks of her life. She'd never been happier.

Vincent was the most considerate of lovers. As well as the most amazing. She'd always known the love shared between husband and wife was special, but until Vincent, she had no idea just how wonderful life could be.

She was loath for their time together to come to an end. They spent their days and evenings getting to know each other. They walked in the beautiful gardens behind Raeborn's massive town house and even spent an occasional afternoon making love.

Often Grace would sit and read while Vincent worked on the ledgers his steward, Henry James, brought to him. He was continually searching for ways to make improvements to what had been passed down to him, and to better the life of the tenants for whom he was responsible. He questioned his steward for hours about the condition of the land and the animals, about the health of his tenants and which homes needed improvements.

Then, in the evenings, Grace would play for him. Each evening she would pick out something special she thought he'd like, depending on his state of mind. Either serious or contemplative or lively and teasing. Sometimes it would be one of Beethoven's more aggressive works. Those she thought he liked best.

When she finished, she'd sit with him in front of the glowing fire, his arm wrapped around her, her cheek resting against his chest, his heart beating contentedly beneath her ear.

When the fire went out and the room turned dark, he would kiss her gently and they would go upstairs to bed.

Not since that first night had he left her at her door. He always came to her bed. Or he would take her to his.

Sometimes they would talk first. He would hold her in his arms and tell her what it was like growing up an only child. And she would tell him what it was like growing up in a crowd of siblings. He would laugh at her stories, and she realized how fortunate she'd been, because Vincent couldn't imagine a life that wasn't solitary.

Then, with a tender sigh, he would pull her beneath him and they would make love.

His lovemaking was always pure magic. Sometimes slow and languorous, sometimes swift and passionate with a desperation she knew stemmed from his fears. Though he constantly fought to hide his demons from her, Grace knew the battle still raged inside him.

She did everything in her power to help ease his fears. But even afterward, when they were both sated and content, shadows darkened his features. She knew it would take more time. She knew it would take the safe birth of their babe.

But she never gave up trying. Never stopped sharing her joy and her elation. Never gave him cause to be anything but happy his babe was growing inside her. Because each morning when she opened her eyes, Vincent's ruggedly masculine face was her first sight. Then his arms held her and his mouth covered hers, and she was happier than she'd ever thought possible.

Unfortunately, happy and healthy were not the same. She was still sick each morning after she arose. This morning had been worse than usual, and she wasn't well enough to join Vincent for breakfast.

If the little maid, Alice, thought anything about her mistress already suffering from a morning malady, she didn't indicate it. But Grace knew her condition was probably a regular topic of conversation among Raeborn's staff. And from the way they doted over her, not one of them was unhappy about it.

They all smiled most warmly when they saw her. Mrs. Cribbage, who worked in the kitchen, was especially considerate. Yesterday morning Alice had brought up a tray with a hot, sweet-smelling drink and some small, wafer-thin toasts on it. Mrs. Cribbage had sent it up because she said it would help with what ailed the mistress.

Grace made a note to thank Mrs. Cribbage for her thoughtfulness. She drank a little more of the hot liquid she'd sent up again this morning and thought perhaps it *had* helped a little.

Grace knew such illness was normal and prayed it would halt soon. She was nearing the end of her third month, and most of her sisters hadn't been ill much longer than that.

She couldn't wait for the sickness to stop. Not for herself so much as for Vincent.

Each morning when she came down to join him, his face seemed as white as hers. His worry was obvious. As if he relived the sickness his first two wives had suffered.

Grace placed her hand on her stomach and smiled. Her stomach was not as flat as before. The babe was growing, and it would soon be obvious she was increasing. It would probably be only two months more and she would have to go into confinement.

Grace finished dressing, having chosen a stylish pink-and-white striped morning dress Alice assured her would brighten her cheeks, and walked to the mirror. She took a final look, satisfied that her face was not so terribly pale, and headed down the stairs.

She walked to Vincent's study, knowing that was where she would find him. She didn't knock but opened the door, expecting him to be behind his desk, busy working on his ledgers. He wasn't there, but stood with his back to her, looking out the window.

Grace silently watched him, her heart thrumming forcefully in her breast. His undeniable masculinity never ceased to affect her.

He'd taken off his burgundy jacket and hung it over the back of his chair. He was dressed only in his white linen shirt, tan breeches, and black boots. His white cravat lay over his jacket, and Grace knew when he turned around, the neck of his shirt would gap open to reveal the dark hair on his chest.

Her body warmed at the thought of running her fingers over his chest and skimming over the taut muscles at his middle.

"A penny for your thoughts."

Vincent turned at her voice. In that briefest of seconds before he could put a smile on his face, she saw the tortured look in his eyes he hadn't been able to disguise soon enough.

"I was just thinking how absolutely beautiful my wife is and that I'm the luckiest man in all of London."

Grace walked across the room and into his outstretched arms. "I think that was not exactly what you were thinking, but I will take the compliment regardless."

He bent down to kiss her, and Grace wrapped her arms around his neck and pressed herself against him.

Vincent pulled her away from him on a laugh. "You play most unfairly, my wife."

She gave him an innocent smile followed by another quick kiss, then looped her arm through his and held him tight. "I can't imagine what you mean." Her voice sounded huskier than it should.

"It's only a little past noon and already all I want to do is carry you back upstairs and have my way with you."

"That does have a certain appeal," she said, then looked up at him with an open smile.

He brushed his fingers down the side of her face and shook his head. "I think not. Our two weeks of privacy are up." He pointed to a stack of cards and invitations on the corner of his desk. "These arrived just this morning. And we are bound to have visitors this afternoon. My guess is that the dowager Duchess of Biltmore will be the first, and with her Lady Pratts and Lady Franklin. They are all notoriously nosy as well as indefatigable gossips. I would hate to have them arrive while we're still abed."

Grace laughed. For the past two weeks she'd felt anything but a serious, thirty-year-old, past-her-prime, on-the-shelf, aging woman. She was unbelievably happy and at times as giddy as a young schoolgirl. Vincent was responsible for this feeling. He was the reason she no longer regretted what she'd done. And she wanted to thank Hannah for matching her with such a perfect man.

"Finding us abed would give them something to talk about."

"In a few months they will have more than enough to talk about. I'd just as soon they didn't start now."

Vincent's words gave her reason to pause. "Does that embarrass you terribly?"

He draped his arm around her shoulder and sat beside her on the floral settee he'd moved into his study so Grace could sit there comfortably while he worked. When they were seated, he kept his right arm around her shoulder while his left hand reached for hers and held it. "Our babe will not be the first in history to arrive less than nine months after the wedding. By the time the news reaches the fashionable drawing rooms, there will be some other scandal that is more important."

She couldn't believe how happy she was. It was as if nothing had ever happened between them to regret. As if the way they'd met had been nothing unusual. As if she could forget that danger wasn't looming in the shadows.

She hesitated, then asked the question that had bothered her since the night of the fire. "Vincent, what are you going to do about Fentington?"

"I don't want you to worry about that, Grace. I will handle the matter."

"But I am worried. There's something not right with him. He does not see things like other men."

"That much is obvious. He's lived with his delusions and self-righteousness so long he's convinced himself he's without faults."

"Why do you think he shot you? And tried to burn the house with us in it?"

"Because I publicly humiliated him. Because his cruelty and perversion are finally out in the open and no one in polite society wants him anywhere near their women or children. He blames me for his ruin. And you were his next victim—until he realized I'd taken your virtue. I ruined you for him."

"Poor Hannah," Grace said, pressing herself closer to Vincent's body as protection. "To have endured living with such a monster. No wonder she hates him like she—"

Grace stopped when she realized what she'd revealed.

Vincent's body tensed next to her. "Hannah…Madam Genevieve is Fentington's daughter?"

She couldn't answer him. She'd promised Hannah. "Vincent, don't. Leave it be."

His brows furrowed and he shot to his feet. "Bloody hell. I should have known. Madam Genevieve is Fentington's daughter Hannah. When she described Fentington with such perfection, I should have realized only someone living under his roof would know so much about him."

"He did that to her," Grace said, remembering Hannah's desperation to escape her home. "Made her what she has become. She nearly died living on the streets, with no one to help her and no place to go. In the end, she had no choice but to become what she is. It was better than living the hell she did every day under his roof. Becoming Madam Genevieve was the only way she could survive."

Tears ran down Grace's cheeks as they did each time she thought of what Hannah must have endured. But Hannah wasn't to blame. He was. The despicable monster Hannah had been unlucky enough to have as her father.

"It's all right, Grace." Vincent pulled her into his arms. "Genevieve has made a place for herself and is content with it. I am glad she was there to help you. I owe her a great debt."

Grace looked up just as his lips came down on hers. Their kiss was warm and tender and destined to turn into something much more intense. Regretfully, Vincent's ardor was interrupted when Carver knocked on the door.

"The Duchess of Biltmore and the Ladies Pratts and Franklin have come to call, Your Graces. And Mr. Kevin Germaine. Are you in?"

Vincent looked at her and smiled, then said, "Yes, Carver. We're in."

Grace tried to hide her flushed cheeks from their butler. There was almost a grin on his face. This was not the first time he'd caught them in an embarrassing display of affection.

"Please, show them to the morning room," Vincent said with a hint of laughter in his voice. "We'll be right there."

"Come, my dear," he said, helping her to her feet. "We'd best see to our guests before they think they interrupted us at something more serious than a simple kiss."

* * *

Vincent led his wife to the morning room. They stopped outside the door and Grace instructed Carver to have Emily serve tea and pastries as soon as possible. Raeborn was glad. The pause afforded him time to resurrect the role he'd played before he married—that of a suitor enamored of the woman he'd chosen to court.

Except, he suddenly realized, playing his role wasn't at all the way it had been a few weeks ago.

He took a deep breath and lowered his gaze to his wife. Her cheeks were a deep shade of red and her breath shuddered when she released it. She was nervous, and he had to smile. He brought her fingers to his lips and kissed them, then nodded to Carver to open the door.

Carver took his cue, and Vincent escorted Grace into the morning room. This was their first time entertaining guests as husband and wife, and it was important that they both appear genuinely happy. He gave their guests a broad smile and led Grace into the room.

He had to stop himself from laughing at the awestruck expressions on the Duchess of Biltmore's, Lady Pratts's, and Lady Franklin's faces. His cousin just looked relieved that someone had arrived to rescue him from three of London's most renowned gossips.

He and Grace greeted their guests most effusively and accepted their well-wishes with open smiles. Then he made sure the three ladies took note when his arm reached behind Grace's waist and he pulled her close. It was important that a closeness in their marriage be acknowledged, that their affection for each other be beyond doubt. The radiant look Grace gave him when he touched her wasn't lost on their guests.

"I'm so glad you've come to call," Vincent said, looking at all three ladies. "My wife and I have been quite preoccupied accustoming ourselves to the routine of married life. I'm afraid we haven't been inclined yet to venture out into society."

Vincent saw the slightest skepticism on the three ladies' faces and their glances drop to Grace's waistline. He'd known that would be everyone's first thought. He'd already convinced himself that what they thought didn't matter to him in the least.

He smiled at Grace and led her to a comfortable love seat, then sat down beside her.

The women were seated on an oversize settee opposite them, and Germaine sat in a chair to Vincent's right. Together the six of them formed a neat little circle.

"You have no idea how news of your marriage surprised us," the duchess said, eyeing Grace as if searching for any sign of reluctance. Perhaps a hint of disappointment.

Vincent cleared his throat. "Yes. We knew the suddenness of our marriage would shock some, and even though Her Grace thought we should wait longer, I'm afraid I was the one who insisted we marry immediately. Wasn't I?" he said, turning in her direction.

Grace's cheeks flushed an endearing pink as she looked at him. Then she gave the perfect response by reaching over to place her hand atop his hand as it rested on his knee and saying, "And I was most wise in agreeing after only a momentary hesitation."

Their skepticism seemed to melt as the Duchess of Biltmore joined in with the sighs she heard from Lady Pratts and Lady Franklin.

"Oh, here is tea," Grace said when the door opened and Emily entered with a serving cart laden with tea and cakes and sandwiches. "I'll pour while you ladies catch us up on all the latest news. And Mr. Germaine, we haven't let you get a word in edgewise as of yet. I can't wait to hear what news you have."

Vincent sat back against the cushion and contentedly listened while Grace conversed with their four guests. Even Germaine seemed to enjoy himself, adding what he knew of the latest happenings.

The afternoon passed perfectly, their guests staying even longer than decorum indicated. In time, though, the Duchess of Biltmore and the Ladies Pratts and Franklin took their leave and only Germaine remained behind.

"I really should be going too," he said, rising to his feet. "I just wanted to be the first to congratulate you again and to welcome you to our family," he said, bowing over Grace's hand. "May I extend my fondest well-wishes."

"Thank you, Mr. Germaine," she said with a trembling smile. "You cannot know how much your kindness means to me."

"And to me," Vincent added. "Here. Let me walk you out. There are a few items I'd like to discuss with you."

Germaine left the room with Vincent behind him. They stopped when they came to the door. "I meant it when I said your wishes meant a great deal to me," Vincent said seriously. "I was afraid after the conditions and stipulations I put down concerning your spending, your feelings toward me would change."

"Nonsense," Germaine said, taking his coat and hat from Carver's outstretched hands. "You only did what you thought best. I realize that now."

"My solicitor tells me you've done an exemplary job running the Castle Downs estate. That you've become a most conscientious landlord and seem to take a remarkable interest in the running of the estate."

His cousin bowed graciously and hooked his cane over his arm. "I am only trying to live up to your expectations, Raeborn. It's not easy walking in your shadow."

"I don't want you to walk in my shadow, Kevin. Your father would not have wanted that either. He would want you to cast your own shadow, to be the best man you are capable of being. I want the same for you."

"Thank you, Your Grace. I appreciate your confidence. Now I bid you good day."

"Thank you for coming."

"I had a most enjoyable afternoon. You are truly fortunate. Your wife is charming. Even though I was sure you would never marry again, I can see you've fit into the role of husband quite well. My congratulations. I am positive that this time you will get the heir you want."

Vincent stepped back while Carver opened the door and watched his cousin leave. Vincent had worried overmuch about the immaturity of his younger cousin. Now he realized his concerns had been for naught. All the reports from his solicitor had been glowing. Perhaps the boy had just needed a firm hand all along and Vincent had been too blind to see it.

He walked back to the morning room feeling very good with the way things had turned out. Feeling very good at the excellent way Grace had handled entertaining their guests this afternoon. At her stunning talent at holding three of society's most notorious gossips at bay. Yes, maybe everything would be all right after all. He'd already discovered it was impossible to keep her from touching his heart. Already found he cared for her much more than he'd intended. And all this in the less than three months it had been since he'd met her.

A smile spread across his face. He couldn't wait to get back to her.

His smile vanished the minute he walked into the morning room and glanced at Grace's slumped shoulders and pale complexion.

"Grace!"

He rushed across the room and pulled her into his arms. Her skin was cold and clammy, and she barely had enough strength to hold up her head.

"Vincent?" she said, her voice shaky. A light sheen of perspiration covered her face. "I'm fine. Just warm."

Vincent held her closer. "I'll get you to bed and call the doctor."

"No, Vincent. I'm fine. Please, just sit with me for a moment."

"Are you sure?"

"Yes. I'm sure."

She lifted her face and smiled, but he didn't believe her attempt was sincere. "Carver," Vincent ordered, and Carver instantly appeared. "Bring Her Grace a glass of water."

Carver quickly brought the water, and Vincent made her drink. He held her hand and sat with her until some color returned to her cheeks.

"There," she said after a while. "I'm much better now."

"Well enough to move?"

"Yes. I'm fine. Thankfully these spells never last long."

His heart skipped a beat. "You've suffered from this before?"

"Of course. It's quite common for women in my condition. Mary suffered terribly for the first few months, but Sarah I think was the worst. This is mild in comparison."

He didn't believe her. He couldn't. Memories of the other times returned to haunt him.

"Don't look so worried, Vincent. I'm fine. Your babe just wants to make certain I don't forget he's there. I think he's going to be a very strong-willed infant." She looked up at him with a teasing glint in her eyes. "Just like his father."

"I think I will be most displeased with him for the trouble he is causing his mother and will tell him the minute I meet him." Vincent struggled to keep his tone light. The panic raging through him was almost more than he could bear.

"Do you know what I'd like, Vincent?"

Vincent held her close, all the while trying to keep his hands from trembling, his heart from racing. "No, Grace. Just ask and it's yours."

"I would like to go for a ride."

Vincent dropped his gaze to hers. She was serious. "Now?" He shook his head. "I don't think—"

"I would like to ride through Hyde Park with the sun shining down on me and the breeze hitting my face. And you at my side."

She reached up and kissed him lightly on the lips. He kissed her back.

"Grace, I'm not sure—"

She pressed a fingertip to his lips. "I am suddenly desperate to go out of doors."

Vincent breathed a heavy sigh. How could he refuse her? "Carver," he called, and the butler instantly appeared. "Have the carriage brought round."

Carver's eyebrows arched.

"See, Grace? Even Carver doesn't think you should go out."

"I know. But Carver is by nature a worrier. Aren't you, Carver?"

"Yes, Your Grace. I do tend to worry overmuch."

"You and my husband." She sighed and shook her head. "I will have to do something about that."

"As you say, Your Grace. I'll have the carriage brought round and instruct Alice to put extra blankets inside. It is only the beginning of spring, and late afternoons can be quite chilly."

"Thank you, Carver," Grace said.

Vincent stood with his arm around his wife's waist while they waited for the carriage to arrive. His turbulent emotions raged through him like an enemy's army attacking from all sides.

"You are worrying, Vincent," she said, leaning into him.

"Only a little, Your Grace."

He felt her shake in his arms and knew she was laughing at him.

"You do not make a very good liar," she said, then pulled away from him and looked up. "Do you remember what

I told you, Vincent? I told you I had enough courage for the both of us. Trust me in this. There's nothing to worry about. I will tell you if there is."

He brushed the backs of his fingers down her cheek. She was soft and smooth to his touch. "You are a rare find, Grace. I don't know how you stayed hidden from the world as long as you did."

"I was waiting for the perfect duke to find me."

Vincent smiled, then bent down to kiss her. She raised her hand to stop him.

"Oh, no you don't. Carver will be back any moment and I'll not have him walk in on us again while we're kissing. Pretty soon the staff will think that is all we do."

Vincent laughed. "No, Grace. They already know that is not *all* we do."

Vincent laughed harder when her cheeks turned crimson red. Then he took her for her ride, knowing he'd lost even more ground in his battle to protect his heart.

Chapter 17

Grace stood before the mirror while Alice fastened the tiny pearl buttons that ran the length of her gown. With each pull from the back, the emerald-green material stretched tight across the front—too tight.

"Enough, Alice. Unfasten it and bring me the peach gown. It is looser."

"Yes, Your Grace."

Grace stepped out of her gown and studied herself in the mirror while Alice went for the next gown. She was only in her fourth month, and already she'd grown so much that hardly any of her clothes fit. Why couldn't she be like Caroline? Her babe would be delivered in less than two months, and only now was she forced to go into confinement. Grace would be lucky to last another two weeks.

"You're going to be late."

Vincent's voice interrupted her from the door that separated their two bedrooms, and she turned.

"Do you want to stay home, Grace?"

Grace looked at him leaning casually against the door frame. He was so handsome it stole her breath. "No. This is Caroline's last evening out before her confinement. I promised her we'd attend the opera with her and Wedgewood."

"You're sure."

Grace smiled. "Of course. I just can't decide what to wear."

"I see." He pushed himself away from the doorframe and stepped into the room.

He was nearly dressed, his pristine white linen shirt molding to his broad shoulders and his white satin cravat tied to perfection around his neck. Grace had to hold herself from walking into his arms.

A frown creased his forehead. "Aren't you well?"

"I'm fine," she said, sliding a smile onto her face. She tried to hold it in place while his gaze moved to her stomach. To her thickening waist.

"I think I'm not going to make it as long as Caroline before I am forced into confinement." The frown on his face deepened. "I think our babe wants the world to know he'll arrive before his time."

Vincent raised his eyebrows and gave her an evaluative look. "I think I will send for the doctor again tomorrow."

Grace's eyes opened wide. "I just saw him last week. All he does when he comes is rock back and forth in his shiny black boots with his hands locked behind his back and ask me a lot of very embarrassing questions. Caroline won't even let the man near her. She says even Anne knows more about birthing a babe than he does, and she hasn't had her first babe yet."

"Yet?"

Grace smiled. "She's not sure, but she thinks perhaps. She has been married nearly five months, after all."

A little of the color drained from Vincent's face. She knew he needed a healthy dose of reassurance. "I'm fine, Vincent. Perfectly fine."

"You're still ill in the mornings."

"Not always."

"More than you should be."

"It won't last much longer. I'm nearing my fifth month. The sickness is almost always gone by then."

"Perhaps we should go to the country?"

"Not yet, Vincent. I want to stay in London as long as possible. Caroline has decided to have her baby here, and I want to be with her when it comes."

Grace saw the shocked expression on Vincent's face, the look of concern.

"I don't know, Grace. I don't think—"

Grace held up her hand. "I have helped with the birthing of nearly every one of my nieces and nephews, Vincent. I'm not about to miss this one. Besides, Caroline promised she would be here when my time came too."

Grace could see the anxious expression on his face, his fear almost palpable. She knew every day of her pregnancy was a torture for him. That he compared her illness and discomfort to what he'd experienced with Angeline and Lorraine. And the comparisons scared him to death.

Oh, she wished her pregnancy would be easier. Francie had two babes and wasn't ill one day with either of them. Why couldn't Grace be like her?

Grace looked at him, at his outward show of bravery. But beneath the surface she recognized his concern and worry. It was almost a tangible thing. His fear a living, breathing monster that haunted him day and night. She'd give anything to erase it, to make it go away.

She knew how hard he tried to separate himself from his fears. How miserably he failed.

Without hesitation, she walked to him, stopping only when her half-clothed body leaned against him. She wrapped her arms around his waist and laid her cheek against his chest. His arms instantly enclosed her in a tight embrace.

"Do you remember my promise to you, Vincent?"

"Yes, Grace."

"I promised to give you a healthy son, and together we would raise him to be a fine young man."

Vincent's heart pounded beneath her ear.

"I also told you not to worry. I promised you I would be fine because I have enough courage for the both of us."

His hands moved down her arms and over her body. She sighed in contentment. "Do not doubt me, Vincent. I need your strength. And you need my courage. Just know this. I have no intention of allowing anything to happen to me. How could I, now that I've found you?"

She held him tighter and let his strength seep into her.

"How did I survive before you, Grace?"

"Very poorly, I'm sure."

He lowered his head and kissed her, his kiss tender and filled with a wealth of emotion. Then he deepened his kiss, and Grace knew if they were to have any chance of meeting Caroline at the opera, she had to push him away.

"You'd better leave now, Vincent. I'm sure Alice is standing on the other side of the door, waiting for you to be gone so she can help me finish dressing."

"We could stay home, you know." There was a gleam in his eyes when he looked at her.

"No, we couldn't. Now leave me."

"Very well." He walked to the door.

"Vincent?" She called out to him, stopping him before he left.

"Yes?"

"Did you find him?"

She saw the surprised look on his face he tried to hide. "Find who?"

"You know very well who. Fentington. I know you went out again this afternoon to find him."

"Who told you I went to find him?"

"No one had to tell me. I know that is what you have been doing for weeks now."

Vincent hesitated, then shook his head. "No. I didn't find him. No one's seen him since before we married."

"Maybe he's gone into hiding."

"Perhaps."

"But you don't think so, do you?"

"I don't know."

He waved his hand through the air as if he wanted their discussion to end. And Grace would let it. For now.

"You'd best get dressed, wife. Before I decide the little you're wearing is to my advantage."

Grace laughed. "Out. I'll be down in a minute."

Grace placed her hand over her stomach and watched him leave the room. She prayed he would never find Fentington. She knew Vincent would kill him if he did. She didn't want Fentington's death on their heads.

But she didn't want Vincent to be in danger. And she knew as long as Fentington was out there, Vincent was.

* * *

Vincent listened to the duet being sung at the end of the second act of Verdi's *Rigoletto*, but he wasn't really hearing the music. He was reliving the scene with Grace in her bedroom before they'd left. Reliving the fear that sucked the air from his body when he noticed how much the babe inside her had grown. And she hadn't even reached her fifth month.

Grace sat in front of him in the Raeborn box. Her sisters, Lady Caroline and Lady Josalyn, sat on either side of her. The men sat in chairs behind them, Wedgewood and Carmody on either side of him. Vincent tried to concentrate on the performance but couldn't. His gaze focused on his wife, comparing her with her sisters. She was the smallest of the three, her shoulders narrower, her build slighter. And yet he'd already seen how big the babe inside her was growing.

A sheen of perspiration broke out on his forehead. He realized again how afraid he was for her. How much he'd come to care for her.

How had he let this happen? How had he let her become so important to him when he swore he would not? He more than anyone knew the risks a man took by giving his heart to a woman. He more than anyone knew the heartache of losing someone you cared for. Yet he'd done it. He'd come to care for Grace even though he'd vowed not to.

He couldn't wait to escape the small enclosure of their opera box. When the act was finished he stood with Wedgewood and Carmody. He needed to step outside to let the cool air clear his head. Grace and her sisters decided to stay above while the men stretched their legs.

"I heard a bit of news you might be interested in, Raeborn," Wedgewood said as they walked down the winding stairs to the lobby below.

Vincent gave Wedgewood a sidelong glance, indicating his interest. When they reached the bottom of the stairs, he led the way out the lobby doors to a less crowded area where they would not be overheard.

"Pinky said he ran into Fentington the other day quite by accident."

Vincent felt his pulse race. Although Baron Pinkerton was not known to stay on the sober side, his facts were usually quite accurate. "Where?"

"Pinky was leaving a less reputable establishment he frequents in a seedier part of town and saw Fentington come out of one of the brothels down by the wharf. Pinky said he looked like the very devil, his clothes shabby and unkempt. As if he hadn't changed in a week or more. Or bathed either."

"Did Pinky talk to him?" Vincent asked, every nerve in his body sharpening.

"He tried. But Fentington was in no shape to carry on a conversation. Just spouted his religious piety and railed a few accusations, blaming society for turning its back on him. You in particular for causing his downfall. Pinky said there was a wild look in his eyes and…"

"Go on, Wedgewood," Vincent said, fighting the anger building inside him.

"Well, he told Pinky you'd get what was coming to you. And he'd be there to see you get it."

"What did he mean by that?" Carmody asked, reaching for a glass of champagne. "That sounds like a threat to my ears."

Vincent reached for a glass too. "It is."

He took a long sip, then told his two brothers-in-law about someone shooting at him and about the fire.

"Bloody hell, Raeborn," Carmody said. "Why didn't you tell someone? We'd all have been looking for the man. He's obviously more dangerous than anyone realizes."

Vincent finished his glass of champagne, listening to Wedgewood and Carmody discuss Fentington's instability, discuss the options Vincent had if he couldn't prove who'd shot him, or who'd tried to burn Grace and him in their sleep. He knew in the end there would only be one choice left to him. The man had already tried to kill him twice. He didn't want to take the chance he'd succeed the next time.

The signal sounded for the start of the performance, and Vincent walked back to his box, barely listening while Wedgewood and Carmody continued to make plans to trap Fentington. When he reached his box, he stepped inside and looked ahead just as Grace turned to glance over her shoulder. Their gazes locked and her lips curved into a magnificent smile. His heart leaped to his throat.

He walked to his chair behind her, but before he sat, he reached out his arm. He needed to touch her. Needed to feel her flesh against his.

He placed his hand on the warm skin at her shoulder at the curve of her neck and saw her cheeks color. Without hesitation, she gently rested her gloved hand atop his. Then slowly turned her hand beneath his, palm to palm, and pressed his hand to her cheek.

Vincent's body reacted with a need that was painful. This was how it always was when he was near her. No matter how hard he'd tried to keep from loving her, it was too late. He wanted her with a desperation he couldn't control.

He sat down in his chair and barely listened to the end of the performance, his thoughts centered on a few hours from now when he'd have his wife in his arms, when he'd be a part of her. A few hours from now when they'd be alone together, just the two of them.

The performance came to a riveting conclusion, and the crowd rose to their feet in appreciation. Vincent was never so glad to have an opera end in his life. He stood and held out his arm for her to take.

"It was wonderful, wasn't it, Vincent?" Grace said as he pulled her closer to him than was needed.

"Yes. Wonderful."

She laughed as if she knew the scant attention he'd paid to the opera. As if she knew where his thoughts had strayed for the last hour or more. As if hers had gone there too.

They made their way down the winding stairway and across the large lobby. The crush waiting outside was huge, as usual, but Vincent led their little group away from the entrance to await their carriage. He didn't mind so much having to wait, as long as he could hold Grace next to him. As long as she was beside him, touching him.

As usual she seemed to have a lot to discuss with her sisters. He was always amazed at how there was never a lull in their conversation when any of them were together.

He looked down the street and saw their carriage approach. He stepped closer to the street and loosened his grip on Grace's arm to hail his driver. His driver signaled, and Vincent stepped back to look in the opposite direction.

A carriage came toward them at a steady pace. Vincent gave it a second glance, then turned back to where his party waited.

Just as he reached for Grace's hand, something pushed him hard to the side. He stumbled and lost his balance.

He righted himself quickly enough, but felt a hard tug on his sleeve where Grace had hold of his arm. He spun his gaze in her direction just as she lurched forward.

"Grace!"

Vincent reached out his hand, grabbing for anything he could get hold of. His fingers clasped the loose-fitting mantle she wore, but the yards and yards of satin went on forever. He couldn't get a tight enough grip to pull her back.

His heart leaped to his throat, his fear nearly suffocating him. Screams erupted all around him, and he fought to gain his footing and pull Grace to safety as she stumbled forward into the path of an oncoming carriage.

Vincent didn't look at the carriage coming toward them. He didn't need to. He could hear the thundering of horses' hooves, felt the threat of tons of horseflesh ready to trample them. He reached out again with a greater desperation and this time felt something solid beneath his fingertips. Her arm.

Vincent wrapped his fingers around her in a viselike grip and pulled her to him, jerking her nearly off her feet. He barely had her safe up against him when the carriage rolled past them.

"Grace!"

Vincent held her in his arms while her sisters fussed around her. His entire body shook and he couldn't breathe. He gasped for air, struggling to make his lungs work.

He could have lost her. The horses could have trampled her to death.

"Vincent."

Or the carriage wheels run over her.

"Vincent."

Or…

"Vincent, I can't breathe."

Vincent released his death grip and looked into her face. "Are you all right?" He ran his trembling hands over her arms and shoulders, then hugged her again, this time taking care not to crush her.

"I'm fine, I think. I'm not sure what happened. I think someone pushed me from behind."

Before she could say anything else, Wedgewood and Carmody ran toward them.

"We lost him in the crowd," Carmody said, gasping for breath.

"Did you see what he looked like?"

Wedgewood shook his head. "It wasn't anyone we recognized."

Vincent took in a harsh breath and looked back down at Grace. Her face was pale and her eyes were still wide with fright, but she looked otherwise unhurt.

"I'm taking Grace home."

"We'll follow you," Carmody said. "I doubt our wives would consider going home without making sure Grace is all right."

Vincent nodded, then helped Grace into their waiting carriage. He sat down in the seat opposite her and pulled her onto his lap. "Are you all right, Grace?"

He heard her shaky breath and felt her nod her head against his chest.

"Do you hurt anywhere?"

She wrapped her arms tighter around him. "The babe is all right. Just hold me."

Vincent held her while their carriage made its way home. He pulled the velvet curtains at the windows open wide to let in any light from the streetlights they passed. He needed to see her. Needed to be able to see her face.

"Perhaps it was an accident," she whispered, but the doubt was evident in her voice.

When Vincent didn't answer her, she stiffened in his arms but said no more until they arrived home. The carriage stopped and he lifted her out, then carried her through the front door and up the stairs to her room. "Do I need to send for the doctor?"

"No, Vincent. I'm fine. I wasn't hurt."

"You're sure."

"Positive."

Before he could ask again, Lady Caroline and Lady Josalyn rushed into the room. They both ran to where he'd placed Grace on the bed.

"You'll stay with her for a while?" he asked, knowing he needed to go down to talk to Wedgewood and Carmody.

Her sisters assured him they weren't going anywhere.

Vincent leaned over the bed and kissed her softly. "I'll be back shortly."

"Vincent, please—"

He held up his hand to stop her from asking him to promise not to do something he had no choice but to do. "You rest. I'll have something warm to drink sent up."

Vincent turned from the room and made his way to the study where Wedgewood and Carmody waited for him. He knew if he saw Fentington tonight, he'd kill him without giving him a chance to defend himself.

The rage inside him was building like a volcano ready to erupt. The terror he'd felt when he saw Grace stumble out onto the street stabbed through him like a pike being thrust through his heart.

He could have lost her tonight. He almost had, because he'd underestimated the lengths to which Fentington's insanity would drive him.

He needed to find the man. Needed to get him before he succeeded and Grace…

He threw open the door to his study and closed it behind him.

"Is she all right?" Wedgewood asked. Vincent saw concern on both their faces.

"Yes. Frightened, but all right. Did either of you see anything?"

"Only what we told you. A small, wiry man in a black tailcoat running through the crowd just after Grace stumbled into the street."

Vincent wiped the perspiration from his brow and started to say something, but spun around when Carver opened the door.

"Mr. Germaine is here, Your Grace. He insists on seeing you."

"Show him in, Carver."

Germaine nearly ran Carver down in his hurry. "How is she, Raeborn? I was at the opera tonight and heard what happened. You left so quickly that no one knew if Her Grace was injured in the mishap or not."

"No. Grace is unhurt. Badly shaken, but unhurt."

Germaine's shoulders sagged in relief. "Thank God. I feared perhaps she'd been injured. Accidents like that can happen so fast."

"It was no accident. Someone pushed Grace into the path of that carriage."

Germaine's jaw dropped. "Surely you aren't serious?"

"I wish I weren't."

"Do you know who?"

"Not for sure. But I think Baron Fentington had something to do with it."

"Word at the club is that Fentington has slipped over the edge," Germaine said, walking through the room to stand with Wedgewood and Carmody. "But I had no idea he'd become so desperate. Being ostracized by society probably did it. He undoubtedly blames you. But what did he expect? Who in their right mind would send him an invitation after you brought his deviant behavior into the open at Pendleton's ball?"

"I'm afraid you made a dangerous enemy, Raeborn," Wedgewood said.

Vincent clenched his jaw, fighting the urge to go out yet tonight and find Fentington. Instead he forced himself to remain calm. "I need your help," he announced to his cousin and two brothers-in-law.

"Tell us what you want us to do," Carmody said, and the others nodded their agreement.

"I want him. I need to find out where he's gone."

"He's obviously here in London," Wedgewood said, walking to a sideboard and filling a glass with brandy. He handed the glass to Vincent. "Someone has to have seen him recently. Someone other than Pinky."

Carmody sipped his brandy as he paced the room. "If I were you, I'd send someone to watch his estate in the country. He has to know you're looking for him now and he'll want to hide."

Vincent clutched his free hand into a tight fist. "I've thought of that. I'll hire someone to go to Fentington's country estate."

"It has to be someone you can trust," Germaine added. "Do you have someone in mind?"

Vincent lifted the brandy to his lips and drank. He needed the liquor to warm his insides. His blood ran cold each time he relived the accident and saw Grace stumble out into the street.

"If you don't," Germaine continued, "I know a man, a Mr. Percy Parker. He used to be Bow Street Runner until they went out of existence. He's got a talent for finding people who have gone into hiding."

Vincent sucked in a deep breath. "Can you get word to him?"

"I can."

Vincent took a long swallow of his brandy, letting it burn as it trickled down his throat. "Good. Send for him as soon as possible."

"The rest of us will keep our eyes open," Wedgewood added confidently. "You have more than just yourself now,

Raeborn. There's not one of Grace's family who doesn't owe her a debt and won't gladly come to your assistance."

Vincent nodded, although the idea of having family at his side was a new experience for him. He'd always been alone. Always had to take care of any problem on his own. Now he had Grace and the family she brought with her. And, he thought with some encouragement, he had his own cousin.

"I have to go to my wife now. Let me know the minute any of you hear anything concerning Fentington."

"We will," they all assured him.

Vincent sent a maid to inform Lady Caroline and Lady Josalyn their husbands were ready to leave, then walked them to the door. He accepted their assurances that Fentington would be found and taken care of so he wouldn't be a threat to Grace again.

Germaine assured him that he'd send Mr. Parker to see him immediately and Vincent thanked them for their assistance.

The minute the door closed behind them he headed for the stairs. He'd done everything he could here, and now he needed to be with Grace. He needed to hold her in his arms and make sure she was all right.

He shrugged off his jacket and pulled his shirt loose from his breeches and his cravat from around his neck, then took the steps two at a time. With each step upward, he vowed not to let Grace from his sight. Not to risk putting her in danger ever again.

It was a promise he had every intention of keeping.

* * *

Grace stood in her candlelit bedroom with a fire still glowing to keep the room warm, but for some reason, she was chilled with a bone-deep cold and couldn't get warm.

Caroline and Josalyn were gone now but had promised to come tomorrow to make sure she was all right. Vincent would be here soon and she was glad. She needed to see him. Was desperate to feel his arms around her and his lips atop hers.

She clasped her hands over her stomach and held them there. The babe was all right. She knew he was, and she said a quick prayer of thanks to God for keeping them both safe. Then added another prayer for God to guard and protect Vincent. She didn't want to think of something happening to him.

"You should be in bed," his voice said from behind her.

She turned around. "I was. But I was lonely without you."

He stepped into the room and shut the door behind him. He still wore his white linen shirt, but it was open around the neck and wasn't tucked in. His hair was mussed as if he'd raked his fingers through it as he was wont to do when frustrated or angry. And the dark look of fury was still on his face.

"It was Fentington, wasn't it?"

He hesitated. As if his first thought was to lie to her. On a heavy sigh he decided it was useless, that she wouldn't give up until she got the truth out of him. "I don't know, but I think so."

"Oh, Vincent. I thought after we married he'd leave us alone. I thought he'd realize he had nothing to gain."

"Evidently not."

"Maybe we should go to the country."

He shook his head. "Running won't help. We can't spend the rest of our lives looking over our shoulders."

A dead weight pressed against her heart. He would go after Fentington, and there was no way she could stop him. Vincent didn't have a choice. Left unchecked, Fentington wouldn't stop until one or both of them were dead.

Grace clasped her hands around her middle to keep from shaking and blinked rapidly to keep the tears from falling. She was so afraid. More afraid now than ever. And not for herself. But for Vincent. For the babe she was going to have. A babe who might grow up without knowing his father.

Tears rolled down her cheeks, tears she'd shed in abundance since she'd begun this nine-month ordeal.

Through her blurry vision, she saw him open his arms to her. Saw him reach out to her, take a step closer to her.

With a tiny gasp, she ran across the room and into his arms.

"Ah, Grace," he said, kissing her eyes, the side of her face, and her cheeks where the tears still ran. "Don't cry. It's all right. I won't let anything hurt you ever again."

"I'm not crying. It's just..."

A smile lit his face. "I know." He wrapped his arms around her and held her close. But she needed to be held closer. She needed to feel him against her, inside her.

"Love me, Vincent. Make love to me."

"Yes. Oh, yes."

With a heavy sigh, he lowered his face toward hers and his mouth crushed down on hers with a desperation equal to her own.

She wanted him more than ever, perhaps because of what had happened tonight. Perhaps because she'd had a glimpse of a future without Vincent in it. Perhaps because her life held everything she'd always dreamed of having and she was desperate to make the most of the gift she'd been given. She thought perhaps Vincent felt the same, realized he had to cherish the gift just as she did. Again and again he kissed her, not with his usual tenderness and gentleness, but thoroughly and completely.

His mouth opened atop hers, his tongue seeking hers, touching hers, battling hers, mating with hers. And he deepened his kiss even more until neither of them could breathe on their own; until their breaths were shared between them, one a part of the other's.

"Love me," she whispered against his mouth.

He lifted her in his arms and carried her to the bed.

From the day she'd forced him to marry her she'd known how hard he'd struggled to keep from caring for her. From the day he'd taken her as his bride she'd known how determined he'd been to protect his heart. And tonight she realized how completely he'd failed.

She saw it in his eyes, in the fear on his face when he thought she might be hurt. In the relief when he realized she was safe. Even if he couldn't bring himself to say the words, she knew the emotion was there. Knew he'd come to love her. And she knew how much that knowledge frightened him.

He moved over her and she ran her fingers over the rippling muscles across his shoulders and down his arms. She lifted her hand and brushed an errant strand of his dark hair from his forehead and cupped her hand to his cheek, feeling the prickly stubble against her palm. It still amazed her. Everything about him still amazed her. And even if he wasn't brave enough to admit his feelings, she was.

"I love you, Vincent. I always will."

Chapter 18

Grace strolled down the path of the garden behind their London town house. This path led to a bubbling fountain next to a trellised archway covered with creeping roses in full bloom. She loved it here. Loved the flowers that bloomed in riotous colors all summer and that now were, in late July, even more plenteous. It was the one place she could come to forget about Fentington and escape the worry that someday he'd find Vincent and hurt him.

It had been two months since anyone had seen him. Two months since the night of the opera, when someone had pushed her into the street, and even though Vincent assured her she had nothing to worry about, she knew it was only a matter of time until something happened. She knew he was waiting until he found the perfect opportunity to strike. The perfect chance to do the most harm.

As if the babe growing inside her felt the same fears, it kicked hard against her side, and she gasped. When the pain subsided, she hooked the basket she'd brought with her over her other arm and reached down to pick some yellow and red carnations. They were in full bloom and called out to her, begging to be a part of the centerpiece for the intimate dinner she'd planned for tonight, just for Vincent and herself.

She picked one red flower, then quickly straightened with a jerk and rubbed her stomach where the babe's feet kicked against her again. Oh, he was an active babe, turning and kicking and moving constantly.

During the night he seemed to be worse. Sometimes the babe was so restless she had to get up. Occasionally she was lucky and Vincent didn't notice she'd left their bed. But often he missed having her next to him and got up with her.

Even though she hated it when she disturbed his sleep, she liked those times best. He'd sit with her in the oversize rocker he'd had brought up to their room and hold her in his lap with his hand resting on top of her bulging stomach. Then, when the babe settled down, he'd lie with her on the bed and hold her close to him.

She felt another strong jab to her side and rubbed her stomach again. She was nearing her seventh month now and was huge in comparison with how big any of her sisters had been.

Her pregnancy hadn't been easy so far. Oh, how she wished it had been. Not for her sake. But for Vincent's.

She knew he was worried. She saw it in his eyes when he didn't think she saw him watching her. His fear was palpable each time he touched her stomach, every time he took note of how big his child inside of her was growing. The anxiety she saw in his eyes was a debilitating emotion, and no amount of reassurance from her made it go away.

Grace placed her hand on her stomach and rubbed the hard mound where feet kicked her again. "You're a strong, healthy babe," she whispered, smiling down at her stomach. "I can't wait for you to meet your father. You'll be ever so pleased with him."

The babe kicked again. "But I am going to scold you a little for all the discomfort you caused me. Quite inconsiderate, you know."

Grace smiled when her stomach settled, then bent over to pick some of the flowers. She only had about half the amount she wanted before she had to stand up to stretch her aching back. That occurred more and more, the bigger she got. Her back ached, and often the only chair that helped was one of the straight-backed wooden chairs in the formal dining room.

Grace rubbed her back with one hand and held her basket with the other, thankful none of the servants were close enough to see her. She knew she was not at all attractive right now. Hadn't been for a month or more.

"May I help you, Grace?"

Grace turned her head to see Vincent sauntering down the walk, the buttons of his jacket loose but his cravat still tied around his neck.

"I'm trying to pick a few more of these flowers, but your son has decided to be extremely active this afternoon. Either that or he hasn't developed a liking for our local flora and will have to be instructed on its beauty."

"I will mention it to him at our first meeting," Vincent said, placing his hands on her shoulders and pressing his mouth to hers.

"I insist that you do," she said, reaching up to kiss him again. "And since you asked, would you please cut some of those pink carnations? I have a special dinner planned for tonight and they will look perfect on our table."

"A special dinner?"

"Yes. For just you and me. With all our favorites."

Vincent laughed. "And what are *our* favorites today?"

"Peach cobbler and rice pudding and cherry pie. And that chocolate dessert Cook makes so well."

"I didn't think you liked peach cobbler."

"Not always, but I'm just suddenly very hungry for it."

"I see," Vincent said, reaching for another carnation. "And what else will you be serving?"

"I don't know. I told Cook to surprise us."

"I see." Vincent laughed, then led her over to the low stone wall surrounding the fountain. "You are beautiful, Your Grace," he said, setting the basket on the ground.

Grace laughed. "I am not. I am monstrously ugly, like a huge whale I've seen in pictures."

"Hardly."

He sat down beside her and draped one arm around her shoulders. He smelled all male, and Grace breathed in the clean aroma of the outdoors and leather from the horse he'd been riding. She knew he'd gotten some information concerning Fentington and was curious as to what it was.

She leaned her head against his shoulder and sighed. "So what have you been doing today?"

"I went to see Madam Genevieve."

Grace lifted her head with a start. "Hannah?"

"Yes. I wanted to talk to her about her father. I wanted to see if perhaps she could give any insight as to where he might be hiding."

"Could she?"

He shook his head. "She said she hasn't seen him or heard from him since the day she left his home fifteen years ago."

Grace felt Vincent's arm tighten around her shoulder.

"I think this Parker fellow Germaine sent to me is right. I think Fentington has left the country. That he's not even in England right now," he said.

"Then maybe he will never come back," she said hopefully.

"Maybe."

"But you don't think so, do you?"

"His home is here. I doubt he will leave it for long."

He held her protectively, and Grace could tell his thoughts were far away. "How is she?" Grace finally asked, pulling him back.

"Hannah?"

"Yes."

"She asked about you. She said she misses you. That for years you met whenever you came to London, but that she hasn't seen you since the night you…"

Grace looked up at him and smiled. "That seems a lifetime away. Going to her was the bravest thing I'd ever done. Having her send you to me was the most wonderful thing that ever happened to me. I have Hannah to thank for how happy I am."

He lifted a hand to her face and brushed the backs of his fingers down her cheek. "Would you like to see her?"

Grace sat up with a start. "Oh, Vincent. Yes. Could I?"

"It could be arranged."

"When?"

"Now."

"Now!"

"Do you feel up to a ride through the park?"

"Oh, yes." She stood as gracefully as her cumbersome body would allow. Vincent stood with her.

"Genevieve tells me you had a system for meeting."

"Yes."

"Then perhaps you will explain it to me on the way. I told her we would meet her at the same place as usual at four o'clock." He reached into his waistcoat pocket and drew out his watch. "That doesn't leave us much time."

Grace reached for his hand and pulled him with her. She suddenly felt as giddy as a schoolgirl. She couldn't wait to thank the person responsible for giving her Vincent. Words hardly seemed adequate.

* * *

Vincent watched Grace shift in her seat as she peered out the window for the hundredth time since they'd left Raeborn House. He wanted to laugh. Grace was so agitated she could hardly sit still.

"We're almost there!" Her voice was filled with excitement. "Tell Barnabas to stop when he passes under that covered bridge," she instructed, peering out the window and pointing a trembling finger.

Vincent shook his head. "I can't believe you want to stop in the dark beneath a bridge and open the door to let someone in."

His wife looked at him as if he'd made the most unintelligent comment in the world.

"Hannah wanted to make sure that no one saw us together. She didn't want to put my reputation at risk."

"Surely you didn't do this while you were alone? How could you be sure it was Hannah who would get in with you and not some lowlife hiding in the dark beneath the bridge?"

"Because Hannah is the only person I sent a note telling what time I would arrive. Now stop tormenting me so I can enjoy my visit."

Vincent laughed. Then he cupped her cheeks in the palms of his hands and brought her lips to his. Their kiss was full and deep, and she ended it on a heavy sigh.

"Vincent..."

He laughed. "I just wanted to put a little color in your cheeks before Hannah arrived."

"You put more than color in my cheeks, you monster. Now stop pestering me until we get home."

"As you wish," he said, then chuckled.

He couldn't wait to see Hannah and Grace together. He couldn't imagine any two friends more different from each other, but he knew how close they were.

Grace needed a friend to talk to right now, a diversion. He'd kept her cooped up in their house for endless weeks while he searched for Fentington, taking her out only to go for an occasional dinner at one of her sisters' homes or when one or more of her sisters came to dine with them. And Grace was not content to be trapped in their house.

She was not like Angeline or Lorraine, who secluded themselves from the moment they realized they were carrying, keeping mostly to their beds, resting and sleeping the days away. Grace wasn't content to pamper herself with idleness but was always working in her garden or practicing a new piece one of her composers had just published.

And every day the two of them walked down every path in the massive garden again and again. He swore she never tired. Swore he would wear out before she did.

But the special times when he took her for a ride were her favorites. She loved the out-of-doors. Loved the fresh air and the sunshine. If it weren't for the birth of Caroline's babe, he would have taken her to the country. But he knew he would have an even harder time watching her there. She would forever be out-of-doors and he would be searching for her.

"Here. Stop here, Barnabas." She peered out the window when their carriage went beneath the bridge.

The carriage stopped. Vincent opened the door and stepped out.

Genevieve came forward as soon as the carriage stopped and stepped inside. The minute they saw each other, the two women squealed and threw themselves into each other's arms.

Vincent ordered Barnabas to drive around the park at a leisurely pace, then stepped into the carriage and took his seat opposite the two women still holding each other in a warm embrace.

He didn't get a good look at Genevieve until the carriage began its drive. The difference between the Genevieve he was used to seeing and the Hannah who was here now startled him.

Her hair was conservatively styled and her gown was plain brown. Everything she wore was very ordinary and nondescript so as not to draw attention. And her face was devoid of makeup. Gone was the enchanting luster and irresistible facade that made Madam Genevieve one of the most alluring women in all of England. In her place was the ordinary Miss Hannah Bartlett, daughter of Baron Fentington.

"I think I have shocked your husband," Hannah said, wiping a tear from her cheek.

Grace laughed. "Yes. I think so. It's the first time since I've known him he's at a loss for words."

They all laughed, then Hannah turned back to Grace and placed her hand on Grace's stomach. "I knew you must be. I'm so happy for you. And for you, Your Grace," she said, looking at him.

Vincent swallowed hard. Genevieve was probably the only person besides Grace who truly understood how terrified he was of having another of his wives go through childbirth.

"Now tell me how you've been," she said, reaching for Grace's hand. "Is Raeborn being the perfect husband? I picked him out special for you, Grace. I expect him to be most exemplary."

Grace laughed through her tears and gave her friend a hug. "Oh, yes. He is. Quite perfect, except for his domineering ways and opinionated notions."

"Here, here, wife. I'll have you know I intend to defend myself, and I've already told Hannah that I'm the ideal husband. You told me so yourself."

"I can see I made a grave error in being so complimentary." Grace laughed, and Vincent sat back against the squabs while Grace and Hannah talked nonstop about Grace's sisters and their families and the babe and Grace's certainty that it would be a boy.

After they'd driven through the park for nearly an hour, Hannah gave Vincent the nod that indicated it was time for their visit to end.

"Go back to the bridge, Barnabas," Vincent ordered, and the carriage took a turn.

"I've been thinking about what you asked," Hannah said when the carriage slowed. "About my father. I remember him mentioning he had a sister who lived in France."

"Do you know where?"

"In Paris, I think. I never knew her."

"Do you know her name?"

Hannah shook her head. "No, just that he had a sister he wanted to go to France to see. He said the two of them had been quite close growing up but that she'd run away."

Hannah's sad gaze locked with Vincent's and she took a shuddering breath. "You don't suppose my grandfather was the same?" She paused. "I'd hate to think of there being two such monsters in the world."

Vincent saw Hannah reach for Grace's hand and hold it, but her gaze remained locked with his.

"You have to find him," Hannah said, the look in her eyes dark and filled with a fear Vincent had never seen in her before. "He truly believes he is one of the elect, sent by God to punish all women for Eve's sins. He thinks he's the only morally upright human on earth and that his righteous piety sets him apart from other sinful mortals. You showed him for the sanctimonious hypocrite he is, and he intends to destroy you because of it."

"Don't worry. He has to come home sometime, and I'll be waiting for him."

The carriage slowed, and Hannah leaned over to give Grace a farewell hug. "Be happy," he heard her whisper.

"I am."

His heart tightened in his chest and he swallowed hard. Those two small words meant more to him than he imagined.

The carriage stopped and Vincent helped Hannah disembark. Without a backward glance, Grace's unpretentious childhood friend walked to the carriage that would whisk her into another life. That of the gorgeous Madam Genevieve—one of the most notorious courtesans in all of London.

Vincent stepped up into the carriage and rapped on the ceiling with his cane. He sat on the cushioned seat beside Grace and took her into his arms.

"Thank you," she said, turning into him and nestling close.

Grace's head rested over his heart. A heart he'd vowed never to risk again.

But had.

* * *

Vincent settled into his oversize, overstuffed chair and listened to Grace play a Chopin polonaise. Her fingers virtually flew over the keys as she immersed herself in the music. Her gaze held the look of an artist lost in her creation. Lost in a world all her own.

He loved to hear her play, loved to watch her work at her craft—the way she leaned forward almost as if the music had the power to draw her into it; the gentle lift of her elbows as she caressed the keys, enticing each one of them to ring with beauty; the strength and power that came from someone so small. It was fascinating to watch her become so totally absorbed in the music that the notes became a part of her.

He loved this part of the day. The time the two of them spent alone together. The precious minutes in which the outside world was not allowed to intrude.

Grace worked the fingers of her right hand through the finishing arpeggio runs, then lifted back from the keys with a swift, sudden completion. Her chest heaved, her cheeks stayed flushed, and her eyes remained focused on the keys in front of her as if some part of her hadn't yet been released from the magic.

She paused. Then her arms dropped to her sides and she turned to him. "Just think what Chopin could have given us had he lived longer," she said on a sigh.

Vincent walked to her and placed his hands on her shoulders. "The world's loss," he said, gently massaging her still-tight muscles. He noticed her hand go to her stomach and rub.

"Chopin did not put him to sleep?" he asked.

She laughed and turned around on the small bench. "I think I should have played Haydn or Brahms tonight."

He helped her to her feet, then sat beside her on the comfortable settee. He pulled her close to him.

"Thank you for today," she said, snuggling against him with her hand over his chest. "I've missed Hannah terribly. I can't tell you how wonderful it was to see her."

Vincent pressed his lips to the top of her head. "Do you feel all right? Are you tired?"

"I'm fine, Vincent. The baby's fine. Here. Feel." She placed his hand on her growing stomach. "See how healthy he is?"

Vincent held his hand there, with hers atop his, their fingers entwined, the life of their child beneath his palm. With her in his arms like this he could almost forget his fears. With her beside him so glowingly healthy, he could almost forget the risk he'd taken. Could almost convince himself he would not be asked to make such a sacrifice again. Would not have to give up someone he loved as much as he loved Grace.

He took a deep breath, struggling to forget how it had been before. Struggling to forget the last time and the—

"You are worrying, Vincent," her voice interrupted, jarring him from his memories.

She turned in his arms and framed his face with her small palms. "Do you remember what I told you?" She brushed her fingers across the stubble on his jaw. "I told you not to worry. That I had enough courage for the both of us. Just look at me." She glanced down at her belly. "There's nothing to worry about. Your babe will be born healthy and I will survive. Trust me in this. I will tell you if you need to worry."

"Oh, Grace."

Vincent leaned over and kissed her, then leaned down to kiss her more deeply. He pulled away at the knock on the door.

"Come in, Carver," he said, knowing only Carver would interrupt them.

"Excuse me, Your Grace. But a messenger just arrived from Lord Wedgewood. He wanted to inform Her Grace that Lady Wedgewood is being delivered of her child and asked for her company."

Grace jumped up from beside Vincent as quickly as the babe she was carrying would allow. She faced Carver with an excited look in her eyes. "Get my wrap, Carver. And have a carriage sent round."

"Very well, Your Grace."

"Grace, no!"

He heard her small gasp and saw the expression on her face turn to one of disbelief. Then unstoppable determination. Carver stopped with his hand on the door.

"You do not have to go with me, Vincent," she said. Her voice was strained, her words pronounced. As if she were forcing herself to remain calm. "But I am going to be with Caroline when she has her babe. You will not stop me in this."

Several long, tense moments passed and neither of them spoke. The defiant glare in her eyes said she would not give up on this. Not without a battle that would have long-lasting repercussions. Finally he moved his gaze to where Carver still stood with his hand on the knob.

"Send for the carriage, Carver. And get Her Grace's wrap—and my cloak as well."

"Yes, Your Grace."

Carver left, and she walked into his arms and pressed a kiss to his lips. "Thank you, Vincent," she said, then rushed from the room.

Vincent followed her.

"You do not have to come with me," she said as Carver placed a cloak around her shoulders. "I can go alone. Or take Alice with me."

He flashed her an over-my-dead-body look and told himself he would survive this night. The woman having the babe was not his wife, after all. Only the sister of his wife and a woman he thought of as a very dear friend.

* * *

They handed their wraps to Wedgewood's austere butler, and Vincent walked to Wedgewood's study while Grace rushed up the stairs. Viscount Carmody was already there as well as the Earl of Baldwin and Wexley.

"Josalyn, Francine, and Anne are upstairs with Caroline," Wedgewood said, handing Vincent a glass of amber liquid. "I expect Hansley and Adledge will arrive shortly."

Vincent looked around the room, taking in the serious expressions on the others' faces.

"I should have known what was up this morning when she ordered the staff to polish the silver," Wedgewood said, raking his fingers through his hair. "Even Mrs. Marble, the housekeeper, knew. She told them in the kitchen to bake extra because there'd be the whole lot of us here before the day was out."

Vincent frowned at Wedgewood, not having the slightest idea why polishing the silver had any significance.

"Francie spends the day in the kitchen. Cook says it's the warm dough. Although I don't know what that means," Baldwin said, shaking his head.

"I don't know what Annie will do," Wexley said. "I guess I'll have to wait my turn to find out."

Baldwin thumped Wexley on the back. "Well, your turn won't be for a while. We'll all be going to Raeborn's next go-around."

Vincent tried to put a smile on his face and hide the fear that weighed down on him like a heavy yoke.

"How long has it been?" Carmody asked, settling in one of the wing chairs scattered throughout the room.

Wedgewood glanced at his watch. "About three hours."

"Oh hell," Baldwin said on a laugh. "She's just begun. Might as well get out the cards."

* * *

The mantle clock in Wedgewood's study struck ten. Then eleven. An eternity later, the clock struck midnight.

Vincent tried to keep his mind from imagining the struggle going on above stairs. But that was impossible when the muffled sounds of Lady Caroline's pain carried down the open stairway. He tried to concentrate on the card game Carmody, Baldwin, Hansley, and Adledge were playing, but he couldn't focus on anything except the vivid memories of the two tragic nights he'd suffered through, waiting word of the birth of his child.

Most of all he tried not to look at the worry and concern on Wedgewood's face. He found that impossible. He knew that fear. Had lived it twice before in his life. Was going to have to live it again.

Vincent refilled his empty brandy glass and made for the open terrace doors. He needed to escape. Needed to breathe in some fresh air and clear his mind of the nightmares eating at him.

He walked outside and braced his outstretched arms against the balustrade. His chest heaved and his head throbbed as he took one gulping breath after another.

He stared out into the blackness. He didn't know how he'd survive it when Grace's time came. He could barely stand to stay here knowing what was going on up above.

"I think it's bloody inconsiderate of them to put us through such torture," Wedgewood said from behind him.

Vincent turned to face his brother-in-law. He hadn't realized Wedgewood was there. Vincent looked at him. Saw the worry. An agony he understood all too well. "How do you do it? This isn't your first. How do you survive the waiting?"

Wedgewood crossed the distance that separated them at a slow, thoughtful pace. "I don't know. There's a time during it when I'm not certain I can."

Wedgewood lowered himself to the railing and sat. He lifted his gaze and stared at the stars. "At times like this, you tend to pray harder than you've ever prayed in your life. You surround yourself with friends and family who know exactly what you're going through. You want desperately to suffer the pain for them because you know it's your fault they're going through this. And you'd gladly trade places with them because you know if something happens you're not nearly so important as they.

"Then, as the hours stretch on, you bargain with God that if He lets her come through this birth safely, you'll never touch her again. That you'll never risk getting her pregnant. But you know you'll never keep your promise because you can't wait to hold her in your arms and make love to her again.

"So you die a little inside with every minute that drags by and pretend to all the world that your nerves are made of iron and you're in control."

Vincent took in everything Wedgewood said and felt the words press against his chest like a painful weight. That was exactly how it was.

"Don't mind me," Wedgewood said, finishing off his brandy. "Blame my maudlin behavior on too much brandy, too little sleep, and too much time to think."

The mantle clock struck one o'clock and Wedgewood pushed himself away from the balustrade. "We'd best get back inside before Adledge loses his country estate to Carmody. The man's deucedly pathetic at cards."

Vincent took a deep breath and followed him inside. Adledge hadn't lost his country estate to Hansley—only his London town house and his firstborn.

Wedgewood made Hansley give back Adledge's heir and told them they could fight over the town house in the morning.

A few minutes later, a servant brought in a tray with hot tea and coffee and plates of sandwiches and the pastries the kitchen had spent all day baking. The hours stretched by with interminable slowness and eventually each of them found a spot to relax and doze for a few hours.

All except Vincent and Wedgewood. The uneasy feeling that overwhelmed them prevented either of them from falling asleep.

* * *

The sky turned a lighter shade of black, then a vapid gray, and finally a riot of pinks and blues and purples and oranges. Vincent didn't know how he'd survived. How Wedgewood had. The deep furrows on Wedgewood's forehead showed he hadn't fared well.

"Bloody hell!" Wedgewood muttered beneath his breath, pacing the room like a caged tiger.

Vincent stood by to offer any assistance that might be needed but knew there was nothing he could do. Knew there was nothing any of them could do.

Wedgewood walked to the two double doors that opened to the terrace and threw them open. The sun was already in the sky, the day having begun. And yet the house was as silent as a tomb. Not even the servants dared to come anywhere near while the master stalked the rooms like an angry predator.

His footsteps echoed to every corner of the downstairs as he paced from the study, across the large foyer, then to the bottom of the stairs where he stopped and waited for someone to come down to give him the latest news.

But no news came.

"What's taking so blasted long?" he demanded, striding back into the study. "It's been twelve bloody hours. It's never taken this long. Never."

"Patience, Wedgewood," Baldwin said, nervously shuffling the cards they'd used the night before.

Carmody rose from his chair and stretched his arms above his head. "Yes. Sometimes it takes longer. Remember my first? I didn't think he'd ever make an appearance."

"My second one was like that," Adledge added, moving a cup from one side of the table to the other. "Thought I was going to lose my mind before it was all over."

"Well, that answers where it went," Hansley said.

"Where what went?"

"Your mind."

They all laughed, but the jovial good humor with which they'd started out the evening before was gone. Now their humor was tinged with caution. Their seemingly carefree attitudes held a hint of wariness. They all knew it had been an exceedingly long time. And no one had come down to check on them or give them any news for hours now.

Tension hung in the room like a black pall. Vincent saw the worry on Wedgewood's face, saw the frown lines deepen, the sunken look in his eyes turn darker. Vincent recognized the haunting fear. He felt it too. Couldn't breathe because of it.

"I can't wait any longer," Wedgewood growled, pushing himself away from the mantel where he'd been leaning. "I'm going up to see what's taking so long."

He bolted across the room and had just neared the doorway when Grace and her sisters, Lady Josalyn and Lady Francine, entered the room. Their cheeks were flushed, their eyes red-rimmed, and all three looked exhausted. Vincent couldn't tell more than that. Their expressions didn't reveal more.

Wedgewood's shoulders stiffened, and Vincent took a step closer to offer support if needed.

"The birth was difficult," Grace said, "but Caroline is fine. You have a daughter, my lord." She dabbed at a tear on her cheek. "A beautiful, healthy daughter."

Vincent heard Wedgewood's cry of relief then watched him race toward the door, stopping barely long enough to give his three sisters-in-law a hasty kiss on the cheek.

Without a backward glance, he ran across the foyer and up the stairs.

Vincent couldn't move. He stood frozen in place as if his feet were cemented to the floor. His blood roared in his head, his heart thundered in his chest, his relief overwhelming.

He looked at Grace and she suddenly seemed so very small and fragile to him. The expression on her face told him that what she'd gone through helping her sister birth the baby had stolen all her strength. That the ordeal had stretched her nerves so tightly she was close to shattering.

He took a step forward and lifted his arms. She ran to him and he wrapped his arms around her and held her.

Her tears flowed harsh and jagged, her body trembled violently. He held her close and let them fall. Let her pour out all her fears, her relief. The two sisters who'd come down with her were doing the same. And his three brothers-in-law whose wives hadn't come down were no longer in the room, but had gone upstairs.

Vincent held Grace and comforted her. When he thought she'd calmed enough, he stepped with her out the doors onto the terrace and held her longer.

"I thought we were going to lose her," Grace said on a shudder. "The babe was turned wrong and nothing we did helped."

Vincent couldn't bring himself to say anything to her. Couldn't bring himself to say the reassuring words he knew she needed to hear. All he could do was hold on to her and tell himself that it wasn't Grace who'd been in danger. That when her time came it would be different.

His heart pounded in his chest and he willed it to slow, but it wouldn't. He fought to push aside the panic suffocating him, but couldn't do that either. It was all too real. He didn't want to think of losing her. Not Grace. He wouldn't survive. He'd come to care for her too much to think of a future without her. He knew he even—

"Vincent."

"Vincent!"

Her voice pulled him back from the black hole into which he'd sunk, from the nightmarish quagmire that threatened to suck him under.

"Look at me. My time will not be like Caroline's. I'm healthy. The babe's healthy."

"So was she!"

"Yes, but I've promised you nothing will happen. And it won't. Do not doubt me in this."

But how did she know she would not be like Caroline? How could she ask him not to doubt she would survive birthing the babe when he knew the risks as well as she?

Vincent held her in his arms and gazed into the sincere look in her eyes. Then he lowered his head and crushed his mouth against hers. He kissed her with a desperation greater than he'd ever felt before. Then he kissed her again.

He couldn't get enough of her, couldn't get close enough to her. She answered each of his kisses as if she felt the same. As if she were desperate to calm him.

But the seeds of doubt and fear had already been planted, and Vincent knew nothing Grace said or did would make them go away.

Chapter 19

Grace paced the whole length of the downstairs—around the circumference of the foyer, past the open staircase on one side of the room, down a short hallway, into the music room, through the connecting door to the library, across another hallway to the dining room, then down a wide corridor that led back to the foyer, and past another open staircase on the opposite side of the foyer. When she reached the middle of the room, one of the footmen would rush forward with a chair so she could sit and rest for a few moments before she stormed through the house again.

The chair was positioned in the center of the foyer facing the entrance so she would not miss him the minute he walked through the front door. The repeated trek through the house was to calm her nerves and cool her temper before he arrived.

Her efforts were not working.

She was as furious with him now as she'd been since Josie and Francie and Sarah left over an hour ago. Since they told her the news they thought she already knew. The news they thought for sure he would tell her.

How dare he.

How dare he!

Grace bolted from the chair and began her trek again.

Carver came up beside her. "Perhaps Your Grace would like to rest in the music room for just a little while," he said, as discomfited as she'd ever seen him. "Perhaps a nice cup of tea would—"

"No, Carver. A cup of tea won't help. Only His Grace's head on a platter will help."

"Y...yes, Your Grace," he stuttered, backing away faster than Grace thought Carver could move.

Grace sat back down in her chair a moment longer. Her feet were swollen, her back ached, and she didn't walk when she moved, she waddled. Each time she passed the mammoth gold-embossed mirror on the foyer wall, she realized she was probably the largest expectant mother in all of England. And she still had at least three, perhaps four weeks until her babe would make an appearance.

What was he trying to do to her?

The change in him was driving her mad. It had begun after Caroline was delivered of her daughter.

Before that night, she'd seen the worry on his face. Saw it in the way he watched her, held her. She knew her pregnancy concerned him. Now his worry didn't reach the surface. He kept his emotions hidden, as if he'd convinced himself his fear didn't exist.

This new course of defense frightened her more. It was as if he'd found a way to separate himself from his fears—from her. His answer was to immerse himself in work. And in his search for the man who'd tried to kill them.

Vincent was a man possessed. Possessed with whatever it took to keep the wall secured around his heart. Well, she wouldn't let him get by with it any longer. Not after what she'd found out today.

She pushed herself from the chair and took two steps to repeat her way through the dining room, then stopped short. The front door opened and she turned.

Vincent swept his hat from his head as he entered the house and looked up. A frown covered his face as he looked first at the chair in the middle of the room, then at Grace.

"Grace?"

His inquiring gaze turned more curious as the footman in charge of the chair almost ran from the room. He looked to Carver, who silently reached for his master's hat, gloves, and cane, then raised his eyes heavenward as a warning to his master.

Grace nearly roared her disapproval, but she held her temper. She didn't want to waste any of her anger on anyone but Vincent.

She waited, her hands balled into tight fists that she propped on her hips.

He waited too, as if he were completely oblivious as to why she might be upset. As if he couldn't imagine what had upset her so. He started to speak, then closed his mouth and opted for silence as his best course.

His silence only made her angrier. She was spoiling for a good fight, and his lack of participation wasn't helping at all.

How dare he!

"Did you have a good day?" she asked, her voice tight, her words clipped.

He hesitated a second before answering, as if debating which answer would be less combative. She hoped he realized it didn't really matter.

"I've had worse."

"So what did you do?"

"I had business to attend to."

"Really? What sort of business?"

He arched his eyebrows as if debating the wisdom of telling her she'd crossed the line in asking about affairs that were none of her concern. "Personal business. Estate business with Mr. James."

"How strange. Mr. James came looking for you while you were out. He had the papers he said you wanted. I left them on your desk."

"Thank you."

"And later I received a message from your solicitor. He wanted to make sure you received the instructions to bring the Marquess of Wedgewood and Viscount Carmody by at your earliest convenience to sign the documents. That the signing must be witnessed in order for everything to be indisputable."

"I'm sorry I wasn't here to receive the messenger myself."

"I'm sure you are."

His shoulders lifted as his lungs filled with air, then he released it on a heavy sigh. He stepped over to her and reached out his hands as if he thought holding her could make her forget all her questions.

He held up his hands in surrender when she twisted out of his grasp.

With another sigh, he walked to his study and opened the door. "Very well, Grace. Perhaps we can discuss this in private. Or would you rather remain here so all the servants can hear our personal business as well?"

Grace walked across the foyer and swished past him, turning to face him the minute the door closed.

"What have you done, Vincent? What do Wedgewood and Carmody have to do with our affairs?"

"It is nothing, Grace. Only business."

She fisted her hands. "Don't tell me it's nothing! I read the papers! I know what you've done. Know that you've put all your properties that are not entailed into my name upon your death, with the stipulation that they go to our child when he reaches maturity. And that you've placed Wedgewood and Carmody as trustees until that time."

His face paled. "I wish you hadn't looked at the papers. They were not your concern."

"Weren't they?"

He slashed his hand through the air. "Is this going somewhere, Grace? These questions?"

"Yes, Vincent. They are." She took an angry step closer to him. "I'd like your opinion. Do you think I'll look good in black?"

His head jerked upward, a muscle at his jaw working furiously.

"Since we're so recently married, I'm sure I'll be expected to wear it the full two years. I just wanted to know what you thought about—"

"Grace, stop!"

"No, Vincent. I don't think so. Did you know I had even more visitors this afternoon?"

He didn't answer, but then she didn't really give him a chance to.

"Yes. Josie, Francie, and Sarah stopped by to make sure I was all right. No," she said, holding up her hand to correct herself. "Actually, they stopped by to make sure *you* were all right. Especially after finding out you'd been shot at again yesterday."

"How did they find out?" he asked, as if that made the least difference.

"Josie overheard Wedgewood telling Carmody that they had to guard you more carefully because the bullet didn't miss you by a foot. Imagine my surprise."

"Bloody hell!"

"What was that, Vincent?"

"Nothing!"

"And after they left, I needed to go outside to clear my head and was informed that you'd given orders I wasn't to go out unless you were with me."

Vincent brushed his hand over his jaw and took a deep breath.

Grace saw the worry on his face and the dark circles around his eyes. She knew he hadn't slept much the last few nights but thought her restlessness was to blame. Now she knew it was only partly her fault. Now she knew his days of endless searching to find the man who'd tried to kill them was taking its toll. She wanted to comfort him but couldn't. She was still too angry.

She took another step closer. "Why didn't you tell me? Why didn't you tell me he was back?"

"What could you have done other than worry?"

She stomped her foot. "I could have forbidden you to go out until he's found. I could have kept you here with me." She paced the floor, then flung her hand through the air in frustration. "I could have taken care of you so nothing happened to you."

He smiled at the absurdity of her declarations. His smile did nothing except wrench her heart and bring closer to the surface the tears she'd so successfully kept at bay. She swept them away with her trembling fingers.

"Why didn't you tell me he was back?" she whispered, and her voice broke.

Vincent shoved a hand through his hair. "I didn't know until yesterday. I've been watching his house every day since the night of the opera. I think he must have left for France soon after that. There has been no sign of him since."

"What happened yesterday?" Her voice trembled and her legs weakened beneath her. She stepped over to the settee and sat.

"Wedgewood was with me. We watched the house for a few hours as usual and saw no activity. When we decided to leave, we drove around through the back, past the carriage house. Wedgewood saw some fresh tracks that intrigued him, and we got out to take a look. Just as we bent down to investigate, a bullet rang past me. It lodged in the wood of the carriage house door to my right. I was not hurt, Grace."

"But you could have been."

He sat down beside her. "Yes, I could have been."

She clenched her hands in her lap and bit at her lower lip to keep it from trembling. She saw him move to put his arm around her, but he stopped when she huddled into herself.

"I went to the authorities and they promised to watch out for him. But—"

"But?"

"There is little they can do without proof. I have never actually seen him. It is just my word that he is responsible."

Grace digested what Vincent said. Everything suddenly overwhelmed her and she feared she might shatter into a million pieces if he didn't hold her in his arms.

"Vincent?"

"Yes."

"Would you please hold me?"

"Yes. I will hold you."

He reached his arm around her shoulders and pulled her close to him, then settled back against the cushions with her in his arms.

"I don't want you to worry, Grace. Getting upset cannot be good for you." He placed his hand over hers where it rested on her stomach, then kissed the top of her head.

"Do you know what frightened me the most?" she said, trying to keep her voice steady. "Even more than the thought of having to spend the rest of my life without you?"

"No."

Huge tears spilled down her cheeks and she wiped them away with her fingers. "It was the thought of having to live out my life knowing that I hadn't told you recently how much I love you."

She heard and felt him take in air. "Grace, I—"

She reached up and placed a finger against his lips. "I don't expect you to say anything. It's not your fault I've fallen so hopelessly in love with you. It's a choice I made with my eyes wide open." She snuggled closer to him, knowing there were things she had to say that couldn't be put off.

"I've known from the first that you couldn't love me back."

"Grace, I—"

"It's all right, Vincent," she interrupted. "I understand why you aren't able to risk your heart. I realize that if it hadn't been for my deception you wouldn't have married again. That I put you in this awkward position."

Grace felt his hold on her tighten, and a lump formed in her throat when he kissed the top of her head. Her voice was barely more than a whisper. The emotion weighed so heavily inside her. "I want you to know I wouldn't change anything if given the chance."

She placed her palm against his chest and held it there. "Now I would like a favor and a promise, Vincent."

"Anything, Your Grace."

"The promise first. I want you to swear you will never keep things from me again. I've led my whole life fearing the unknown. Living with my father was trial enough. I learned I could deal with anything as long as I knew what I was up against. Will you promise me that, Vincent?"

She heard him chuckle. "I have underestimated you again, haven't I? I should have remembered the courage you keep telling me you have."

"Yes, Your Grace. You should have remembered."

Grace shifted in Vincent's arms and lifted her hand to cup his cheek. "Now, my favor." She rubbed her thumb across his lips. "I would like my husband to take me upstairs."

She saw the doubt on his face.

"Are you sure, Grace?"

"Oh, yes. I'm very sure."

Vincent lowered his head and captured her lips, kissing her deeply and desperately. She matched his kisses, then let him help her to her feet. With his arms around her, they walked out of the study and across the foyer. Grace refused to acknowledge the grin on Carver's face as she and Vincent made their way up the stairs.

Just as she refused to think about the papers Vincent had had drawn up and the reason he thought they were imperative.

* * *

She loved him.

Vincent stared at the papers on his desk in front of him without really seeing them. Instead, all he could think of was what Grace had said four days ago when he'd held her. What she'd repeated as she lay in his arms. She loved him.

He looked up to where she sat in the overstuffed chair he'd brought in for her. She sat as gracefully as a very pregnant woman could sit and leaned her head against the side of the chair. Her eyes were closed, but he knew she was only resting. The minute he moved, her eyes snapped open as if she needed to watch him to make sure he was safe.

Oh God, but he loved her. More than he thought it was possible to love anyone. And it scared him to death.

He looked at her small, fragile body, then down at the mound that was his babe. He broke out in a cold sweat every time he thought of her trying to birth it. The fear he felt forced him to struggle to take a breath.

She turned and moaned. Then clutched her hand to her side. He knew she was uncomfortable, but not once did she complain.

"Grace," he said, walking over to where she sat. "I have a little more work to do here, but I want you to go upstairs and rest until I'm finished."

"I'm fine, Vincent."

"No. You're not. You need to lie down. Besides, I can't get any work done with you here. I'm too tempted to sit beside you and kiss you until neither of us can think straight."

"Mmm. That sounds delightful." Her mouth lifted to a warm smile.

"To you, maybe. To me it's just damned uncomfortable."

She laughed, and the sound filled the room like sunshine on a cloudy, dreary day. "Go on, now. I'll be up to check on you as soon as I'm finished."

She let him help her to her feet. "Very well. I don't know why, but I am quite tired today."

"Then you should rest." He kissed her on the forehead, then walked with her toward the door. They stopped as Carver entered on a knock.

"Mr. Germaine and a Mr. Percy Parker are here to see you, Your Grace."

"Show them in, Carver."

Carver left, and Grace turned to face Vincent. "Perhaps I should stay, Vincent. Perhaps they've heard something about Fentington."

Vincent put his arm around her shoulder and escorted her toward the door. "If it's anything important, I'll tell you."

She worried her lower lip. "Promise me you won't leave me. I don't want to be left alone, Vincent."

"I'm not going anywhere except to take you to your room."

Vincent wrapped his arm around her and led her to the door as Germaine and Parker entered.

"Your Grace," they both greeted.

Grace nodded politely. "Mr. Germaine. Mr. Parker."

Parker went into the room, but Germaine lingered. His gaze lowered to her protruding stomach. The look on his face was one of surprise, but he recovered quickly and reached for her hand and brought it to his lips. "May I say you look radiant?"

"How kind of you, Cousin," Grace said on a laugh. "As you can see, I have blossomed since we last visited several months ago."

His gaze moved back to her stomach. "I see it won't be long before you present Raeborn with his heir. Much sooner than I anticipated. My most heartfelt congratulations to you both."

Grace smiled. "Thank you. We are both looking forward to the event."

"I'm sure you are," Germaine said on a polite bow.

Grace looked toward Vincent, then back to Germaine. "It was nice seeing you again, but if you will excuse me, I was about to retire."

"Of course. Good day, Your Grace."

Vincent ushered Grace to the door. He was annoyed with the way his cousin had looked at her with a belittling expression because Grace was so close to delivering. As if the fact that Grace had conceived their babe before their wedding lowered Germaine's opinion of her.

"Please, make yourselves comfortable," he said, looking over his shoulder to the side table where several crystal decanters of liquor sat. "I'll escort Her Grace upstairs and return shortly."

"Of course, Raeborn. Take your time."

Vincent walked Grace to her room and assured her he had no intention of leaving the house, then walked back to the study where his cousin and Parker waited.

"What have you found out?" Vincent sat in the chair behind his desk. Percival Parker sat in the wing chair in front of him to his left, and his cousin sat in the chair to his right.

"We found him, Your Grace," Mr. Parker said, a smile of satisfaction on his face.

Germaine leaned forward in his chair. "He's been hiding in a house on Border's Lane."

The muscles in Vincent's jaw tightened.

"He's been staying with a Mrs. Jordean," Parker added. "She runs an establishment that caters to gentlemen who have peculiar tastes."

Vincent's stomach turned. "Is he still there?"

"He left that establishment a few hours ago. I followed him on foot until he reached the market area, then he hired a hansom cab and I lost him. But don't worry. We know where to find him now. He can't hide for long."

Vincent slid back his chair and looked out the window behind his desk. An uncontrollable fury grew inside him, fury increasing every time he thought of the attempts on his life and on Grace's.

"What are you going to do, Raeborn?"

Vincent slowly turned to face his guests. "I'm not going to give him a chance to try to kill me again. Hire as many men as you need, Parker. But I want that house watched twenty-four hours a day. The minute he shows up, I want to know it."

"Do you want us to go in after him?"

"No. I want to be there. I'll wait to hear from you."

Both Parker and Kevin smiled, but Vincent didn't. How could one smile when it was likely that before the sun set on tomorrow he'd be responsible for a human being's death?

* * *

Grace woke the next morning with a nagging backache. She attributed her restless night to Vincent, Baron Fentington, Kevin Germaine, and Mr. Parker. They were all responsible for her fitful sleep.

Perhaps that was why she felt so strange today. Too little sleep, too much worry, and the premonition that something she could not control was about to happen.

Grace finished her morning routine and went in search of Vincent. She didn't know why, but she felt an overwhelming need to be close to him. To keep him close to her. It was just another phase of this pregnancy she couldn't explain. Her sharpened awareness that something was not right.

She'd felt it from the moment Germaine and Parker left yesterday. Vincent had been quiet and withdrawn, but each time she asked him what was wrong, he answered that it was nothing. Only that Parker had seen Fentington, but that he'd lost him. Nothing to be concerned over.

Grace walked into the dining room. Vincent sat at the table, a half-filled plate still in front of him.

"There you are." She walked to him and accepted the kiss he placed on her cheek.

"Good morning, Grace. You look especially lovely today."

Grace smiled. "Thank you. Alice and I had to work a long time. It's difficult when your body is shaped like a clumsy barge sailing down the river instead of a sleek clipper ship. Caroline always looked so regal with her babes. Even just before she delivered she didn't look as cumbersome as I do now. And I still have over a month to wait."

"Perhaps it is because Caroline is several inches taller than you. She has more room to hide a babe."

Grace sat at the table with a heavy sigh. "That must be it."

Vincent took her plate to the sideboard and filled it. "Do you want eggs this morning?"

Grace nodded. "And one of those oat muffins and a fruit pastry. And a meat pie."

Vincent looked over his left shoulder and raised his eyebrows. "You must be hungry."

"It's your son. He's got quite the appetite."

Vincent smiled and placed her heaping plate in front of her. He sat in his chair and sipped his coffee while she ate.

"Perhaps you'd like company today, Grace? Perhaps Lady Josalyn or Lady Francine could visit this afternoon?"

"I'd rather spend the day with you." She ate another bite of coddled eggs with her toast and orange marmalade. "The nursery is almost finished. I want you to see it."

"Perhaps tomorrow, Grace."

Grace lifted her gaze to his. She put down her fork when she saw the serious expression on his face. "What's wrong, Vincent?"

"Nothing. I just thought you might like company is all."

A stabbing unease rushed through her body. Her breath caught and she clutched her hand to her stomach where a pain shot through her. She forced herself to take several deep breaths until the stitch in her side went away.

Vincent frowned. "Are you all right?"

"Yes," she said after the pain eased. "It was just a catch. I think I've been sitting too long. I need some exercise. Perhaps we could walk in the garden?"

"I'd love to. As soon as you've finished."

Grace ate a little more of her breakfast but didn't have the appetite she had before. Something was wrong. Even the babe felt it. Another cramp caught in her side.

Grace finished her tea, then walked with Vincent in the garden. She told herself it was her imagination that he held her closer than usual while they walked. And her imagination that when his fingers twined with hers, there was a greater urgency in his touch. And her imagination that he studied her face as if memorizing her every feature.

He stopped before the small pond in the center of the garden. A beautiful swan sailed gracefully across the quiet water, and several ducks swam back and forth, from side to side. She and Vincent sat together on a stone bench and watched the peaceful scene; then he kissed her.

She knew the desperation she felt in his kisses was not her imagination. It was real.

They stayed out-of-doors longer than usual, both of them hesitant to go inside. Both of them reluctant to have this perfect day end. But Grace needed to rest. The ache in her back was not lessening but increasing. And the stitch in her side refused to go away but darted through her with regularity.

"Are you ready to go in?" he asked a little later.

"Soon. I want to sit with you a little longer."

Vincent smiled at her, then lifted his gaze to the path when Carver came toward them.

"Mister Germaine is here, Your Grace. He seems to be in a—"

Vincent's cousin was fast on Carver's heels, nearly knocking the butler to the ground. "Raeborn! He's back. Parker's watching him."

Vincent stiffened beside Grace, and the blood in her veins turned to ice. A fear greater than any she'd ever known twisted its gnarled fingers around her heart.

"No, Vincent. Don't go. Leave him be."

"I can't, Grace. You know I can't."

"Then send for Wedgewood and Carmody. Don't go until they can go with you."

He didn't answer but pulled her into his arms and pressed a hard kiss to her mouth. "I'll be back soon. Don't worry." He dropped his arms from around her.

"Vincent, no." She couldn't keep the fear from her voice. Couldn't keep the panic from stealing the air she needed to breathe.

Vincent paused.

"Hurry, Raeborn!" Germaine bellowed. "Or you'll lose him."

"I have to go, Grace."

Vincent pulled her into his arms and pressed a last kiss to her mouth.

Grace was frantic to hold him and not let him leave. But one look at the determined expression on his face and she knew it was useless. She lifted her face and kissed him with all the passion she felt. With all the love she had for him.

He dropped his hands from around her and Grace hugged herself, the absence of his body from hers a loss that nearly took her to her knees.

"Carver."

Carver was instantly at their side.

"Take care of your mistress."

"With my life, Your Grace."

Vincent turned and was gone, the sound of his footsteps fading to silence.

Grace stared after him, fighting to keep the tears from consuming her. She hugged her arms around her bulging stomach and sucked in a gasp as another sharp pain stabbed through her.

Chapter 20

Grace paced Vincent's study like a caged animal. She needed to be here, in this room, where she felt closest to him. Where she could see him at his desk, breathe in the clean smell that always reminded her of him. Where she could close her eyes and hear the deep sound of his voice.

She rubbed her hands over their babe and fought the tears that wanted to fall. There had to be something she could do. She didn't know how she'd survive if something happened to him.

A picture of Vincent lying on the ground flashed through her mind, his face pale, his blood soaking into the dirt. She clamped her hands over her mouth to stop a cry from escaping. She never should have let him go. She should have done something to keep him here. At least until Wedgewood and Carmody arrived.

She continued pacing, then stopped when another sharp pain gripped her.

"Cook sent a tray," Carver said, opening the door for one of the downstairs maids to carry in hot tea and pastries. Deep worry lines etched his forehead. "Is everything all right, Your Grace?"

Grace took a deep breath and straightened her shoulders. "Yes, Carver. Tell Cook thank you."

"Of course, Your Grace."

Carver closed the door behind him and left her alone. Grace looked at the tea service and thought how routine and familiar the gold-leafed teapot with matching cups looked sitting there. The antithesis to the turmoil raging through her. She looked again to his desk, expecting to see him sitting there. She started when the door opened.

A breath caught in her throat. "Mr. Germaine?"

"Good afternoon again, Your Grace."

Her heart raced. She reached for something to steady her. "Is something wrong? Where's Vincent?"

"He's fine. Probably taking care of Fentington at this very moment."

"Then why have you come? You should be with him."

"Your husband was worried about you. He insisted I return to stay with you."

Grace tried to stamp down the questions that crowded her mind. What was wrong with Vincent that he'd send his cousin back here? She wasn't the one in danger. He was. "I'm perfectly safe, Mr. Germaine. Please go back to help Vincent."

He softly closed the door and walked into the room. "I'm afraid I promised I'd protect you." Germaine stopped beside the tray Cook had sent up.

"I see you were about to have tea. That sounds wonderful. Would you mind if I joined you?"

Grace's mind spun in confusion as Germaine sat in one of Vincent's oversize chairs and stretched out his legs. He smiled while he waited for her to pour, as if this were the most ordinary of days.

* * *

Vincent dismounted more than a block away from the house where his cousin said Fentington was hiding and made his way through the alley so he wouldn't be seen.

Vincent knew he should have gone for his brothers-in-law first but hadn't wanted to take the time. He was glad when Germaine volunteered to go for them. He wasn't sure what exactly would happen when he confronted Fentington and preferred to have Wedgewood and Carmody with him.

He didn't want to kill him if there was any other way. But Fentington hadn't left him any other option—except one. To force him to leave England and never come back.

Vincent pulled the gun from his pocket and stepped behind a hedgerow. He stayed protected as much as he could while he moved forward. Finally the house came into view.

Parker stood behind a large elm tree to the right of the house and nodded when he saw Vincent. Vincent nodded in return, then closed the gap between them.

He followed the walk, crouching low to get his best advantage, then froze when Fentington's voice bellowed from inside the door.

"Both of you! Step out where I can see you."

Vincent stood, his gun still hidden in his jacket pocket. He couldn't see Fentington, only the gun pointed at him from a crack in the door.

"Tell your lackey to step out, Raeborn."

Vincent lifted his hand and motioned for Parker to come forward.

Parker hesitated, then moved from his hiding place. When they were both in sight, the door opened and Fentington stepped out of the house.

His clothes were dirty and disheveled, and his hair was overly long. His face was shadowed by stubble that hadn't been shaved for weeks. For the first time ever, he wasn't in his usual white, but in black breeches and a dingy gray waistcoat and jacket. His shirt may have been white at one time but wasn't any longer.

"Come in," Fentington ordered, throwing open the door. "I'd offer you tea, but I'm afraid I gave the servants the day off."

Vincent walked through the door and stepped to the other side of the foyer.

Parker reluctantly followed.

Fentington lifted his pistol and pointed to the center of Vincent's chest. "Drop your guns to the floor and kick them over to me."

Vincent hesitated, then reached in his pocket and dropped his gun. Parker did the same, and they both kicked their weapons across the wood-paneled floor.

Fentington reached to pick up the gun closest to him, then turned. In one fluid motion, he raised the gun and fired.

Vincent jerked, then turned to where Parker had been.

His limp body dropped to the floor, a bullet hole in the center of his forehead, his eyes open in a deathly stare. The gun he'd attempted to pull out of his pocket was still clutched in his hand.

Vincent swallowed hard, then turned to face Fentington.

"Are you surprised?" Fentington asked.

Vincent steeled himself. Unless he could find a way to get Fentington's gun, it wouldn't be long and he'd be as dead as Parker. "Hardly. You forget. I've already been the recipient of one of your bullets."

Fentington frowned as if he wasn't sure what Vincent was talking about. Then a smile spread across his face. "Oh, yes. The bullet you took on your way to meet your lover."

Vincent sucked in a deep breath but held his tongue.

Fentington walked from one side of the room to the other, all the while keeping his gun aimed in Vincent's direction. "What would you say if I told you I didn't shoot you?"

"I'd probably call you a liar."

Fentington stopped in front of Vincent and stared at him, the look in his eyes turning darker, a muscle in his jaw twitching. "Look at him." He pointed at Parker's lifeless body lying on the floor.

Vincent turned his head and looked, then turned back toward Fentington.

Without warning, Fentington lifted his gun and fired over Vincent's shoulder.

Vincent felt air brush against his cheek, the bullet barely missing him. The shade on a lamp sitting on a table at the far side of the room shattered. Fentington pulled another gun from his pocket.

"If I had shot you, you'd be dead. I wouldn't have missed."

Vincent was confused. The first uncomfortable doubts rose to the surface. "I saw you. I saw your white horse," he said accusingly.

Fentington smiled. "I didn't say I wasn't there. I said I wasn't the one who shot you."

Fentington paced the room, and Vincent used the time to try to decipher what he was saying.

"Have you ever considered someone else might want you dead, Your Grace?"

Vincent glared at him. Fentington was forcing him to consider a possibility more reprehensible than any he could imagine. His mind rejected such a thought. "I saw you. Why else would you have been there?"

Fentington smiled. "I was watching her—your whore. I was supposed to marry her. I would have—until I found out she wasn't pure. That she'd already given herself to someone else." He flailed a hand through the air. "I could hardly take a harlot for my wife. Someone who'd given away what should have been mine."

Fentington waved his gun between them. "I wanted to know who she'd given herself to. So I followed her and waited. I knew her lover would eventually come to her." He laughed. "You can't imagine my surprise when I discovered it was *you*."

Fentington paced in front of him. There was a wild look in his eyes, a desperate expression on his face. This was a man who'd lost everything, including his self-respect. A man who would do anything to retaliate, to punish anyone he considered responsible for his fall.

Vincent's heart beat faster.

"How long had she been spreading her legs for you, Raeborn? Weeks? Months? More?"

The blood roared in Vincent's head.

"How rude of me to ask." Fentington gave a sadistic laugh, a demented laugh. "I can hardly expect you to tell your dirty little secrets, can I?"

A malicious grin lifted the corners of Fentington's mouth.

"You cannot imagine the joy I felt when I saw you get shot. Someone else was doing what I'd only dreamt of doing."

Fentington stepped closer. "You deserved to die. You'd stolen the woman I was supposed to marry and embarrassed me in front of the *ton*. My reputation is ruined! I wanted you dead. Oh, how I wanted you to suffer for the damage you'd caused." He shook his head. "But I didn't have the courage."

Vincent tried to digest what Fentington was saying. He wanted him to believe he hadn't fired the gun, but it *had* to have been him. It *had* to have been.

"And do you know why?"

Fentington paced in front of him again while Vincent studied his actions. His movements were jerky and agitated. He caressed the gun in his hand as if it were a precious keepsake. Vincent's breaths became shorter. His fear more pronounced.

"Do you?"

Vincent shook his head.

"Because no matter how great I thought your sins were, no matter how vile and insignificant I thought you were in God's eyes, or how much I despised you, killing you would have lowered me to your level. Killing you would have made me no better than the power-wielding creature you are.

So I turned to prayer. I prayed God would snuff your life out like you had snuffed out mine."

Fentington stepped close to Vincent and pressed the gun beneath Vincent's chin. "Just that swiftly, I thought my prayers were being answered. While I watched you ride to meet your lover, God sent someone else to do what I was not brave enough to do. God sent another of your enemies to kill you."

Fentington walked to the far side of the room and glared back at Vincent. "I was going to leave after he shot you. But when he stayed, so did I."

"You saw who shot me?"

Fentington smiled. "Of course I did."

"Who was it?"

Fentington ignored him as he continued his story. "Later, I watched him barricade the doors and set fire to the house."

He waved his gun through the air. "I thought for sure you would all die. But you were spared again."

The expression on his face turned harsher, more intense. "That's when I realized that I was in as much danger as you."

Vincent tried to follow Fentington's reasoning but couldn't. "How so?"

"Don't you see? The killer wasn't satisfied with just your death. He intended to kill your wife too." Fentington shook his head. "He confirmed my suspicion the night he pushed her out in the street in front of that carriage." He dragged the back of his hand across his forehead. "For as much as I wanted you dead, I didn't want her to die too.

If something happened to her, the world would reach the same conclusion you did—that I was to blame."

Vincent was desperate to try to make sense of what Fentington was telling him. "Why would anyone want to harm Grace?"

Fentington barked a loud laugh. "Because of the child, Your Grace."

Vincent took a step away from Fentington. He didn't want to understand what Fentington was implying.

Fentington laughed again. "You want it to be me, don't you? You want me to be the one who has repeatedly tried to kill you and your wife so you don't have to admit there is someone who hates you more than I do?"

"It *is* you!"

"Oh, Raeborn. Surely you can think of someone else who can't let you or your heir live."

Blood thundered inside Vincent's head. His chest ached as he struggled to breathe. What if Fentington was telling the truth?

"Think, Your Grace. Who is the only person who would benefit from your death? The only person who will lose everything once your heir is born. *If* the child is a boy?"

Vincent shook his head.

Fentington paced the floor, then stopped beside Parker's body. "How did you learn about Mr. Parker's talents, Your Grace?"

Fentington laughed. "Let me guess. I'll wager your cousin, Mr. Germaine, suggested him. Am I correct?"

Vincent swiped at the perspiration streaming down his face.

Fentington looked around the room. "Where is your cousin? He seems to be missing."

Vincent swallowed hard. "He went for help. To get Wedgewood and Carmody, in case I needed them."

"They should be here by now. Don't you think?"

Vincent's knees weakened beneath him.

Fentington pointed to the door. "Go ahead. Look. They've had more than enough time to arrive. Do you see them?"

Vincent didn't go to the door. He knew he wouldn't see them. Knew Fentington was telling the truth. That his cousin was the one who'd tried to kill him. That if Germaine wanted the Raeborn title and wealth, he would have to make sure Grace died before she could present him with an heir.

The blood drained from his head. Nothing had prepared him for the debilitating fear he felt thinking that Grace might be in danger—that he might lose her.

Vincent looked into Fentington's face and knew beyond a doubt who wanted him dead. His heart fell like a rock to the pit of his stomach.

Fentington shook his head. "I thought I wanted you dead—but I don't. I thought I wanted *her* to suffer for making a fool of me, but I don't." He paced the room, then stopped. "I visited my sister," he said, facing Vincent. "She made me realize how unbalanced our father was. Then she made me see how closely I resembled him. The comparison made me sick. I don't want to be anything like him. I've already done enough damage."

Fentington held out his pistol for Vincent to take. "You'd best hurry. He can't afford to let her live."

"Thank you," Vincent said as he grabbed Fentington's gun and ran from the house. His lungs burned, the breath froze in his chest. What if he was already too late?

Chapter 21

Grace didn't know why, but an uneasy feeling gripped her and refused to let go. "How did you get in here? Why didn't Carver announce you?"

Vincent's cousin stood, then walked the length of the room, his footsteps slow and cautious. "I'm afraid he didn't hear my knock, so I took the liberty of letting myself in. I hope you don't mind?"

Grace knew there had been no knock. Just as she knew that whatever reason Vincent's cousin had for being here was not good. "I think I prefer to be alone, Mr. Germaine. I'll ring for Carver to show you—"

He held up his hand to stop her from rising. "I'm afraid I can't allow you to do that."

She took a closer look at him. His handsome face was tinged with hard lines she hadn't noticed before; the look in his eyes had turned cold and dangerous. Her pulse raced. "Why are you here?"

The smile he gave her sent shivers down her spine.

"To stay with you while your husband takes care of the evil, sinister Baron Fentington. Of course, Raeborn thinks I've gone for help. To get the authorities and Wedgewood and Carmody. He'll discover soon enough I haven't."

Grace stood, then took one step away from him, but Kevin Germaine reached out his hand and grabbed her upper arm to stop her from getting too far from him. Fear raced through her as she looked at his hand squeezing her arm painfully.

"I want you to leave, Mr. Germaine."

"I'm afraid I can't do that, Your Grace. Not until I've accomplished what I came to do."

"And that is?"

"Why, kill you, of course."

Grace stumbled backward. Full terror gripped every part of her body when she looked at him. He was serious.

Grace twisted to the side and his fingers lost their grip. Her arm burned where he'd held her. "Get out! Car—"

He pulled a gun out of his pocket and held it where she could see it. "If you don't want to see Carver die in front of you, I suggest you keep quiet, Your Grace."

Grace took several deep breaths, then nodded that she understood.

"Very good." Germaine dropped his hand and looked at the tea service still sitting on the table. "It's regrettable we don't have time for a cup of tea. It would be enjoyable to sit here and visit a while before you suffer your unfortunate accident."

Grace clutched her stomach as another pain shot through her. She wished they would ease. If only she could lie down for a few minutes, she was sure they would. "Why are you doing this?"

He walked to a small table with three crystal decanters on it and poured a little brandy into a glass. "The money, of course. *All* of Raeborn's money. The money that should have come to me, but now will go to…" Germaine drew the back of his hand over his mouth and pointed to Grace's stomach. Her hands instinctively reached out to protect her babe.

He laughed. "I was so sure he would never take another wife. I didn't even see it coming until it was too late." He emptied his glass and glared at her. "How did you do it? You obviously spread your legs for him long before you married. You must have realized getting his child in you was the only way you could force him to marry you. I just can't believe he was such a fool he didn't realize what you were doing."

Grace felt her cheeks burn.

"Oh well, it doesn't matter now. Your accident will solve my problems."

"Surely money isn't worth killing an innocent babe?"

"Isn't worth it! Bloody hell, woman. Do you know how much wealth is involved? Enough to keep me in style for ten lifetimes."

Germaine held the gun on her with one hand and sloshed more brandy into his glass with the other. "Instead, your bastard husband has condemned me to the life of a *country farmer*. Told me if I managed the pittance he gave me well enough, I'd have more than enough on which to live."

Grace watched Germaine's face turn a mottled red, his features distort in anger.

"What kind of a fool does he think I am? How does he think I can exist on the measly quarterly allowance I've been allotted? That pitiful amount isn't substantial enough to support me for one week of the life I am accustomed to living. And what's even more astonishing is that he honestly believes he's being generous!"

"Perhaps if you talk to him he'll—"

Germaine slashed his hand through the air. "I want it all! It should have been mine. It *could* have been. Except that Raeborn's father was born just minutes before mine."

"But it still won't be yours," Grace argued. "Even with me dead, the money is still Raeborn's."

"I'm counting on Fentington to solve that problem for me. With Mr. Parker's help, of course." He took another sip and smiled. "You are probably a widow already, Your Grace. It is highly unlikely Raeborn will survive his confrontation with Baron Fentington. But then..." He laughed. "I swear your husband has as many lives as the proverbial cat. But this time I've taken care of things myself. If Fentington doesn't rid the world of your husband, Parker will."

Grace felt light-headed. "It was you?" she whispered as if she couldn't believe what her mind was telling her. "*You* tried to kill Vincent?"

"I only regret I didn't get the job done before he married you. Then it wouldn't be necessary for me to kill you, too. But..." He shrugged his shoulders.

Grace saw the evil determination in his eyes and knew words would do no good. There was no way she could talk him out of killing her. She slowly edged her way to Vincent's desk.

She knew the gun Vincent kept in the drawer was no longer there, but perhaps there was a knife of some sort. Anything she could use to protect herself.

She tried to stall him. "You won't get away with this. Vincent will know it was you."

Germaine smiled and walked the length of the room. "No, he won't. He won't even suspect me. Even if he somehow escapes Parker, the shock of finding you and his heir dead will put him in a state of depression. He loves you, you know? I'm not sure if he loved either of his other wives, but anyone who sees the two of you together knows he loves you. It's a shame, really." He slowly sipped his brandy. "For Raeborn to finally have it all and lose it."

Grace slowly opened one drawer just a crack and glanced down. Nothing. Then another. Kevin continued as if lost in his reverie. Lost in the delusion of his perfectly laid plan.

"No one will even question it when he's found with a bullet to his head. Perhaps Fentington will get credit for Raeborn's death."

Grace placed her hand on the papers strewn on the top of the desk. Perhaps beneath one of them…

Her hand closed over a letter opener.

"I couldn't believe my stroke of good luck when Raeborn assumed Fentington was the guilty party." A smile brightened Germaine's face. "He didn't suspect me for a moment, did he?"

Grace jerked her head up. "No. Not for a moment."

A frown covered Germaine's face. "Enough! We've wasted enough time. Come with me, Your Grace. I'd like for us to take a stroll in the garden. I seem to remember a lovely pond somewhere near the center. In my youth, I was always warned to be careful and not get too close to the edge. The water's quite deep, you know."

Grace clasped her hand around the letter opener just as another pain ripped through her body. She couldn't hide it. She leaned heavily against the desk and gasped for breath.

Germaine's eyes opened wide. She saw his first sign of nervousness. "I see I am almost too late," he said, wiping a sheen of perspiration from his forehead. "You and Raeborn would have really shocked society with an arrival this early."

"Please," Grace begged, holding her breath until the pain eased. "It's not too late. If you leave now, I promise I'll—"

"No! There cannot be an heir. That babe you are carrying will inherit everything, and I'll have nothing again. Nothing! Just like I've had my whole life. Always left to beg for the money I need to live. I deserve it. I've always deserved it. And I'll not let a babe steal it from me."

Grace stared at him. Bitter hatred tinged every word, vile jealousy shot from his glare. He truly hated Vincent. Why hadn't she seen it before? Germaine's greed was a living, breathing cancer destroying his mind, body, and soul. His loathing was so intense he actually believed the Raeborn title and wealth belonged to him.

Germaine held out his hand. "Why don't we take that walk, Your Grace. If anyone asks, you can tell them you need some fresh air. I am merely accompanying you."

Grace shook her head.

"Now!" he bellowed, lifting the gun in his hand and taking a step toward her.

Grace grabbed the letter opener and tucked it into the folds of her skirt. She'd wait until they were out of the room before trying to make her escape. Surely Carver would hear her and help, or one of the gardeners or footmen?

She stumbled as he pulled her toward the terrace doors, his grip on her arm biting into her flesh. Then another pain overtook her, this one so severe she doubled over from the strength of it.

Grace clutched her hand to her stomach as her first cry echoed in the room.

Oh, the pain. This couldn't be happening. It wasn't time. She couldn't have her babe yet. Not for at least four more weeks.

Another spasm gripped her, and she knew.

So did Germaine. The panic on his face terrified her. "Move! You'll not have his babe!" He jerked her arm and dragged her across the room. When they reached the French doors, he pushed them open and pulled her onto the terrace.

She knew if she had any hope of escaping, she'd have to do it before the next pain came. They were already too severe. And too close. Another warning that something was not right. A warning that the babe she'd promised Vincent would be birthed without problems was going to turn her into a liar.

"If you'd be so kind as to hurry, Your Grace," he said, his grip on her arm tightening.

"Please, Kevin."

"Don't waste your breath, Your Grace. It won't do you any good. It's much too late to change what's about to happen."

A frightening chill shattered her self-control. He seemed so calm, his voice terrifyingly pleasant, the serene expression on his face frigid. When he looked at her, the malevolent glare in his eyes told her he would not hesitate to kill both her and the unborn babe she carried. And Vincent later, if Fentington and Parker didn't do it for him.

Grace crossed the terrace and stopped at the steps. She held on to the cement railing with her left hand and the letter opener with the right, waiting for the opportunity to use it to escape. From her precarious foothold on the steps, she knew her best advantage would be when she reached the bottom.

She took the first step, then the second, planning her every move, anticipating any problem.

Grace tightened her grip around the handle of the letter opener, turning it so that when she brought it down, she would have the leverage she needed to do the most harm. She took her last step and stopped.

"Is something wrong, Your Grace?"

Grace turned her head to look into Carver's worried face. The butler walked across the terrace, his protective determination propelling him into danger.

"Is everything all right, Your Grace? Would you like me to send for Alice?"

"I…uh. No, Carver. I was just…"

Carver didn't stop but continued toward them.

Germaine's fingers clasped around the arm she had anchored on the railing and squeezed. The air caught in her breast, and a terrorizing fear as powerful as a raging thunderstorm shot through her. She prayed Carver would stop. Prayed he'd leave before—

"Please, allow me to escort Her Grace, Mr. Germaine," Carver said. "I'm afraid I didn't hear you knock or—"

Without warning, Germaine turned and fired his gun. Grace screamed, then watched the expression on Carver's face turn from surprise to disbelief before he slumped to the stone terrace. Blood darkened the front of his pristine white shirt and he lay motionless.

"Carver! No!"

Grace reacted with uncontrollable fury. She raised the letter opener and spun around. A picture of Carver's injured body flashed through her mind as she lifted her arm and brought it down with all the force she could manage.

Germaine didn't anticipate her attack, and by the time he reacted it was too late.

Grace sank her weapon into him as far as she could push it. Cloth ripped, skin tore, and she felt the grind of metal penetrating muscle.

Germaine bolted, then stared at the pointed opener sticking out of his shoulder. He flashed her a look of disbelief before he pulled it out of his shoulder, then yanked her down the path, through a flower bed to the pond's edge. Nothing would save her if he pushed her in.

She struggled, but the pains robbed her of any strength to fight him.

She was going to die without ever seeing Vincent again. Was going to die before she held her babe in her arms. Was going to die before she saw the look on Vincent's face when he saw his son for the first time.

Another white-hot stab of pain speared through her and she lost the little strength she had left.

She fought to stop the scream but couldn't. The pain was too great. One clutching grip after another reached deep inside her and blocked out all sense of reality. She couldn't fight both Germaine and the pain any longer.

She clutched her stomach and cradled the child that would never be born.

Chapter 22

No!

Vincent sped onto the terrace as Grace's pain-filled scream rent the air. He raced past the spot where Carver lay on the stones and ran toward Grace's cry for help. Every breath of air left his body when he saw his cousin pulling his wife toward the water's edge.

"Germaine!"

Germaine spun around, jerking Grace closer to the pond. Vincent knew with just a push she'd fall into the water.

"Let her go!"

Vincent raced toward Grace.

"Stop right there!" Germaine ordered, pulling Grace in front of him to use her as a shield. "Don't take another step or I'll push her."

Vincent raised his hands in surrender and stared at the agony in Grace's eyes. There was a pleading in her gaze that wrenched his heart from his chest. "It's over, Germaine. You can have it all. The money. The estates. Everything. Just let her go."

Germaine laughed. "How generous of you, Raeborn. Now that it's too late."

"No. It's not too late. I'll have my solicitor sign everything over to you. It will all be yours. Everything. Just let Grace go."

Germaine glared at him, the demented look on his face so hate-filled it sent shivers down Vincent's spine.

"Let her go? And then what? You will just forgive and forget this little misunderstanding?" Germaine laughed, but there was an unnatural sound to his laughter. "You still don't understand, do you? Your wife will not live, Your Grace. And neither will you."

Germaine tightened his grasp and brought Grace closer to the water.

She was losing her foothold on the loose dirt near the edge, and clods of earth fell into the pond with a dangerous splash.

A malicious grin changed Germaine's features with each spatter, and he raised his right hand and pointed his gun at Vincent's chest. Vincent knew he was going to die. Grace must have known it too.

With a tortured cry, she turned sharply and hit Germaine's wounded shoulder.

He cried out in pain and lifted his uninjured arm. His hand connected with Grace's cheek and her head snapped back from the force of the blow. Vincent saw red. White-hot fury erupted inside him.

He heard her scream, then saw her double over in pain. Her sudden movement pushed his cousin off-balance, and when Grace twisted to the side, Vincent raised the gun Fentington had given him and fired.

Germaine stared with horrified disbelief at the growing circle of blood that covered his chest, then jerked forward and fell headfirst into the water.

"Grace!"

Vincent rushed toward the edge of the pond and knelt beside her. His hands trembled as he reached out to touch her. He was afraid she'd shatter if he moved her.

She was lying on the ground, her body curled into a tight ball, her hands clutching her stomach. He knew something was terribly wrong. Her face was white, her skin hot and clammy, rivers of perspiration already dampening her forehead and cheeks. And she was in pain. He could see it in her eyes.

"Grace?" He placed his hand on her shoulder and turned her. He stopped when she cried out. "I'm here now, Grace. You're safe."

She gasped, her breathing harsh and labored. "He shot Carver. He's hurt."

"It's all right, Grace. We'll take care of Carver. Are you hurt? Did he hurt you?"

"It's the babe…Vincent. The babe's…coming."

A vicious blow jabbed him in the gut and he sucked in a harsh breath. He squeezed shut his eyes as he tried to keep his heart from leaping from his chest.

She gasped again and clutched her stomach when another wave of pain hit her. "It's not time…Vincent. It's too…soon."

"It's all right, Grace. I'll send for the doctor."

"No. Caroline. Send for…Caroline. She'll know what to do."

"Alice!" Vincent yelled, but Alice was already there, tears flowing down her pale cheeks. "Get your mistress's room ready and have someone see to Carver."

"He's already being looked after, Your Grace," she said, then raced back into the house.

Vincent cast a quick look down the path and saw a crowd of servants staring down at him, ready to do whatever he commanded.

"Someone go to Lady Wedgewood's and tell her to come immediately. Make sure she knows to hurry. And someone get a doctor for Carver."

Two footmen raced back into the house.

Vincent turned his attention back to Grace. Her breathing was rapid and shallow, her chest heaving as she struggled through the pain. He held her until her breaths came more easily, then placed his arms behind her. "I'm going to move you now, Grace. Put your arm around my shoulder."

Grace nodded and placed her arm around him. Her grasp seemed so weak; her chest heaved with exertion. He picked her up, thinking she'd weigh much more than she did. Her lightness was another reminder of how delicate she was. How fragile. How easily he could lose her.

He'd only taken a few steps before another wave of pain racked her body. He held her tight while she rode out the worst of it, then carried her into the house and up the stairs.

He thought he knew fear. Thought he'd become immune to the helplessness. But nothing had prepared him for this. And the babe was coming too soon.

He wasn't ready to lose her yet. He hadn't had enough time with her. Enough time to love her.

He took huge, gasping gulps of air and held her.

"Vincent."

"Yes."

"You're worrying."

"No, I'm—" He swallowed past the lump in his throat. "Yes, perhaps a little."

"Have you forgotten my promise?"

"No. I remember what you told me."

"Then you know there is no need for you to worry. I will be…fine. I have enough courage for…both of us."

Vincent fought to keep his worry from showing. "I will try my best to remember that."

They reached the room they'd shared since they were married. Alice met them at the doorway. "Stay with me, Vincent. There are some things I want to say before there isn't time."

Vincent nodded, then helped Alice get Grace out of her dress and into a gown. Twice they had to stop. The pains were coming with more frequency and more severity. When each attack was over, she collapsed back against the mattress, gasping for breath. He held her close, needing to touch her. To be alone with her.

"Alice," he said over his shoulder. "Go down and wait for Lady Wedgewood. Bring her up the minute she arrives."

"Yes, Your Grace." Alice bobbed a curtsy and ran off.

"I would go through this for you if I could," he whispered, cupping her face in his palms.

She laughed, but it was a pain-filled laugh. "I think I would let you." She looked at him, then clasped his hand and held tight as another spasm took her.

His blood ran cold. He didn't think the pain would ever ease, but finally she breathed a sigh and lifted her head.

"Would you kiss me, Vincent? Please. Before the next pain comes. Before Linny gets here."

Vincent lowered his head and kissed her with all the passion he felt for her. She kissed him back, and he couldn't mistake the desperation. The fear.

He cupped her face in his hands and kissed her again. Then looked at her. "I love you, Grace."

She tipped her head and there were tears in her eyes. "I've known for a long time that you did. But I'm glad you told me."

He kissed her again, this time slowly and tenderly.

"I've prayed that someday…you'd be able to look past how I deceived you…and learn to care for me. For a long while…I told myself it wouldn't matter if you couldn't. But it does. Because I love you so desperately. I couldn't bear to think that you couldn't love me…just a little."

"I do love you, Grace. More than a little. More than life itself. Promise me you won't ever forget that."

"I won't—" she started, then ended in a cry when another pain hit her.

"I think…I'd like…Caroline to…hurry," she gasped, sagging against him as the pain eased.

"Grace?"

He turned toward the doorway to see Caroline rushing into the room. She wore a concerned expression she tried to mask with a smile.

"Linny. I think my babe…has decided he wants to be born sooner…instead of later."

"It's all right. There's never been a mother yet who's had a say in when her babe comes."

Lady Caroline took charge of the room, ordering Alice to stoke the fire and have plenty of blankets warmed. Then to keep water warm in the kitchen and to show Her Grace's sisters up the minute they arrived.

Alice scurried from the room, issuing orders to the servants waiting to be of service.

"You'd best go down now, Your Grace," she said, turning to Vincent. "Grace will be fine. We'll all see to it."

Vincent stood at the side of the bed where he'd been sitting and let loose of Grace's hand. "I love you, Grace," he said, kissing her once more.

"And I love you."

He moved to step away from her then stopped. "I need a promise, Grace."

She looked at him through pain-filled eyes.

"Promise you will not make me wait too long. I don't think I can survive it if you do."

"I will try my best, Your Grace. And I need a promise from you too."

"Anything."

"That you will not worry."

He tried to smile. "I will try my best," he answered, knowing neither of them had the power to keep the promises they'd just made.

"And take care of…Adledge. Don't let him…wager any of his children tonight. Mary was terribly upset…when she found out they'd lost Timothy…to Hansley."

"I will try my best."

* * *

She'd lied to him.

She was making him wait a long time. Longer than he thought he could stay sane.

All six of his brothers-in-law were here with him, had been here for the past eight hours. They'd stood by him while he explained to the authorities what had happened, then Hansley and Baldwin had taken Germaine's body to his town house to be laid out.

Vincent checked on Carver and was assured by the doctor that with sufficient rest he would heal. Then he went back to the study to begin the endless torment.

He knew he should be grateful to his brothers-in-law. They did their best to keep him occupied, to entertain him and immerse him in topics they knew interested him. But nothing helped. He couldn't keep his mind on anything but Grace suffering upstairs.

What if she lost the battle? She was so damn small. How did he expect her to birth his babe? And the babe wasn't even supposed to come yet. It was more than a month early. Even he had recognized the worry on Caroline's face when she entered the room. The risks of delivering a babe safely were that much greater when it decided to come early.

Bloody hell! He couldn't lose her. He couldn't live without her.

He rubbed at the back of his neck and paced the room again, ignoring Carmody's attempt to include him in their conversation. He couldn't take this much longer. If he didn't hear soon, he'd—

He turned around and stopped short when Lady Sarah entered the room. Her hands were clutched in front of her and there was a smile on her face that didn't quite reach her eyes. Her face was pale and her worry was obvious. But the optimism he heard in her voice let him hope she was not bringing him bad news.

"The babe's not here yet, Your Grace. But Grace sent me down to tell you she's sure it won't be long now."

"How is she?"

Lady Sarah started to give him a glowing report of Grace's condition, then paused as if she realized only the truth would suffice. "She's tired, Your Grace."

Vincent thought he would be ill. His heart lodged in his throat. He stood rooted to the spot, yet wondered how he managed to stand unassisted. His knees didn't seem strong enough to hold him.

"She wanted me to come down to assure you she was all right and to remind you of your promise. She wants your word you will not worry. Your son will be here soon."

Vincent dragged his hand across his jaw and swallowed past the lump in his throat. "Please remind my wife that she promised it would not take overly long. Tell her I think it has been far too long already. I would like this finished."

Lady Sarah smiled. "I'll tell her, Your Grace."

Lady Sarah gave her husband a concerned look, then turned to go back upstairs.

Lord Hansley followed his wife out of the room, and Vincent heard the two of them whispering quietly before she climbed the stairs.

"I'm sure it won't be long now," Hansley said when he came back into the room. "It just seems so terribly long because there is nothing we can do to help."

All the other husbands agreed, and Vincent prayed that what Hansley said was true. Because if it wasn't over soon he was going to lose his mind.

* * *

Four more hours passed, and Vincent knew something was terribly wrong. Mary came down after Sarah to reassure him everything was going as it should, then Francine an hour or so later.

No one had come down for almost two hours now and he knew why.

Grace was dying. Birthing his babe was taking her life.

He paced the room from one side to the other, willing the frantic fear to calm, but it wouldn't. He couldn't lose her. He couldn't. He loved her. Loved her more than he thought it possible to ever love a woman. And he found himself doing exactly what Wedgewood said when Caroline was being delivered of her child. He prayed harder than he'd ever prayed before and promised God that if He brought her safely through this, he'd never touch her again. He'd never risk her life by getting her with child again.

Except Vincent meant it. If God would just let Grace live, he swore he'd never plant his seed inside her again.

If only she'd live.

The weight of his fear pressed more heavily against him, and Vincent couldn't take any more. He had to know what was going on upstairs. Had to be with her. If she was going to die, he didn't want her to die alone.

Vincent turned, then stormed from the room. Wedgewood called after him. Or perhaps it was Carmody. He didn't stop to see who, but kept walking. He raced across the foyer and took the stairs two at a time.

He didn't hesitate but threw open the door and entered her room. He was greeted by a loud, agonized moan, a cry for release as terrifying as any he'd ever heard.

His heart stopped for longer than just one beat and he feared it would never start again.

"Grace?"

Grace's sisters turned, their expressions filled with surprise.

"Your Grace. You shouldn't—"

Vincent walked past Lady Francine, who was the first to speak. He went directly to Grace and took her hand from Lady Josalyn's grasp, then sat down beside her. She looked exhausted, her hair wet and plastered to her head, her face drawn, her complexion pale. She was in the midst of a violent contraction, her body heaving in pain. Vincent ached so he wanted to cry. Oh, what she was enduring for him. For their babe.

The contraction ended. Another followed.

"Grace?"

"Vincent…you shouldn't…have come."

She was panting ferociously, the pains one right after another now. One of her sisters wiped her face with a cloth. Another stood by with a blanket. Another with more towels.

"I couldn't stay away any longer. I thought perhaps you might need me."

She smiled a weak smile and panted faster. "I will always need you, Your Grace."

He held her hand as she cried out.

"Push now, Grace," Lady Caroline ordered, moving to the foot of the bed. "Push!"

Grace cried out and pushed.

When the severity lessened, she sank back onto the pillows, her chest heaving with exhaustion.

"Your babe's almost here, Grace. This next time will do it."

"Vincent!" Grace cried out and clutched his hand.

Her scream rent the air, the blood-curdling agony of it a pain he felt to his toes.

"Push, Grace. Push!"

Grace's head lifted from the bed and she pushed harder.

Her hand squeezed his, and Vincent looked down as his son made his way into the world.

The babe was small and red and wrinkled, but the most beautiful sight Vincent had ever seen. The babe gave a lusty cry, and Vincent's heart burst with joy.

"Your son, Your Grace," Lady Caroline said, working to free the child. "You have a healthy baby boy."

Vincent felt such relief he could barely contain himself. "Grace. Did you hear? We have a boy. A healthy baby boy."

"Yes, Vincent," she whispered, lifting her hand to wipe the tears streaming down his face. "A son."

He leaned down and kissed her. "I love you."

He couldn't explain the emotions raging through him. The joy. Elation. Euphoric jubilation. Relief.

Love.

He brushed his hand over Grace's damp face. "I love you, Grace."

She breathed a heavy sigh and turned her face into his palm and kissed him.

Vincent looked to Lady Caroline and the rest of Grace's sisters. All of them had tears in their eyes as they cared for Grace and the newborn babe.

"Thank you," he said to no one in particular. To all of them.

"You're welcome, Your Grace," Caroline answered. "Why don't you give Grace a few minutes' privacy so we can freshen her up? You can come back in a few minutes to formally meet your son."

Vincent stood and looked down at Grace. Her face was still pale and the expression she wore still etched in pain. "Are you all right, Grace?"

"Fine. There's nothing to worry about now, Vincent. See? I told you everything would be all right."

Vincent nodded, but he wasn't convinced. The memory of the terror he felt was too recent. The nightmare he'd just endured too familiar. Even though Grace assured him she was fine, the look on her face didn't say the same.

"I'll be outside the door. I'll come back when you're ready."

She smiled, and he leaned down to kiss her again, then walked to the door. He barely had his hand on the knob when another piercing scream stopped him cold.

"Grace!"

He saw the worried looks on her sisters' faces as they rushed to where Grace lay, her face contorted, her body heaving in pain.

He stayed back, knowing his intrusion would be more of a hindrance than a help. His fear was so great he couldn't overcome it.

His elation had been premature. All the fears and terrors rushed back to haunt him. Something was wrong. He could see it in the panic-stricken looks on everyone's faces, hear it in their voices.

"What is it, Grace?" Lady Caroline said, her hands and eyes quickly examining Grace.

"Vincent!"

Vincent rushed to her side, clasping her hand, helping her ride out another pain. He wouldn't let her die now. Not after she'd given him a son.

"What's wrong?" he asked, looking at the fearful expression on Lady Caroline's face.

She shook her head.

Vincent felt every fear come back in full force. Surely God would not ask him to trade one life for another. Surely not...

Another pain stopped his thoughts as Grace clutched his hand. He looked at Caroline again and saw her features soften.

"When the next pain comes, Grace, push as hard as you can."

"I'm tired, Linny," Grace said, her voice weak, her pain-ravaged body near exhaustion.

"I know, Grace," Caroline said, pressing her hand to Grace's abdomen. "But you have another babe who wants to be born."

Vincent felt the air leave his lungs when Grace arched from another pain.

She pushed once, then twice, and a second babe made its way into Lady Caroline's arms.

"You have a daughter too, Your Grace. A very beautiful daughter."

"Did you hear, Grace? We have a daughter."

Tears streamed down Grace's cheeks, and he wiped them away with his fingers, then pressed his lips to her forehead.

"Is she healthy, Caroline? Why hasn't she cried?"

The babe chose that moment to utter her first very loud, healthy cry.

Grace breathed a heavy sigh and closed her eyes. Vincent looked at the babe Lady Josalyn held in her arms.

His daughter was smaller than her brother but looked perfect. Even her delicate cry was perfect.

* * *

Vincent sat in a chair beside her bed and watched Grace sleep. Her sisters had bathed her and put her in a pretty satin gown sprigged with dainty yellow embroidered flowers and trimmed in lace. Even though dark circles rimmed her eyes and her face was still pale, she was the most beautiful woman in the world. She was his wife. The mother of his children.

He loved her with such fierceness it frightened him.

Josalyn and Anne were in the next room with the babes. He could hear their low whispers as they cooed over the newborns. God's miracles.

Sarah and Francine would come later, and Caroline and Mary tomorrow. They would all watch closely for the next few days to make sure Grace didn't come down with a fever.

Vincent would keep his own watch. He wouldn't let anything happen to her ever again.

He dropped his head back against the chair and stared up at the ceiling. He couldn't believe it was over. Couldn't believe Grace had survived his cousin's attempts to kill her. Couldn't believe Grace had given him not one, but two perfect babes. Vincent knew he was the luckiest man on earth.

He silently thanked God again for blessing him so and vowed anew to keep his promise. Even though he knew it was a terrible penance to pay, he would never risk losing Grace with another pregnancy.

"If I didn't know better, I'd think you were still worrying, Vincent."

Vincent sat forward in his chair and reached for Grace's hand. "That isn't worry you see, my love. That's the humble look of a man who has just been given the world. I have just returned from looking at them again. They are beautiful, Grace. You have made me the happiest man alive."

Vincent lifted her hand to his lips and kissed her fingers. "I didn't know it was possible to feel such love. Both for the children I never thought I'd have and for the wife I am so blessed to have. I love you, Grace."

"And I love you," she said, touching her palm to his cheek. "Have you chosen a name for your son?"

"I think Edward," he said, watching her reaction. "After my father." She smiled, and he gave her the rest of their son's name. "He will be Edward Andrew Vincent Germaine, twelfth Marquess of Hayworth."

"That sounds perfect."

"And what name have you chosen for your daughter, Grace?"

She hesitated, then said, "I would like to call her Hannah."

Vincent smiled. "Yes. I think Hannah would be very pleased to have our daughter named after her. She is, after all, responsible for her being here."

"Thank you," Grace said with tears in her eyes.

Vincent leaned forward and kissed her tenderly, then pulled away at the soft knock on the door.

"The servants are here to remove Your Grace's things," Alice said, holding the door open.

Vincent nodded. "Send them in."

"What's happening, Vincent?"

"Nothing to concern yourself over, Grace. For now I think it's best if I move to another room so you won't be disturbed."

"No, Vincent."

He heard the disappointment in her voice and saw the frown deepen on her forehead, but ignored it. He had no choice. He'd never be able to stay in the same room with her, let alone the same bed, and not touch her. "You need the rest. I would only bother you."

He nodded for Alice to show the servants in and take everything that was his out of Grace's room. Before Grace could question him further, Josalyn and Anne came into the room. They each carried one of the twins in their arms.

Vincent helped Grace to sit and propped some pillows behind her back.

Josalyn reached the bed first. "Your son is already showing quite an independent streak, Grace. He isn't shy at all in letting us know when he wants to be fed." Josalyn placed a fussing Edward in Grace's outstretched arms.

"I can see already he's going to take after his father," Grace said, smiling up at him.

"And your daughter already shows exquisite manners and a quiet, calm temperament," Anne said, holding a contented Hannah.

Grace looked at him with a gleam in her eyes. "She's obviously going to take after me."

Vincent laughed and waited until the servants were out of the room before soundly kissing his wife, then leaving her to feed the babes. The minute he left the room he breathed a sigh of relief. Thanks to the babes, he'd escaped an argument. He knew it wasn't over, but for now, any concerns Grace had about his moving out of her room were, if not forgotten, at least delayed.

Chapter 23

Grace listened to the mantel clock below strike two in the morning, then slipped out of bed and lowered her feet to the cool wooden floor, long chilled from the dying fire in her room. With a slight shiver, she lifted her nightgown over her head and tossed it across a chair. The cool night air brushed against her bare flesh and she shivered again before slipping into the thin satin robe she'd painstakingly laid out before she'd gone to bed.

The material did little to warm her, but warmth was not her intent. Not now. She'd be plenty warm later on.

She smiled to herself and looped the tie at her waist just tight enough to hold the satin together, then walked to the door. She was off to wage a war, to fight a battle, to defeat the enemy. She smiled a broad smile and shivered a third time as a rampaging wave of desire swirled low in her belly.

She was off to seduce her husband.

She walked down the hall and stopped before the door to the room he'd moved into six weeks ago, on the night their twins had been born. She'd known his intent from the first, had known he was distancing himself from her because of his fears. Fears he'd battled since his first wife died. Fears he'd struggled to defeat even before he knew for sure she was carrying his child. Fears he was convinced he was not brave enough to face again.

Grace was aware of his nightmares, just as she knew he foolishly thought he could be content never to resume the private side of their marriage. And since there'd been little she could do until now to counteract such an absurdity, for six weeks she'd let him think she was in agreement with his decision.

Nothing was further from the truth. It was time to show him she was not satisfied merely holding hands or sharing a chaste and polite kiss. Time to show him she would never be content with a marriage that lacked physical intimacy. Time to find a release to the building desire that grew increasingly intolerable by the day. Time to end the self-imposed separation he foolishly thought would keep her safe.

She no longer worried that the *ton* would speculate that she'd gotten pregnant in order to trap Vincent into marrying her. Because she'd been carrying twins, and because of the tragedy that had occurred the day the twins were born, the babes' early arrival hadn't even been noticed. Now, no one would count months when they heard she was increasing again.

She smiled and opened the door to his room, not bothering to knock. Not bothering to give him warning.

She expected to find him in bed, but the covers were thrown back and the bed empty. He was obviously spending as restless a night as she.

She looked around the room. Her gaze found him staring out the window, his gaze locked onto the darkness, his hands clasped behind his back. No wonder each morning he looked like he hadn't slept the night before.

She wanted to laugh. At least tomorrow morning there would be a reason for his tired look.

Grace knew the minute he realized she was there. He turned and took one step toward her, then stopped. Concern etched his features. "Grace? Is something wrong with the children?"

"No, Vincent. Edward and Hannah are fine. In fact, they are perfect." She took a step closer and worried her lower lip to keep from smiling. "It's me."

"You?" Vincent crossed the distance that separated them in two anxious strides and clasped his hands around her upper arms. There was real fear in his eyes. "What's the matter, Grace? Are you ill?"

"Not exactly," she answered, trying to stop the shiver his touch caused. "It's more an ache. And it won't go away. In fact, it seems to be getting worse and worse."

Deep worry lines crossed his forehead and Grace felt a momentary pang of guilt for worrying him so. She quickly brushed it aside.

He rubbed his hands up and down her arms, then pulled her closer to him. "Where do you hurt? Do you want me to send for the doctor?"

She shook her head. "No. I'm afraid a doctor can't help me."

He touched his fingers to her cheek, then his palm to her forehead. "You don't seem to be fevered."

"Oh, yes. I think I am."

He felt her face again, then leaned his forehead to hers. The feel of him so close sent waves of molten heat spiraling to the pit of her stomach, then lower.

"Would you please hold me?"

"Of course," he said eagerly. "Do you want to lie down?"

"Not yet."

"Very well. Where does it hurt?"

Grace pulled at the belt around her waist and pushed her wrapper from her shoulders. "Here," she said and lifted his hands to her breasts.

Vincent's breath caught and he shuddered.

Grace heard his breath catch and considered the raspy sound of his breathing the first sign of surrender.

* * *

Vincent knew what she was doing. Knew what she intended would happen tonight. Bloody hell and damnation! Didn't she know he couldn't allow it? Didn't she know the risk they'd be taking?

His heart skipped a beat and he fought to move away from her. But his feet refused to move. He could do nothing but stand there with her breasts nestled in the palms of his hands. Bloody hell! This was torture of the worst kind.

"Yes, Vincent. Touch me."

"Ah, Grace…"

"Please. Hold me."

Her voice was soft and held a pleading quality to it he couldn't resist. The battle raged fiercely inside him, and his only victory seemed to be a compromise. Maybe he would just hold her. But he vowed he would do no more.

Vincent wrapped his arms around her and touched her soft, satiny skin. A thousand spirals of heat swirled in vicious circles all through his body. A molten whirlpool of desire rushed deep in his gut and he grew uncomfortably heavy. He squeezed his eyes shut and sucked in a deep breath.

He swore he would stand here for just a few moments, then let her go. Swore he would. But of their own volition, his hands moved in slow, gentle circles over her flesh.

"Yes, Vincent. Now lower."

He drew his circles lower on her back.

"Lower yet, Vincent."

His hands moved lower, and she sighed when he touched her. He was hot, hard, uncomfortable. He needed to stop. Needed to push her away from him. But he couldn't.

Then Grace lifted her head and said, "Kiss me, Vincent. Please."

And he was lost.

His mouth lowered to hers and his lips touched hers, tasting her, drinking from her. And she answered his kiss with the same desperation that surged through him.

He opened his mouth atop hers and met the boldness of her tongue as she came in search of him. They touched and parried and battled until neither of them could breathe. Then, with an agonized moan, she wrapped her arms around his neck and pulled him closer.

Vincent knew he was lost. Knew if he looked down, his resolve to never make love to her would lie shattered at his feet.

"Ah, Grace…"

"Shh, Vincent. Just love me."

He gasped a sharp intake of breath. The feel of her against him sent fiery heat spiraling low in his belly. Then she pressed a kiss against his flesh where his robe gaped open and it was nearly his undoing.

"Grace?" His voice sounded heavy and strained even to his own ears.

"Don't talk, Vincent."

She kissed him again, then rained kisses over his face and neck and chest. And all the time, her hands worked frantically at his flesh, touching him until he was on fire.

"I…we…" His back arched and his head dropped back on his shoulders. "Ah, hell."

"No, Vincent. But I'll promise you heaven." Grace slipped his robe from his shoulders and let it puddle at her feet. Then she went willingly into his embrace.

His breathing was raspy and labored; his chest heaved as if he had to struggle to control his breathing. He couldn't take much more of this. Couldn't let this go much further. Yet he didn't have the willpower to stop.

His breaths shuddered. If he didn't want her so desperately he might have the power to push her away from him. But he wanted her too much.

He made the mistake of looking into her eyes and almost laughed at the raw desire that stared back at him. The same look he was sure he wore.

"Touch me, Vincent. Please."

The moan that escaped him was rife with torture and agony, but Vincent wrapped his arms around her and held her as if he were desperate never to let her go.

"We shouldn't be doing this," he said, burying his face in her loose hair. "I swore I never would." He gasped for more air. "Swore I'd never risk losing you again."

"You're not going to lose me," she whispered, touching her lips to his flesh. "You're going to love me." She kissed him again. "And love me."

She touched his cheek with her hand, then tilted her face and kissed him again.

He fought as valiantly as any warrior had ever fought, but lost the battle with every kiss. He knew he couldn't hold off much longer.

"Love me, Vincent. Make love to me."

He moaned as if calling on every ounce of willpower he possessed. But he knew it was futile. He'd waited so long. Dreamed of loving her so many nights.

On a heavy sigh he gave up the battle and stared at her with all his raw pain and fear exposed for her to see.

"You're going to force me to risk it all, aren't you?"

"I have to."

She lifted her mouth and kissed him on the lips.

He moaned softly, then kissed her back. "I can't fight this any longer."

"You're not supposed to fight it, Your Grace. You're supposed to enjoy it."

She kissed him again. Then again.

"Grace, I promised. I—"

She pressed her fingers atop his lips and stopped his words. "We'll talk about your promises in the morning."

"By then it will be too late," he said on a gasp.

She smiled. "It's already too late, darling. Now please. Love me."

With a moan of resignation, he picked her up in his arms and carried her to the bed.

Their lovemaking was a melding of passion and desire. Their need for a connection that bound them to each other was a beautiful culmination of love as it was intended to be.

After he floated back to earth, Vincent cradled her to him, marveling at the perfect feel of her in his arms. He stroked her flesh, then kissed each spot where his fingers had touched her.

"I love you, Grace," Vincent said when his breathing had calmed.

"Almost as much as I love you," she answered.

Vincent thought of the night she'd deceived him and smiled. He never thought her deception would turn out so perfectly.

He tucked her close beside him and lowered his mouth to meet hers. "I should have known it was impossible to fight you."

She smiled as her hand cupped his cheek and rubbed her fingers across his jaw. "Impossible. From the first."

She wrapped her arm around his neck and brought his mouth down to hers. The kiss they shared was a fusion of emotions neither of them could deny.

At last, his mind understood what his heart had known all along. That the love they shared was strong enough to conquer all his fears. Strong enough to endure a lifetime… and beyond.

About the Author

❦

Laura Landon taught high school for ten years before leaving the classroom to open her own ice-cream shop. As much as she loved serving up sundaes and malts from behind the counter, she closed up shop after penning her first novel. Now she spends nearly every waking minute writing, guiding her heroes and heroines to happily ever after. She is the author of more than a dozen historical novels, and her books are enjoyed by readers around the world. She lives with her family in the rural Midwest, where she devotes what free time she has to volunteering in her community.

Made in the USA
Charleston, SC
25 November 2012